Endorsements

I recently was taking a trip back to the North East and needed a few books for my long flight from Reno. After hearing about *Bonners Fairy* through Elizabeth's husband Dave, whom I work with, I was intrigued. He gave me a copy before I left, and after reading the first one I was hooked! Soon to follow, I was anxious to start the second book, *A New Kind of Battle*. Once I got my hands on a copy, it took me less than 24 hours to read. I was eager to find out what our favorite characters were up to, and how things were panning out in Bonners Ferry and Roan. Shortly after completing this, I found out Elizabeth had finished the third book, *Mischief and Mayhem*. To my surprise I was given a copy of the manuscript to read before it even went to the publisher! Talk about luck!!

The third piece to the *Bonners Fairy* series is my favorite so far. With each turn of the page, the story unveils new and exciting turns and twists. The anticipation to find out what happens on the next page is so strong; you cannot put the book down!

Elizabeth has a great way of telling a story. The imagination used to even begin this series is something I can only dream of having. Even down to the dancing fire fairies, everything in Roan holds so much magic and wonder it truly just makes the reader want to jump in the story and take some cruises around the woodlands with the rest of the characters.

I am ecstatic that I was able to get my hands on the manuscript so I could continue my journey with Haley and Henry. I cannot wait for the fourth book to be done so I can see what new and exciting adventures the twins find themselves involved in!

-Amanda Nolan
South Lake Tahoe, California

Also by Elizabeth A. Patterson

"Bonners Fairy"
Book One

"A New Kind of Battle"
Book Two

Elizabeth A. Patterson

Mischief and Mayhem

A Bonners Fairy Novel

Have fun :)

Elizabeth Patterson

iUniverse, Inc.
Bloomington

Mischief and Mayhem
A Bonners Fairy Novel

iUniverse books may be ordered through booksellers or by contacting:

iUniverse
1663 Liberty Drive
Bloomington, IN 47403
www.iuniverse.com
1-800-Authors (1-800-288-4677)

ISBN: 978-1-4759-3794-7 (sc)
ISBN: 978-1-4759-3795-4 (e)
ISBN: 978-1-4759-3796-1 (dj)

Library of Congress Control Number: 2012912459

Printed in the United States of America

iUniverse rev. date: 07/11/2012

Dedication

For my Father, Gerald,
My Inspiration

Acknowledgements

Thank you to my husband, David, my rock.
Special thanks to Nora Douglas, a brilliant woman.

Contents

Chapter 1
Intruder Alert

It was a cold and dark afternoon. Thunder and lightning crashed outside. The storm moved in quickly bringing fierce winds and bitterly cold temperatures. A mixture of rain and snow beat against the estate on Blue Bell Glen.

Haley Miles bedroom tower was cold, and she shivered as the lights flickered. The pot-bellied stove in her room couldn't seem to give off enough heat. She added another log and pulled up a chair.

Odd things had been happening lately which put her on edge. Since she and her twin brother Henry had returned from Roan, a hidden world full of fairies, witches, and all manner of creatures.

After they met Prince Valian and his sister Sersha, who lived in the hidden realm in the land of Wisen, their lives had not been ordinary to say the least. Sersha had pleaded with them to aid in the rescue of Zebulan Bonner, founder of Bonners Ferry in Idaho, and a group of captured fairies.

They accepted and had seen firsthand a real world beyond their wildest dreams. They discovered fairy tales weren't just the product of someone's wild imagination. They truly existed in another realm. A place, if you were lucky enough, that revealed itself through hidden portals.

The legend of Bonners Ferry, which had been a fun topic of discussion around a midnight campfire or at a slumber party on a stormy night, was a real and tragic event in human history, though the true ending of the story turned out to be quite different.

No one knew what happened to Zebulan Bonner or his family centuries ago. They had disappeared and were presumed dead. Speculation varied from one person to another and always seemed to change the more often it was told.

Circumstances beyond their control forced the twins to introduce the fairy world to their parents, Paul and Carol and the prince and princess took an instant liking to them as they spent one relaxing morning regaling the group with the details of Haley's and Henry's adventures in the land of Wisen. They had astounded her parents when she and Prince Valian disclosed their plans to marry in three year's time.

Just when all seemed right in Haley's world, the blue stone that was given to Prince Valian by witch Hilda, broom Hilda as the twins liked to call her, the friendly witch who lived in the outskirts of Roan, suddenly began to vibrate, sending out electrical shocks; meaning trouble, a summons for help.

Valian quickly looked at the others.

"I gave my stone to our guardian Theodore," Sersha whispered anxiously.

"We must go," Valian said urgently, standing to leave.

Haley stood, feeling uneasy.

"You and Henry stay here," he added.

Haley opened her mouth to protest, but he stopped her.

"No. Not this time. Sersha and I will deal with this. It's our problem, not yours."

As Valian and Sersha walked out the kitchen door, he turned and kissed Haley's hand.

"Don't worry, we'll keep you informed."

The pair spread their wings and descended the tall bluff, disappearing into the sun.

A week passed and the twins still hadn't heard a word from the fairy world. Haley was getting restless and had to fight the urge to go to the *other side*. Valian had been very clear in his instruction to stay behind, but she didn't like it and the weather did nothing for her spirits. It was spooky.

She kept remembering broom Hilda asking Queen Lilia; Valian and Sersha's mother, what was up with all the weird storms they were experiencing, and the queen's bewilderment and lack of any explanation.

She threw another log on the fire and moved her chair closer to the stove.

Then there was the fact that their creepy neighbor, Ike Seers, had seemed to simply vanish.

Ike was a desperate man who as a young boy, accidently discovered the land of Wisen, and had become rich from the gems he stole from the other side.

He was obsessed with finding another portal to enter that realm to continue building his wealth and was willing to do anything, He even went as far as holding Princess Sersha captive in his attempts, but disappeared after her rescue.

Ike's soon to be ex-wife Judy, brought their sons, Ike Jr. and Ernie, for a visit and found their beautiful home across the valley from the Miles' estate deserted. Ike wasn't to be found.

Ike Jr. was the twins' age and a troublemaker. He was an overweight boy with hayseed colored hair who thought everyone was beneath him and took pleasure in making the twin's life miserable.

Ernie was three years younger and totally the opposite. Same hair, but extremely thin, and barely said two words to anyone. Judy and the boys had been staying at the house ever since.

Rumors spread that Ike Sr. had met the same fate as everyone else that had disappeared from Bonners Ferry throughout the years. Drowned in the river, gone mad and lost in the forest, attacked by Zeb Bonner's ghost perhaps.

Then there was school. Haley and Henry had only attended school briefly before being whisked away to the *other side*.

Princess Sersha had modified the memories of anyone who would miss the twin's. Not even the Seers boys remembered them when they returned to school, which suited them just fine.

The announcement was made for the upcoming autumn festival and Halloween party, but Haley wasn't as thrilled about it like she was the year before. She did have a great idea for a costume though. She would unveil her wings and go as a fairy. She grinned at the thought.

Broom Hilda was planning to invite the Bonner family to the festival. The twins had helped the fairies rescue the family and knew they were currently alive and well, living on the other side these past two hundred years. This thrilled Haley.

She got up and began to pace the floor. Her mind continued to wander back to what happened with Violet. That meddlesome little fairy had tried to steal Valian away from her by using a witch's spell that promptly backfired and caused her to grow tentacles from her forehead.

Haley smiled at the memory of Violet's reaction when she found out Valian had asked Haley to marry him.

Violet had somehow managed to get rid of the protrusions and had shown up at Ike's place. She had gone from a pretty little lovesick fairy to being devious; obsessed with becoming rich and powerful.

She thought about Valian's display of emotions. Valian was a species of fairy called Manwan, which were incapable of experiencing the kind of emotion so prominent in humans. It was blind luck that they discovered the reason behind it.

The given gem each fairy wore suppressed displays of emotion. Once the gems were removed, the fairies couldn't handle the power of what they were experiencing and broke out in fights.

It was a real eye opener, and Haley planned to use this new found knowledge to train them how to use emotions to their advantage.

She walked over to the window. Looking out, she half hoped to see Sersha sitting on the ledge waiting for her. With a heavy sigh she went back to the chair.

Her parents and Henry had left that morning for Spokane to shop for some new appliances, and the storm had her worried. It didn't look like it was going to let up any time soon. The power kept going out, and she kept hearing noises as the wind beat against the estate.

It continued to grow darker as the storm front moved in. The lights in her room flickered and went out. She waited several minutes hoping they would come back on. When they didn't, she lit a couple candles.

She was really into aromatherapy and soon her room smelled like pumpkin spice.

She began to pace again. Frustrated, she decided to go down to the kitchen for some hot chocolate.

She put on her fuzzy red robe and slippers and took a candle to the door. As she stepped through, the candle flickered and almost went out. She hadn't realized how drafty her home was.

She cupped the flame and descended the west tower stairs. As she walked down the hall toward the grand staircase, her eyes began playing tricks on her.

The eyes in the portraits seemed to follow her, watching her. The tapestries fluttered ever so slightly as if a breeze had passed by.

She walked slowly, listening. They say when a house settles, it creaks and groans, but this was no new house. It had been on these grounds for almost two hundred years.

The hair on the back of her neck began to prickle.

She stopped at the top of the grand staircase and looked down into the foyer.

Lightning lit up the room and for a split second she could have sworn she saw a figure, silhouetted by the front door.

She waited for the next flash and found nothing there.

When she was half way down the stairs she heard a loud bang. She stopped suddenly, wondering what to do.

She thought about her sword, but that was up in her room, and she was too un-nerved to turn around and go back.

Another banging sound came from the right, toward her father's office in the west hall.

Summoning up the courage, she continued to the bottom of the staircase and slowly crossed the foyer and peeked around the corner. The hallway was empty and dark except for the occasional lightning.

She moved quietly down the hall, stopping and listening at each door, afraid to look inside at what she might find.

Bang!

She jumped and almost dropped her candle. The noise came from the room at the end of the hall. It was the study where she and Henry did their homework.

She put her hand on the knob, turning it slowly and eased the door open. Her eyes darted from one end of the room to the other. The curtains were flapping in the large northwest window as a strong gust of wind blew rain and snow into the ice cold room.

She set the candle down and hurried over to close the window. She slammed it shut, bolting it quickly, and drew the curtain.

For the first time in her life she was really frightened. She began to rationalize the situation. "There's no reason to be afraid," she said to herself. "Henry probably left it open. It's just the wind."

Lightning cracked again causing her to jump.

"For goodness sakes," she said aloud. "Don't be such a baby."

She picked up her candle and started down the hall. Just as she got to the foyer she heard a crash in the kitchen.

She froze. Goosebumps crept up her arms as she struggled with what to do. She spotted the closet door and quietly tiptoed over. Then she realized the front door was unlatched and ajar.

Lightning lit up the foyer again, and she gasped at the wet footprints leading across the floor to the kitchen.

A wave of terror traveled through her body like a blast of cold wind. Her heart thundered in her chest as she tried desperately to remain calm.

She reached over and pushed the front door closed and locked it. She searched inside the closet for anything she could use as a weapon. She spotted Henry's hockey stick.

She grabbed it and crossed the foyer.

She paused at the kitchen door, listening. All was quiet except for the clap of thunder. Slowly easing the door open she stepped inside.

Suddenly the lights flickered. A dark figure stood at the sink and spun around.

Haley screamed, blowing out her candle.

"Estelle! You scared me half to death!" she cried, at the sight of the Miles' housekeeper standing at the kitchen counter. She dropped the hockey stick and put her shaking hand to her heart. The strength left her legs and she sank to the floor.

Estelle hurried over, her hand on her own heart as well. She bent down.

"I'm so sorry my dear. I didn't think anyone was here. Are you all right?"

Haley could barely speak. She just sat there trying to catch her breath.

Estelle Grimsworth was a sweet, gray-haired lady that came with the house. A plump woman with a soft voice and bright eyes. She was a witch who had lived on the estate for almost two centuries. In their last visit to Roan the twins discovered to their surprise, she was also broom Hilda's sister.

"Oh Estelle, I've never been so scared. I heard noises and the front door was open and the window in the study..."

"It's just the storm," said Estelle with a soft smile, helping Haley to her feet and over to the table.

"Oh my goodness," she said, her legs shaking as she sat down.

"You're all right. You get comfortable and catch your breath; I'll make us some hot chocolate."

"That's what I came down here to do when I heard all those noises," Haley said with a sigh.

"Obviously, I came in the front door, and you know your brother. He can be forgetful sometimes. He probably forgot to close the study window."

"Yeah, you're probably right," Haley said, rolling her eyes. "It's funny how your imagination gets away from you," she laughed half heartedly.

"Doesn't it though?" Estelle agreed. "Then of course I knocked these pans off the counter when I put my bags down."

The lights went out again as a tremendous crack of thunder rattled the windows.

Haley jumped again.

Estelle hurried over to a kitchen cabinet and felt around for some candles.

"Darn these power outages," she muttered.

"I have a candle here," said Haley. "Do you have any matches?"

Her candle suddenly came to life.

"Wow, I didn't know you could do that," she said, walking over to Estelle.

"That's easy. It's one of the first things witches learn how to do," Estelle replied as she pulled more candles from the cupboard and lit them with a wave of her hand.

"How do you do it?" Haley asked. "I mean, is it something anyone can learn?"

"I don't really know. No one has ever asked me that before. I suppose anyone could if they concentrated hard enough. It's all in your mind."

"Kind of like the force?" Haley smiled, thinking of a movie she had seen.

"Yes, that's it exactly."

"Could you teach me?" she hopefully asked.

"Of course I could."

"Wow. That would be so cool."

Just then the telephone rang. Haley answered.

Estelle went to the fridge and pulled out a gallon of milk while Haley talked to her mother. She was busy stirring the pot when she hung up.

"Well, they're spending the night in Spokane. The road is closed because of the storm. I guess it's snowing pretty bad there."

"It looks like it's just you and me tonight," said Estelle as she poured hot chocolate into a couple of large mugs.

"I guess so," Haley replied, taking a sip. "Why are you home?" she asked. "I thought you were spending the weekend with Hilda."

"I was, but she is busy trying to round up Violet with the guardians; so I thought I'd get some pre-winter cleaning done. I guess I'm a little late," she chuckled.

"Violet? She got away from the infirmary?"

"She never made it there," Estelle answered. "Guardians Theodore and Troy, as you know, were in charge of taking her back to the other side to stand before the royal Lords and Ladies for her crimes against a human. Well, they were both knocked unconscious before they could get her through the portal. She somehow managed to tie them up and pushed them through, and then she disappeared."

Haley sat wide eyed, a sick feeling in the pit of her stomach.

"That's why I haven't heard from Valian. Maybe I should go…"

"No," Estelle interrupted. "Valian was adamant that you and Henry stay here."

"I know. I just feel so helpless sitting here. It's nerve wracking."

"I know it is, but you know how dangerous the other side can be. You're better off waiting until his return. He would feel horrible if something were to happen to you."

Haley sighed. "Well I hope it's soon. I hate waiting."

"Let's go make a fire," said Estelle, picking up a candle.

In the den she waved her hand and a fire sprang to life. Haley watched, fascinated as Estelle pointed at one of the leather chairs and directed it to move in front of the fireplace.

"Have a seat," she said, pointing to another chair. "Let's get comfy and have a chat."

Haley settled back in her chair and sipped her cocoa. "Umm this is good. Tell me something Estelle, what do you think happened to Ike?"

"Who can tell? My guess is he found a way to the other side, using Violet perhaps. After all, they were in cahoots together."

Estelle paused for a moment, thinking. "Once she escaped from Troy and Theodore she probably went back and got Ike."

"That makes sense," Haley agreed. "So they are back on the other side, making plans to conquer the world," she continued discouraged. "All they care about is being rich."

"More than that," said Estelle. "I get the impression that Ike is after more than riches. He craves power and that is a dangerous combination. People that are that obsessed can become desperate. I've seen it before," she added with a sigh.

The thunder continued to roll through the valley as the afternoon pressed on.

Haley and Estelle enjoyed an early supper in the kitchen as the wind whipped fury outside. Snow began to pile up on the window sill and the stunning outdoor view was swallowed up in the approaching darkness.

Estelle began preparing a steaming pot of homemade chicken soup. Dozens of candles added cheery warmth to the room that reminded Haley of Christmas. She watched Estelle as she waved her hand and pointed, causing the onions, celery, and carrots to peel and chop themselves.

"That's what I'd like you to teach me," she said.

"Hum?"

"To make things move."

Estelle turned and looked at Haley with that familiar twinkle in her eye.

"That's a good place to start," she replied.

"So, what do I do first?"

"Well… you have to prepare your mind."

"Prepare my mind? How?"

"Do you remember when you drank the elixir and grew wings, how Valian taught you how to fly, to control them, and after you ate the dwindle drops he gave you, how you controlled your size?"

"Yes."

"You have to have that kind of concentration, but more. You not only have to picture it, you have to feel it deep down in your stomach. That desire has to be strong enough to course through you. You'll feel it in your entire body right down to your fingertips. Try it with this napkin here," she said, placing it in front of Haley. "Now concentrate. Feel the urge."

Haley stretched out her finger and pointed to the napkin, her forehead creased in concentration. The napkin remained still.

"Try again," Hilda instructed, "with feeling."

Haley tried again and again, but the napkin didn't budge or even twitch.

"Well, keep practice…"

Bang!

Haley shot Estelle a look.

"See," she whispered.

"Come on," Estelle said quietly. "Let's go check it out."

Haley nodded and picked up Henry's hockey stick.

They left the kitchen and walked into the foyer. They heard a muffled sound coming from the hallway to Paul's office.

Haley pointed in the direction of the study. They quickly and quietly hurried down the hall. Haley's heart was hammering in her chest.

Estelle threw the door open and lit every sconce in the room at the same time. The room was empty and quiet except for the same northwest window which stood open. The curtains had been sucked out the window by the storm and flapped in the heavy winds.

Haley stood frozen. Her entire body had become one giant goose bump. "That's the window I closed and locked," she whispered.

Estelle hurried over and checked the area. She shut the window and drew the curtain. "Come and look," she motioned.

There was a lone footprint in the snow that had blown into the room.

"Someone is here," Estelle said quietly.

Haley shuddered.

"Who?"

"Good question. I don't imagine they are friendly, sneaking into someone's home. Stay close to me."

"Don't worry, I will!"

The pair left the study. They checked Paul's office and the library which were both empty. They stopped at the entrance to the foyer and listened. The only sound was the wind blasting its way around the house.

"I don't like this," Haley whispered.

Estelle didn't reply. She cocked her head and went toward her bedroom. As before, she threw the door open and candlelight flooded the room. They caught just a glimpse of someone passing into the gloomy reflection of a storm, into Estelle's private postern, an entrance to the other side.

"Darn," Estelle blurted in frustration, "just missed them."

"Shouldn't we follow?" Haley asked.

"It would be a waste of time," Estelle answered. "They could be anywhere in Roan."

"Please," Haley begged with a pleading look. "We need to find out who that was and why they were in our house."

"All right, but we have to be extremely careful."

Haley grinned, putting aside her fear.

Estelle quickly grabbed a couple wide brimmed hats and rain jackets and together they entered the postern.

Chapter 2
A Surprising Reunion

It was storming on the other side, though not as severely as at the Miles estate. They emerged at the creaking waterwheel next door to Mathilda's restaurant. The darkness pressed in on them, cold and empty.

They checked the area around them. Not a soul was out and about. The outskirts were deserted. The lamps up and down the cobbled streets glowed dully as the rain covered them in a thin obscuring layer.

All the shops stood silent and dark except for Mathilda's and the old, run down pub down the street. A lone light told them the restaurant was locking up for the night.

Estelle eyed the pub curiously. "I wonder," she said to herself. "We'll go in the back way."

Haley followed her around the corner to the alley. They quietly slipped in the back door. Nothing had changed since the last time Haley had been there. It was fairly dark inside. Small, wall mounted lamps glowed red as she and Estelle took a seat at one of the tables. Estelle motioned to Haley to keep her head lowered to hide her face.

A tall, thin man with a long, bushy beard and gray hair stepped out from behind the bar and ambled over. Haley recognized him as the pub keeper.

"What'll it be?" he asked, stooping slightly to get a look at their faces.

Haley lowered her head even more. "Rainbow dew," she mumbled, deepening her voice slightly.

"I think I'll have one of your watered down ales," Estelle grumbled sarcastically.

The pub keeper grunted and shuffled back to the bar.

Haley looked around the room.

A small group sat at the bar talking quietly and didn't give them a glance.

"What are we doing here?" Haley began just as the pub keeper brought them their drinks.

She sat quietly as Estelle flashed an old iron medallion at the pub keeper. He seemed startled for a moment as he recognized it and turned back to the bar.

"What is that?" Haley whispered.

"It is the witches crest," she answered. "It is like... having a tab; you know, service now, pay later. Here, here's one for you," she said, pulling another medallion from her pocket. She waved her hand and a chain appeared. "Might come in handy."

Haley nodded and put it around her neck.

Just then the front door opened, and a hooded figure entered wearing a dark cloak. He was hunched over and slowly limped over to the bar and took a seat.

The pub keeper took his order and delivered a smoking stein and shuffled back to the group on the far side of the counter.

Haley and Estelle watched, silently holding their drinks up to hide their faces.

The hooded figure reached out a shaking hand and picked up the stein. Haley drew in a breath. His arm was bloodied from deep open gashes. It was a horrible sight, half scabbed over, and it looked infected. She noticed his pant leg was just about shredded and stained with blood.

As he bent forward to sip his drink, they saw the gleam from a black stone hanging from the chain around his neck. Obsidian stone.

Obsidian was a stone that had a powerful evil influence on whoever wore it. It was a tool used by the evil presence in the land; Molock the Merciless. He was a being that lived under a dead mountain in a realm

13

far from Roan, a being that relentlessly tortured and tormented the fairies for thousands of years for no apparent reason.

Haley flashed a look at Estelle. Estelle nodded. There was no mistaking it. It was Ike.

Estelle motioned for Haley to follow and they slipped out the back door. "Come," Estelle said quietly.

They went up the street half a block to a narrow doorway. Haley followed her up the steep stairs.

Estelle knocked. After a few moments light flooded the stairwell as a man opened the door.

"Good evening, Norman."

"Well, Estelle, nice of you to drop by. What brings you out in this weather?" he asked, ushering them inside.

"Norman, the guy in the portrait at Hilda's place?" Haley thought to herself. The picture of the young couple had reminded her of someone, but she didn't know who.

Norman's chestnut hair hung loose in long waves. He was tall and lanky and his eyes were bright.

Haley was immediately drawn to him.

"Mable, we have visitors," he called to his wife.

Mable came in and gave Estelle a big hug.

She had the most beautiful, golden blonde hair. Her green eyes were so vivid they reminded Haley of the bright green apples she had seen at the fairy farm. She was a plump woman with a kind face.

Norman and Mable looked at her curiously.

"This is Haley Miles," said Estelle. "She is Prince Valian's betrothed."

As they shook hands, again Haley had a feeling like she'd met them before.

"Haley is from Bonners Ferry."

Mable cocked her head momentarily.

"Well, it is certainly nice to meet you, Haley. Come in by the fire and get warm," she said, ushering them down the hall into a small, cozy but modestly decorated living room.

Estelle and Haley took seats by the fire as Mable disappeared into the kitchen and reappeared with a small tray.

"I was just making tea, would you like a cup?" she asked, setting the tray down, taking a seat next to Estelle. "So, what brings you out in such nasty weather?" she asked.

Norman stood by the fire, lighting his pipe. He took a long draw, eyeing Estelle and Haley questioningly.

"We have just come from Bonners Ferry on the trail of an intruder," said Estelle as she poured herself some tea.

"An intruder?" Mable asked with concern.

Estelle explained what happened at the estate and that they had just come from the pub where they believed the culprit was.

Norman and Mable leaned forward, listening intently.

"So," Estelle continued, "we were wondering if we might watch the pub from your place."

"Absolutely," Norman replied, getting up to open the shade in the guest bedroom.

"Excuse me," said Haley. "I hope you don't mind my asking, but what is your last name?"

"Seers," Norman answered as he went to the shade.

Haley's eyes grew wide as she realized who she was talking to. She exchanged glances with Estelle. She couldn't believe it. These were Ike Senior's parents! She had heard somewhere that Ike's parents had died in a fire when he was a small boy and that he was raised by his grandparents. She remembered Hilda's story of how Norman and Mable had been found wandering the border of Woodland realm, and that they had no memory of what happened to them or where they came from. Now she understood their familiarity.

"Oh my goodness," she thought to herself. "Should I tell them? Would it be too much of a shock? How will they react when they found out about Ike?" Her mind was swimming with questions as she looked over at Estelle.

Estelle, as if reading her mind, subtlety shook her head no. "Come, let's have a look down the street," Estelle suggested.

She and Haley walked over to the window in the other room.

A fog began to roll in, painting the main street a hazy blur. They could just make out the dull red glow from the pub window.

Haley glanced back toward the living room. She could see Norman stoking the fire as Mable sat quietly sipping her tea. She looked at Estelle.

"Shouldn't we tell them?" she asked. "They have a right to know."

"I know they do," Estelle answered. "I don't know that this is the right time."

"There is never going to be a right time," Haley suggested stubbornly.

Estelle was quiet as she looked out at the pub. They watched the deserted street for several minutes. She seemed to be struggling, drumming her fingers on the sill. Finally she looked at Haley with concern. "You're right. I would want to know if it were me, but let's not say anything bad about him. This is going to be enough of a shock."

Haley nodded. "You want to tell them or should I?"

"Let's do it together," Estelle answered.

"What about…" Haley began, motioning toward the pub.

"Later," Estelle said quietly. "We know he's here, we'll catch up with him."

With a deep breath, Haley followed Estelle back into the living room.

Mable looked up as they neared. She almost looked afraid, as if she had a feeling they were going to tell her something she didn't want to hear.

Estelle opened her mouth to speak but Mable cut her off.

"I know what you're going to say," she began.

They looked at her slightly surprised.

"We've known for some time."

"Known what?" Estelle asked, wondering if she was referring to Ike.

"That we are from Bonners Ferry," Mable answered with a sigh. "We are so comfortable here and I just don't think we could handle living back there. How would we explain what happened to us? Everyone thinks we are dead."

Haley hadn't thought of that. They couldn't possibly reveal anything about Roan or Wisen and the outskirts. People wouldn't believe them and would think they were a couple of kooks.

"There's more," said Estelle.

Norman and Mable looked positively frightened.

"Your son," Estelle began.

Mable was on the edge of her seat.

"Ike?" she whispered.

"He's here… now, in the outskirts."

Mable, shaken, got to her feet.

"He's here? Is he all right? Where…?"

"He's at the pub," Estelle interrupted. "He seems all right, but we don't know why he's here."

"I must see him," Mable said excitedly, going for her wrap. Norman stood there with a blank expression. He was pale and seemed at a loss for words. "Come on," Mable said, giving him a poke. He grabbed his coat and hat.

"Now you need to prepare yourselves," Estelle said quickly. "As I said, we don't know what he's doing here…"

Norman and Mable rushed past her as though they didn't hear her, heading for the door.

Haley and Estelle hurried into the rain after them, wondering if they made the right decision and what they'd gotten themselves into.

Mable threw open the door to the pub and stood in the doorway dripping wet, panting, and looked around the room in anticipation. The occupants all turned, startled.

"Mable?" said the pub keeper. "You ok?"

As her eyes traveled over the group, they fell upon a hooded figure sitting alone, hunched over as if oblivious to what was going on. Mable slowly approached the stranger. She stood behind him, trembling. "Ike?"

The figure turned slowly. He removed his hood and stared at her, his eyes glazed over. His face was full of scratches and he had a deep gash on his neck.

Mable gasped in horror. "Ike, what's happened to you?" she whispered. He sat there as if nothing registered.

"Ike, talk to me?" Mable said desperately. She reached out and put her hand on his shoulder.

He jerked back suddenly and put his arms up as if shielding himself, terror in his eyes. "Who… who are you?" he asked as he tried to back away.

Mable's face sank as tears flooded her eyes. "I… I'm your mother," she answered half sobbing.

Ike sat there. He didn't seem to quite catch what she said. "How do you know me?" he asked as he stood, inching his way away from her.

"Ike, it's me, it's your mother!" she cried. She took him by the shoulders and shook him. "Ike… look at me. Look… its mother."

Ike's forehead creased in a scowl. He shook his head as if he still didn't understand.

Mable reached up and gently put her hands on his cheeks. She spoke softly. "Ike sweetie… it's momma." She looked deep in his eyes. Tears rolled down her cheeks.

Ike looked back. It was as if a veil was lifted from his eyes as a spark of recognition registered there, briefly. He stumbled backward and landed on the floor, staring up at his mother in disbelief.

Haley watched mesmerized, tears in her eyes at this touching reunion.

Norman stepped forward. "Son," he said softly as he knelt down in front of Ike.

Ike looked back and forth at his parents.

"He's in shock," Estelle said quietly.

Ike looked at Estelle and Haley. It was as if he was trying to put two and two together, but with much difficulty.

Haley stepped forward. She was taking a chance, but she had to do it. "Ike… here," she said, reaching out. "This will help." She slowly began to lift the chain from around his neck.

Ike flinched and grabbed the chain quickly, a shadow crossing his face.

"No…" she said softly, "it'll be all right."

Ike, calmed by her gentleness, let her pull the chain over his head and she handed it to Estelle.

The second he was free from the obsidian stone, his face softened. He looked at his parents. "Mom, Dad?" he said as if he thought he were seeing things. "Is it really you? Am I dreaming?" The tears of an eight year old boy streamed from his eyes as he began to shake and sob. Norman and Mable sat on the floor, embracing their son.

Years of suppressed emotion and loneliness flooded the pub as the onlookers sat silent, staring at the wondrous scene before them.

Haley's heart, felt enlightened and warm.

The pub keeper asked if there was anything he could do.

Estelle gave him a soft, sad smile. "No, let them be," she answered quietly. "Do you have anything hot to drink?"

The pub keeper grinned.

Haley marveled at the pub keeper. His eyes seemed to light up and the lines on his face seemed, not so hard anymore.

He hurried into a small room behind the bar and came back with a steaming cup of tea. "My specialty," he said, handing it to Estelle. "Nobody ever wants tea anymore..." his voice trailed off as he went back behind the bar.

Estelle knelt down and handed the tea to Mable.

Mable gave her a grateful look and offered it to Ike who took it with a shaking hand. He slopped it all over as he tried to take a drink. Mable steadied the cup and he took a small sip and looked at his parents in wonder and the tears again began to fall.

"Let's get him home," said Norman. He and Mable helped Ike to his feet.

Back at the apartment, Norman piled on the logs in the fireplace as Mable helped Ike to the sofa.

Haley grabbed a hand crocheted blanket and handed it to Mable, who promptly tucked it around Ike then quickly left the room and came back with a wash cloth, a small basin filled with warm water, and a box full of bandages.

"We must clean up these cuts," she said softly and proceeded to wipe the wounds gently.

Ike sat silently drinking his tea and staring at his parents.

When Mable was finished she smiled at him. Her love permeated the room. Everyone could feel it, especially Ike. A contented look crossed his face and he sighed.

"Are you hungry, darling?" Mable asked.

Ike nodded as his eyes began to droop.

"I've got it," said Estelle. "Haley, can you give me a hand?"

Estelle led Haley from the apartment. Minutes later they were several blocks away at broom Hilda's door. Surprisingly, she answered. "Blessed be," she greeted them. "What are you doing here? I was just on my way out."

They quickly relayed the incredible events that had just taken place. Hilda was flabbergasted.

"We came to get some of your special soup," said Estelle.

Hilda waved her hand and removed a bubbling caldron from the fridge and handed it to Estelle.

Haley shook her head. "How do you do that?" she asked. Hilda smiled and winked. All three left for Norman's.

"Ike..." Mable said softly. "Have something to eat."

He sat up and acted as if he hadn't eaten in days, making a mess with his shaking. Hilda, Estelle, and Haley sat quietly as Mable cooed and fussed over her son. When he finished he had some of the color back in his face.

"Do you feel up to telling us what happened to you?" Norman asked, pulling a chair next to the sofa.

"I... don't know where to start," he replied.

His voice croaked and cracked like he hadn't spoken in some time. He cleared his throat and took another sip of tea.

He began by telling how he grew up with his grandparents on their potato farm in Bonners Ferry and how they died. He told how he had come into some money, although he didn't elaborate, and built his house, married and had two sons.

"I have grandsons?" Mable asked excitedly. "Norm did you hear that?" Without waiting for a response she continued to pummel Ike with questions.

Ike tried as best he could to answer, but soon he began to get frustrated trying to remember everything. He seemed to go into a fog every so often and there were periods of time where he couldn't recall anything.

Haley thought she'd ask him a couple questions and raised her hand. Everyone looked at her, waiting for her to speak.

"Ike, do you remember me?"

He nodded.

"Do you remember taking gems from here, back to our side?"

He hung his head and nodded again and looked up at her with a pleading expression. "We were so poor. I just did it so we could have better lives, but then I couldn't tell anybody about it. It wasn't until Grandpa and Grandma died that I did anything with them. Then it wasn't enough. I had to have more, so I came back, but I only found just a few loose stones. When I tried to come back the second time, I couldn't get in. Then I came across a diary that said there was a map, but I couldn't find it until I saw you and your brother at the post office. I saw the map he was hiding behind his back. Then when I went to your estate, she…" he said, motioning to Estelle, "told me you weren't there. You were out exploring or something."

He paused for a moment, taking a deep breath as he sorted it out.

"It was me chasing you on the snowmobile," he said, looking at Haley.

"I know," she answered.

"I followed you."

"What?" Haley was astonished. "We didn't see you."

"When you disappeared, I knew there was a portal there and I kept my eye on that spot and waited a few minutes before I went through. I was actually surprised I was able to enter since I couldn't see it."

"What happened to you then?" she asked.

"I followed you. I walked through the forest as you made your way to that pub, and watched you leave with that big fairy and go to that brick house. After that I don't remember anything except waking up in my horse corral with my pockets jammed with jewels. From then on things have been hazy."

"Do you remember how you came by your necklace?" she asked.

Ike's forehead creased as he thought about it. "No, all I can think of is feeling dark inside, lost."

"Did you just come from the estate?" Estelle asked.

"No, I have been hiding out here." He cocked his head a moment. "I remember… being by water and spinning, then…" A horrified look crossed his face. "I was in a swamp. Something was biting and tearing at me," he sobbed. "I think it was trying to kill me," he continued, trying to catch his breath. "It was a horrible, horrible creature. I fought it and dragged myself up the bank, but it was slippery and I kept sliding backward. It kept tearing at my legs until I kicked it in the face; that's how I got away," he shuddered.

"Heime," Haley replied.

"Yes," Estelle agreed.

"Heime?" Ike asked.

"The swamp hag," Haley said, rubbing her arms. "Heime was a traitorous fairy that was banished and cursed to live out her life as a hag. She has a portal in her swamp and is able to reach into the human side."

"You were lucky," said Hilda. "She eats human flesh."

Ike's eyes grew wide. He looked at his parents. "And what about you? You left when I was little. Grandpa and Grandma said you died in a fire."

"I remember the fire," said Mable sorrowfully. "Your dad and I had both been sick. You were in school at the time. Something woke me, I don't know what, but the house was filled with smoke. I woke your dad and we ran down the stairs and out the back door. The smoke was so thick we both collapsed not far from the house. I remember the wind was blowing so hard we were pelted with sticks and leaves and when we woke up we were here. We didn't know how we got here, and neither of us could remember anything. It wasn't until a few months ago I started having these dreams, nightmares really. Bits and pieces began to come to me. I mentioned it to Norman and he was having the same dreams. Together we pieced it all together," Mable sighed. "I'm sorry for not being there for you, Ike. It must have been so hard for you."

"I'm sorry too," Ike replied. "I haven't been a very good example for the boys or Judy." Ike looked miserable and defeated. "Now I've lost them because of my greed."

Everyone sat quietly.

"It's not too late," Haley said quietly. "It's never too late to make amends. When Judy finds out what's happened, you being under the influence of a powerful stone, she's bound to understand," she smiled.

"Do you really think so?" Ike asked hopefully.

"Sure. If she's any kind of decent human being, of course she will."

This seemed to cheer Ike up immensely. He looked at Haley, remorse on his face. "I'm so sorry for all the trouble I've caused. I'm not a bad person; I've just been very mixed up lately."

"Lately?" Haley grinned.

Ike grinned back and everyone smiled.

"Ales all around," said Norman with a clap. "Except for you two," he said looking at Ike and Haley, "hot chocolate or tea for you."

Estelle helped Mable get the drinks together and the group all raised their glasses in a toast.

"To new beginnings," said Norman.

Chapter 3
Ruena's Redemption

The atmosphere at Norman's and Mable's was one of celebration. The group relaxed and spoke of all their adventures. They sat in front of the fire, swapping stories and enjoying their first meal as a family again. Haley couldn't have been more delighted.

Outside the storm raged on as afternoon turned to evening.

Mable had made up a bed for Ike in the spare room and tucked him in as if he were eight years old again. He didn't seem to mind and looked as though he enjoyed it. She turned out the light and left the door ajar and joined the others by the fire.

Everyone seemed at a loss for words at first, sitting quietly, listening to the rain and the crackling fire. Ike's snores were a comfort to Mable.

"I can't believe it's him," she said, staring into the fire like she was somewhere else. "He looks so much like you Norman," she smiled at him.

Norman smiled back, tapping his pipe. He looked over at Haley. "Tell us... what happened to him? What's he like?"

"It's pretty much just like he said," Haley began. "Valian and Sersha said he had a good heart... at first, but it's as though he became consumed with the desire for wealth. It's not hard to get sucked in with the possibility of riches. They say money makes the world go round, but they also say the love of money is the root of all evil. I guess it's true. A lot of people in the world have more than they could possibly need yet some of them are miserable. They have everything they've ever wanted,

24

but somehow it's not enough. I don't think they desire more money, I believe some of those folks just feel empty inside, like they're searching for something."

"What?" Mable asked.

"Fulfillment, purpose and direction. I think perhaps some are looking for love and acceptance."

The others sat listening quietly as she went on. "I think so many things make love real. A connection between two people and compassion for others, that's what makes a person feel whole and fulfilled. It gives them joy in their hearts. That's love you can't buy no matter how much money you have."

Hilda and Estelle nodded and looked at Haley curiously.

"Those are wise words," said Hilda.

"It's just how I feel," said Haley. "That's what I think may have happened to Ike. He felt empty perhaps and thought he could buy things to fill that void. He became something he's not, deep down, obsessed. And that stone didn't do him any good either," she said in disgust. "Can I see it?" she asked.

Estelle pulled it out of her pocket, holding it up and away from her, like it was a stinking, putrid rag. The stone dangled and shone innocently in the firelight.

"What is it, this stone?" Norman asked.

"It's obsidian," Haley replied, taking the chain. "I don't know its properties, but it's bad."

She held it up to her eye and examined it closely. She saw nothing out of the ordinary, but she sensed it was cold, empty and controlling somehow.

"I don't think it's the stone in itself, but what's behind it. Maybe it's cursed."

She looked at the others.

"I saw this stone when we went on the hunt for Zeb. It covered the ground in Molock's realm. Jagged pieces of it stuck out of the ground everywhere."

"What is the name of this realm? Is it near here?" Mable asked in a whisper.

"I don't know the name, but it is a long way from here. Molock has obviously done something to the stone. He's put a spell on it or something so he can use it to control others. This needs to be destroyed, less some unsuspecting fairy or other creature pick it up."

"Who is this Molock?" Norman asked.

"I can't answer that because I honestly don't know. The only thing I know is what Sersha told me. It's an evil presence that has been here since the beginning I think. It's a being that wants control, to rule, to enslave, I don't know. The fairies have been searching for a way to defeat it for forever, and now supposedly it has an apprentice."

The room got quiet again.

Norman put another log on the fire, and Mable began to fidget nervously.

Hilda and Estelle exchanged glances. The mood had turned somber.

Haley could see this and she felt a sense of sadness. After several minutes she sighed.

"Listen everyone; we'll just have to find a way to defeat it. We'll band together. We will train up and go to war against this intruder. It doesn't belong here. We will cast it into the sea."

The others nodded in agreement. Their faces grew defiant and determined.

"Here, here," said Hilda, raising her cup, "to the downfall of Molock the Merciless."

The others joined her in the toast.

Haley grinned. "We're gonna kick his butt!"

"We should probably be getting back," said Estelle. "We need to get you home before Valian finds out and kicks *my butt*," she smiled.

"As soon as Ike is well enough, we'll need to get him back to the other side," Estelle said to Norman and Mable. "Fare thee well," she added giving everyone a hug.

Haley put her hat and rain jacket on. "I'm happy for you," she said, taking Mable's hands into her own. "Enjoy getting to know him," she smiled.

"I will," said Mable, "and thank you."

Estelle put on her hat and followed Haley to the door. "We'll see you in a few days," she said over her shoulder.

Haley opened the door and gasped in surprise.

Valian was standing there with his hand raised to knock. He wore a scolding look on his face. Haley flashed a half hearted, innocent smile up at him. Before she could speak, a smile began to take shape as he looked upon her. As he embraced her, she felt warm and safe in his arms.

"I've heard," he said. "I stopped in at the pub and they told me what happened."

"Amazing isn't it?" said Haley.

"I thought I told you..."

"You haven't heard the whole story," she interrupted.

"Prince Valian, do come in," said Norman, taking him by the arm and steering him over to the fire where he stood warming himself while the group told him all that had happened.

Valian shook his head in wonder. "I'm impressed," he said, giving Haley a look of admiration and respect. "You never cease to amaze me."

She looked at him questioningly.

"Taking that necklace from him was pure genius."

"I wouldn't go that far," she giggled.

"Let me have it," he said in a more serious tone. Haley pulled it from her pocket. He took the necklace and put it in the pocket of his tunic.

"I shall smite this stone and all it stands for," he said in earnest. "So, what else is new?" he asked changing the subject.

Haley and Estelle explained what happened back at the estate.

"Curious," Valian replied when they finished. "If it wasn't Ike, then who could it have been?"

Estelle and Haley shook their heads and shrugged.

"Hey, what about you?" Haley asked. "What's happening with Violet?"

"Not a thing," Valian answered with a sigh. "There has been no trace of her. It's like she vanished. The last thing we're sure of is she overpowered Theodore and Troy. How she managed that, I'll never know. Then she just disappeared."

"Estelle and I thought she may have met back up with Ike, but as you can see, he's here... wait a minute, wait a minute," Haley continued excitedly. "Maybe she did meet up with him."

"What do you mean?" Valian asked.

27

"Maybe she went back to Ike's after getting rid of Theodore and Troy, talked him into coming here and steered him into Heime's swamp to get rid of him."

Valian nodded. "That's possible. Is she really that far gone as to try and get someone killed, just so she can have her way?" He shook his head.

Haley thought for a moment. "Violet said something that night in Ike's shed when she captured Sersha and Henry, about not needing you anymore," she said, glancing at Valian.

"Sersha told me about it. She said Ike promised her riches. Maybe she decided she didn't need Ike either. She can go back and forth, bringing as many jewels to our side as she wants. You know what kind of value they hold…"

Valian shook his head.

Haley looked at his creased brow. "What?"

"She can't go back and forth."

"What do you mean, why not?"

"She can't see the portals on your side. She is not a Manwan. She can only see them from this side."

"You mean she's stuck there?" Haley began to laugh. "That just made my day."

Valian gave her a grin. "Now my sweet, where's your compassion?"

"I'm slightly lacking in that department just now, thank you," she smiled back. "You reap what you sow you know."

"What of her wings?" Hilda asked. "Can she shroud them?"

Valian's smile grew wide.

"No, only Manwans can bestow a shroud, and I don't believe my mother has given that honor to anyone but Haley and Henry."

"Ha!" said Haley. "The tables are turning. Fortune has smiled upon us. She's messed that up royally. Did we ever find out how she grew tentacles out of her forehead?"

Valian gave her a bemused look.

"I'm embellishing a little," she said rolling her eyes.

"As a matter of fact," said Hilda, "it was a love potion gone awry."

Haley gave Valian an innocent smile as if to say "see?"

"Where did she get a spell from?" Estelle asked.

"We don't know," Hilda answered.

"My guess is Maximillion," Valian replied.

Immediately a vision of Prince Sorcerer, Maximillion flashed across Haley's mind.

He was an extremely handsome witch who tried to steal her away from Valian and even went so far as to fight Valian for her.

She smiled as she remembered shooting Maximillion with cupid's arrow, which stopped the fight and allowed them to escape.

A look of shock passed between Hilda and Estelle.

"The sorcerer?" said Estelle. "Why would he…"

"He's been after Haley ever since they met," Valian interrupted.

Haley blushed slightly. "How did you come to that conclusion," she asked.

"I felt it," he answered. "I felt his… longing for you at the secret witches' council meeting and again on the island when we were searching for Mother. He is enamored with you."

Queen Lilia's disappearance from the palace amidst all the chaos of emotions the fairies were experiencing had been extremely stressful, and still they were no closer to finding her or her guardians. The trip to the islands held no clue as to her whereabouts.

Haley gave him a look of shock.

"Let's face it, you are captivating," he smiled, "but you're mine."

Haley's heart gave a little flutter as she looked up at him. He was beaming.

"We would be hard pressed to prove it though," he continued. "I can't see Violet ever confessing to seeking out another species magic. It would make her look bad and incompetent, not to mention embarrassed by the way she apparently flubbed it all up."

Haley laughed. "She sure did! Oh, sorry," she said looking at the others, "couldn't help it." She cleared her throat. "So what's the plan?"

"Well, I'm thinking it may have been Violet who broke into your estate. Who else could it have been? No, I think we'll let Violet stew on your side for awhile."

"Yes, but I don't want her in my house," Haley said with disdain.

"We'll set a trap for her," said Valian with a growing smile. "And once she's been captured, she will be escorted to our side personally by me, and will be brought before the Lords and Ladies of the high court and tried for her actions."

Haley nodded in agreement.

"Shh," Hilda whispered. Everyone looked at her. "Listen!"

Everyone was quiet, straining their ears to hear.

A mournful wail was barely audible.

"How did you hear that?" Haley whispered.

Hilda didn't reply.

It came again far off in the distance.

Goosebumps began to creep up Haley's arms even though she recognized the sound.

"It's Ruena," she said, remembering the day the wailing willow showed up just outside the estate claiming to be Heime the swamp hags sister and cursed to live out her life as a willow tree.

She was searching for Henry and Haley to offer her help in finding Princess Sersha. She turned out to be instrumental in capturing Ike as he and Violet tried to discover a way back into the fairy world.

"We need to take her before the Lords and Ladies," said Valian. "She went out of her way to help us and has proved her loyalty. Let's do it now so we can concentrate on other matters."

Valian and Haley bid everyone goodbye. "We'll be back later," said Valian.

They left the apartment and headed up the foggy street. It was just drizzling now and growing darker. By the time they met up with Ruena, they were drenched.

Ruena greeted them with a sorrowful wail as she bent low in a bow.

Valian wasted no time.

"Come, Ruena, we shall go before the royal court now." He waved his hand in front of her and she was zapped so small, she was barely visible. Her wailing was just a squeak, and Haley smiled at how cute she was.

Valian picked her up and held her in the palm of his hand as they took flight. They changed size as soon as they disappeared over the canopy of the forest and arrived at the beautiful palace above the trees minutes later and went into the dining hall.

The fires were blazing and warm and several guardians stood warming themselves and quickly stood at attention.

"Summon the Lords and Ladies at once," said Valian, placing Ruena on a table top.

She shuddered as she let out another wail, throwing water from her tiny dripping branches.

It didn't take long for the Lords and Ladies of the court to arrive. Some were dressed in their pajamas, scratching their heads at this unexpected summons. As soon as everyone was present, they sat staring curiously at the minute willow in the middle of the table.

"I call this meeting to order," said Valian as he toweled off.

He quickly relayed the events of Ruena's aid during the rescue of the princess, and how she captured Ike as he tried to flee.

The Lords and Ladies were impressed with her actions.

"I propose Ruena to be restored to fairy kind and take her rightful place again. Agreed?"

There were nods of approval from everyone.

"So shall it be," said Valian turning to Ruena. He gently picked her up and placed her on the floor.

"Everyone… now."

The entire court waved their hands at her.

Haley watched in awe as Ruena began to transform.

Her long willow branches began to rise and became long auburn hair. Her limbs began to take shape. Legs and arms formed, and two beautiful wings began to unfold. It was the most amazing thing Haley had ever seen.

The bark on her trunk changed into a long, brown, flowing gown. Several of her willow branches looped themselves around the outline of her wings and shined emerald green with off white speckles.

She had beautiful rosy cheeks and extremely long dark lashes. Her eyes looked like doe's eyes, large, brown and shining.

As everyone looked on, tears rolled down her face. When she opened her mouth to speak, a mournful wail came out at first and gradually became a voice, high and soft.

She stood there trembling before them and slowly rose to the same height as everyone else.

She bent down on one knee before the court. "Thank you," she said between sobs. "I am in your debt."

"Welcome back," said Valian putting his hand on her shoulder.

"Thank you Your Highness," she answered still trembling.

Her hair was all wet from the rain and she shivered.

"Come by the fire," said Haley taking Ruena's arm.

All the room applauded. Everyone had to reach out and touch her in welcome as she walked by. She was all smiles as she passed through the crowd.

Haley pulled a couple chairs by the fire and sat down next to her.

"Thank you all for coming," said Valian dismissing the court.

The group left in twos and threes, back out into the dreary evening.

"Thank you, Milady," Ruena said looking into Haley's face as if she'd just made a new best friend. "I'm so happy to be free."

Haley smiled softly.

"I am glad to meet the real you," she said.

"My sister..." Ruena began.

"Your sister will stay where she is I'm afraid," said Valian sternly, but compassionately.

"I know... I must go to her."

"Why?" Haley asked.

"She is dying," she wept softly.

"Dying?" Haley whispered.

"She has been injured somehow. I don't think she has much time left."

"I'm sorry, Ruena," Haley said sadly.

Valian stood listening.

Haley could tell his heart was heavy. She could see it in his eyes. He looked like someone had let all the air out of his tires.

He sighed.

"Would you like us to come with you?" Haley asked.

"I would appreciate that," she answered. "But we need to go now if possible," she said in a pleading voice.

Haley nodded and looked up at Valian, searching his face. He nodded his head.

"Let's get you some dry clothes and we'll leave." Haley took her to her room and gave her one of her own gowns to wear. They put on warm, long sleeved cloaks, pulled up their hoods, and met up with Valian in the dining hall.

The trip to the swamp was cold, wet and miserable.

They flew under the canopy as much as possible to avoid the rain. It began thundering as they arrived.

The water in the swamp was still except for the large raindrops sending ripples across the surface. The dragonflies and water bugs were gone. The scene seemed peaceful and innocent.

They landed on the bank and scanned the area for any sign of Heime.

Ruena seemed desperate as she trudged along, hovering briefly and touching back down like a bird flitting from flower to flower.

She suddenly shot across to the other side of the swamp.

There Heime lay on the bank, half in and half out of the water. Valian and Haley landed beside her and looked down upon the wretched creature. Her hair hung in matted wet strings across her face, which had been caved in on the left side.

Haley realized that must have been where Ike had kicked her.

Her mouth was half open, revealing sharp little teeth. There were gray gaps where she had lost most of them. She almost looked like a dead animal lying there, half decayed.

Haley was sure they were too late, but Heime's chest rose slightly.

"Heime," said Ruena desperately.

Heime's eyes fluttered momentarily.

"Heime," she said again.

Heime opened her eyes slightly. They were unfocused at first then slowly her sight became clearer.

She looked up at Ruena and made an attempt at a smile.

"Oh, Heime," Ruena said sadly as tears streamed down her cheeks.

Heime let out a moan as she tried to move and made gurgling noises, her eyes becoming watery.

Haley could tell she was weeping.

As she coughed, blood began to ooze from the corner of her gaping mouth, her voice croaking as she tried to speak.

"I... m... so... sorry... Rue... Ruena. You... did... didn't deserve... any of this...you weren't guilty."

"I am sorry too," Ruena cried, "I am so sorry. I love you Heime..."

Heime took a final breath and her eyes went blank.

Ruena bent over, wrapped her arms around her sister's frame and sobbed.

Moments later Heime began to transform. What was once a hideous and grotesque creature now became the silhouette of what she used to be.

Heime looked much like her sister, rosy cheeked, with long, beautiful red hair and glorious wings. She looked peaceful lying there, but was just an empty shell.

Valian and Haley stood, their arms looped around each other, standing in the cold drizzle, silently watching Ruena in her grief and despair.

"I'm so sorry, Ruena," Haley said softly.

"At least I got the chance to see her before she was gone," said Ruena as she lovingly smoothed Heime's hair from her face.

"It is a sad day," said Valian, "my condolences to you, Ruena."

"Thank you, Prince Valian. I know she did wrong deceiving the queen, trying to gain power, and I don't blame the queen for her punishment. I just wish she would have seen the error of her ways and not gone downhill."

"I think she did see it," said Haley, "in the end. Now she can rest in peace."

Ruena walked a short distance away and rolled a dead log over, retrieving a long, green, rolled up, leathery looking thing, and brought it back to her sister's lifeless body.

Seeing Valian's and Haley's puzzled looks, she explained. "This is a wide leafed Campion. It is said, if you wrap the dead in its leaves, and bind the head and feet of the body with the bark, in a certain bow before burial, the dead will be reincarnated. Can you help roll her over?"

Valian and Haley gently turned Heime so Ruena could roll her in the long leaves, and watched her carefully tie the bark around her head and feet. She stood, looking down at her sister and whispered goodbye waving her hand over her. Heime slowly sank into the ground and became one with the earth.

She turned toward Valian and Haley. "Let's leave this place," she whispered.

The flight back was somber and quiet. When they reached the palace, Valian had a room prepared for Ruena and after a quick bite to eat, she retired for the evening.

Valian and Haley went to the blue room. Valian sat down on one of the sofas and was quiet for quite awhile. Finally he spoke. "I believe that Ruena was innocent," he said sighing. "Heime on the other hand… I feel something, like empty inside."

"That," said Haley, taking him by the hand, "is sorrow."

"I don't like it," he said, his forehead creased, a small frown on his face.

"It'll pass," she said softly. "It's a normal thing to feel grief at the loss of someone, even someone that has gone astray. It is even harder when it's someone you love. Unfortunately death is something that will happen to us all, eventually."

"I know," said Valian shaking his head.

"You know the best way to deal with this is to remember the good times and the joy you once shared. Celebrate the things that made the person special."

Valian gave her a sad look. "I never shared any joyous moments with Heime, I barely knew her when she and Ruena served at the palace."

"You can share Ruena's wonderful memories of better times. They don't have to be your own."

Valian smiled half heartedly. "Thank you, my sweet. I'm glad you're here to help me through this maze of feelings. And it's not only Ruena and Heime that troubles me, it's the disappearance of my mother and Violet's treachery, guardians going bad, deserting their duties and taking part in this, this… I don't know what to call it."

"I know it's overwhelming, but think of the good that has been achieved. Ike is free from the obsidian stone and reunited with his parents. Ruena got to see her sister before she passed. Good things have happened and they always outweigh the bad. They have to, that's what keeps us going. Come on; let's get a good night's sleep. Things will be a little better by the light of day."

35

Valian kissed her hand. "What about Hilda and the others?"

"They'll understand. We'll see them in the morning and explain what happened."

They said goodnight and went to their rooms.

As Haley lay on the bed, everything that happened that day played through her mind like she was watching a movie. So much occurred in such a short period of time it was almost overwhelming to her, too.

She wondered how poor Ruena would be able to carry on without her sister, what Heime might come back as, what would happen to Ike and his family, and who in the world had entered her home.

She thought about Violet and what she may be capable of, and most of all, she wondered what had happened to Queen Lilia. Haley was also worried about the identity of the new apprentice the witches had discovered supposedly working for Molock.

All her jumbled thoughts were giving her a headache, and she found it difficult to sleep. Eventually she drifted off, but spent a restless night tossing and turning.

Chapter 4
A Visit to the Infirmary

By morning Haley woke up exhausted. She wished she could take the advice she'd given Valian. Things didn't look better by the light of day. She felt under the weather and didn't want to get out of bed and drifted back to sleep.

The next thing she knew, she woke up in a room she didn't recognize. She tried to sit up, but her back ached terribly.

She looked around the room. Nothing was familiar, but she had a strange feeling she'd been there before.

She lay there for what seemed like hours but was actually only about a half hour. Then the door to her room opened and a very chubby fairy with black hair waddled into the room.

"Good morning Milady. It's good to see you awake."

"Where am I?" Haley asked.

"You're at the infirmary. You were totally out of it when they brought you in, but you're doing much better now."

"Who brought me here and what's wrong with me, and why does my back hurt so much?"

"Prince Valian and a couple guardians brought you here yesterday. You had a high fever according to Doctor Gretta and you lost your wings. That's why your back hurts."

"I lost my wings?" Haley exclaimed, trying to feel behind her back, but the pain was almost excruciating.

"Yes, if you don't take the elixir on a regular basis, you lose your wings, but not to worry, Milady. Prince Valian will remedy that when he arrives," she said fluffing Haley's pillow. "He would have taken care of it yesterday, but you had that high fever, and of course you can't take the elixir if you're asleep."

Haley sighed. "Does everyone have the same reaction?"

"No, that's just how it affects humans."

"Did the prince say when he'd be here?" Haley asked.

"Well, he mentioned something about someone named Henry, which made no sense to me, and he would be back later this afternoon."

"Henry," she whispered. "Valian must have been worried about Henry losing his wings," she thought to herself.

"Here, have something to eat," said the nurse pulling in a small cart on wheels from the hallway, and rolling it up to the bed.

She placed a tray across Haley's lap. It contained something which looked like chicken soup, crackers, cooked carrots, and applesauce. She scowled at the meal and gave the nurse half a smile.

"I'm Geri by the way. Is everything all right?" she asked seeing the look on Haley's face.

"It's nice to meet you, Geri. It's just I could really go for a cheeseburger and fries."

"Milady?"

"Never mind," she said with a sigh, picking up her spoon.

"If you need anything, just rap the stone and I'll be here in a jiffy," Geri instructed turning to leave.

Haley spotted the stone on her bedside table. It looked very similar to the stone broom Hilda had given them before their little excursion to the Islands, to summon help if they ran into trouble. She ate most of her soup and one of the crackers. "Hospital food," she grumbled. "No better here than our side."

Her eyes grew heavy and she fell asleep without touching the rest of her food. An hour later Valian stood beside her bed, looking down on her as she slept. Alongside him were Henry, and her parents, Carol, and Paul.

Valian gently picked up her hand and held it to his heart. She stirred and opened her eyes. She gazed into his pale blue, loving eyes and smiled happily.

"Hello, my sweet," he grinned. "How are you feeling?"

"I've been better, but not too bad. My back is killing me though."

She looked at her family gathered around her. "You're here!" she exclaimed. "Oh, my goodness, you have wings! I'm so glad, but I wish I could have been there when you went through the portal. I would love to have seen your faces."

"It was great," said Henry grinning. "You should have heard mom shrieking."

"I didn't shriek," said Carol with a wide smile. "I was just expressing my joy." Paul laughed and Carol turned red.

"Isn't this place fabulous?" Haley asked excitedly.

"It's a wonder," Carol replied. "It's so fresh and clean here."

"Let me see your wings," asked Haley, her eyes shining brightly. Carol and Paul turned so she could get a good look. "Oh, how beautiful you look," she said running her hand down Carol's wing. "And that gown looks wonderful on you."

Carol grinned. "Oh, my goodness, Haley, what an experience, taking the elixir and growing these. They feel just like a part of my body. I can feel it when I touch them! And the dwindle drops that let you change size…"

"Now that was a trip," said Paul.

"They were like kids in a candy store," Henry laughed. "You should have seen them learning to fly!"

"Oh, I wish I could have been there," said Haley with a sigh.

Just then Geri came in with Dr. Gretta. Everyone stepped aside as she checked Haley for fever.

"Well, Milady, there's no fever. You should be fine to take the elixir," Dr. Gretta pronounced, glancing at Valian.

Valian pulled out a familiar small stein. "Can you sit up?" he asked.

With the help of Paul and Valian, she was able to sit up just enough. She grimaced at the smell and drank the liquid quickly.

Immediately her back became warm as the elixir traveled through her body.

Her parents stood wide eyed as the small humps on her back produced little protrusions that slowly grew, wet, sticky, and deformed looking. Carol's mouth hung open in amazement as Haley's wings got bigger. Beads of sweat formed on Haley's face and she bent forward, taking in deep breaths, trying to get rid of her light headedness.

The process only took a couple of minutes and Valian began to examine her wings as soon as they unfolded. "Good as new," he smiled, standing back satisfied.

"Wow," said Haley. "My backache is gone!" She bent forward and backward without pain.

"Now you just sit there quietly while they dry and harden," said Dr. Gretta. "As soon as you're ready, you can leave." She turned and left the room with Geri behind her.

"Can you stand?" Valian asked holding his arm out for support.

"I think so," she replied.

"That was the neatest thing I've ever seen," said Carol.

"Isn't this place cool Mom?" Haley asked. "I can't wait to show you all around Roan and the outskirts."

"Oh, by the way," said Carol. "While we were shopping, Henry mentioned that you wanted to buy two baby dolls that could walk and talk. He wouldn't say why, but I bought them anyway. It wasn't until after Valian arrived, I mean the prince... Prince Valian," she corrected herself.

"Valian, please," said Valian, looking at Carol affectionately.

"Valian," she said blushing with embarrassment. "Yes, Henry told me then why you wanted them, so... I brought them with us."

"Outstanding," said Haley enthused. "I can't wait to see their faces!"

"Whose faces?" Paul asked completely out of the loop.

"Zeb and Sarah Bonner's little girls. I told them about dolls that could walk and talk and promised I would bring them one when I came back to visit. Susan and Rosie will be thrilled I'm sure."

"Oh yeah, I forgot about the girls," her father said, embarrassed.

"Well, let's get you out of here," said Valian helping her stand. "We're all going to Hilda's for lunch."

"Oh, wait until you see Hilda's place," said Haley. "She lives in the outskirts. Where is Estelle?" she asked.

"She's at Hilda's, cooking," said Henry rubbing his stomach with a big grin.

Haley laughed and rolled her eyes. "Some things never change."

"The Bonner's have been invited… and the Seers family," said Valian.

Haley gave him a look that plainly said, "I love you," as she took her first steps. "I'm feeling better already," she sighed.

Valian handed her a warm wrap to wear. While Carol helped her into it she began thinking about Ruena. "How is Ruena doing?" she asked.

"She's gone on retreat to Julius's place," Valian answered.

"Good. That's just what she needs."

They left the infirmary flying single file through the continuous rain, Henry bringing up the rear. Valian called for everyone to change. Five flashes of spark briefly lit up their surroundings like little firecrackers, and they all grew.

They landed in the outskirts and walked down the main street. Haley pointed out all the familiar spots excitedly. Minutes later they were in Hilda's kitchen where everyone was talking at once. It was like a family reunion. They all gathered together reminiscing, busying themselves preparing food. Introductions were made to broom Hilda and she made Haley's parents feel welcome with her hugs.

Estelle got a loving, knowing glance from Carol. They discussed the secret Estelle kept so well for centuries, being the caretaker of the estate for almost two hundred years with no one the wiser.

Henry took Paul into the living area and made a fire. Paul couldn't get over the tiny flame fairies as they leapt and danced among the flames.

The sound of the gargoyle knocker announced the Bonner's arrival. As soon as Susan and Rosie spotted Haley, they squealed with delight, rushing over, almost tackling her. They climbed all over her and she was elated.

Hilda introduced Paul and Carol to Zeb and Sarah. The four had been looking forward to meeting. Hugs were abundant among the women. Zeb and Paul shook hands as though they knew each other already and immediately began discussing the old homestead and all the changes.

Carol couldn't get over the resemblance between Sarah and Haley. "Oh my goodness, it's uncanny," she remarked wide eyed. "You could be identical twins."

"See, I was right," said Estelle grinning. "I knew Haley would be the key to everything."

Hilda began passing out smoking mugs to everyone. "This is one of my special brews," she commented as she handed one to each. "It has a punch and will warm you right up."

"Umm," said Carol as she took a drink. "Cold. It's very refreshing. I can't quite figure out the flavor." She took another sip. "What is this? It's wonderful." Hilda just gave her a wink as she passed by and went into the living area to serve the men.

The gargoyle sounded again. "I'll get it!" Haley called out Norman, Mable, and Ike stood dripping and shivering at the door. Haley smiled widely. "Come in, come in," she said grabbing Mable's arm.

"Welcome," said Hilda warmly. "Come in by the fire," she said, ushering them into the room. Hilda left momentarily and returned with three more mugs.

Haley was all smiles and gave Norman and Mable a hug. When she turned to Ike, his head was down slightly as if embarrassed. She took his hand in hers. "Welcome," she said giving it a squeeze. "It's good to see you looking better."

"Thank you," he replied. "I'm sorry about..."

"There's no need," Haley interrupted. "That's past now." Ike looked at her in amazement. "Thank you."

"Everyone slips up now and then, I'm just glad you got through it all right. And now look," she said motioning to Norman and Mable, "you have your family back. What a wonderful gift."

"Yes," said Ike, "I never would have believed it."

"How do you feel?"

"Like a great weight has been lifted from my heart."

Haley gave him a huge smile. "Not many people get the chance to start over. I'm so glad for you."

Valian sat on one of the sofas watching his beloved. He had a look of complete satisfaction on his face. Haley looked over at him, her eyes shining. He got up and walked over. "It's nice to see you looking so much better," he said shaking Ike's hand.

He turned to Haley and kissed her hand. "You're amazing. Wisen seems to suit you, Ike," he continued.

"Thank you Prince Valian. It is nice to have a clear head. I must say, I think I was in a pretty bad way and I'm lucky for the way things turned out. Something had a hold on me…" he said, lowering his voice, "besides being greedy, something dark and sinister."

Valian motioned Ike to the other side of the room and sat down. "I think it may have been Molock," said Valian quietly.

"Molock?" Ike asked.

Valian briefly explained the presence of the evil being living in a realm far off from Roan. How it tormented those that happened to wander into its territory, and the grip it had had on Zeb. "We've been looking for a way to defeat it for centuries, now we have found out it has an apprentice. We don't know who, but we've got to find a way to stop it from doing any more damage or becoming more powerful."

While Valian and Ike talked in low tones, the rest of the household was busy laughing and talking in the kitchen. Carol sat at a small butcher block table making a salad and watching Hilda and Estelle in amazement as they pointed and directed. Hilda made it clear she was proud to have made a roast the "old fashioned way", by baking it in the oven.

Haley giggled at that statement and sat down by her mother. They fanned their wings as they cut up tomatoes and shredded the lettuce. "I can't believe this place, or them," said Carol watching the activity around them.

"I know," said Haley grinning.

Henry was busy getting in between Hilda and Estelle, stealing bites of whatever he could get his hands on while Susan and Rosie continued to get under foot.

Haley glanced at her mother excitedly. "Where are the baby dolls?"

"Oh, I forgot about that. They are in a bag by the front door."

Haley jumped up and retrieved the bag. "Girls, I have something for you," she called.

Susan and Rosie hurried over. Their eyes grew wide as she pulled the baby dolls from the bag. For the first time since she met them they were speechless and carefully took the dolls into their arms. It was like watching two kids trying to carry a spoonful of water without spilling it.

They went into the living room cradling their babies in their arms like treasures.

Sarah walked over and put her arm around Haley. "Thank you. They've been asking about those baby dolls ever since you mentioned them."

"You're welcome. Actually my mother picked them up." Sarah went over to thank Carol while Haley joined the girls.

The dolls couldn't walk but came with baby bottles.

Haley showed them how they cried until you put the bottles in their mouths. They were elated and sat playing quietly until it was time to eat.

Hilda looked around her large kitchen and shook her head. "Tsk, tsk, tsk. This won't do," she said.

Everyone in the kitchen looked on as Hilda raised both hands and pushed as if pushing on an invisible wall and watched the kitchen grow in size by twenty feet. Carol's mouth dropped open as Estelle pointed at the kitchen table and waved her arm, drawing an invisible line. The table also grew in length with enough room for everyone to be comfortably seated.

The sister witches then began pointing here and there. Magically, dishes and silverware began coming out of their cupboards and drawers. Placemats, napkins and candles flew through the air and landed in front of each chair.

"There. That looks great," said Hilda satisfied.

"All right everyone, time to eat!" Estelle called.

Lunch was wonderful. Conversation and laughter dominated the meal. After everyone had their fill and left the table for the living room. Hilda clapped her hands and told the dishes to clean themselves. As she joined the others, the kitchen buzzed with activity as instructed.

The girls played with their dolls while the others began a more serious discussion about the strange weather, Molock's apprentice, Violet, and the missing queen.

As the afternoon wore on they were no closer to finding any answers. The girls became restless so Zeb and Sarah decided to get them home, but promised to visit the Miles' estate, and attend the autumn festival.

Ike talked Norman and Mable into coming to his place on the other side to meet Judy and the boys. They left Ike at Hilda's and went home themselves.

The rest of the group sat comfortably by the fire.

"I've been thinking," said Valian to the others. "If indeed it was Molock that had such a powerful hold on Ike… that might work out to our advantage."

"How so?" Haley asked.

"Molock doesn't know Ike's current condition. He probably thinks Ike is still under his control. We may be able to use him to get the upper hand, gain some insight into what he is up to."

"I don't know," said Haley, frowning. "Do you think he is up to something like that? He may be too vulnerable so soon…"

"No," Ike interrupted. "He almost destroyed my life, in more ways than one. I want to help. Get some of my self respect back, redeem myself so to speak."

Haley studied Ike's face. "Are you sure?" she asked.

"Absolutely," he answered.

"I'm sure an opportunity will present itself," said Valian. "If we could fool him into thinking you still belong to him maybe we will discover who this apprentice is. As far as Violet is concerned, I believe she is stuck on your side. She can't get into much trouble there. She sticks out like a sore thumb. She doesn't dare show herself to anyone and she knows it. I think we'll let her stew for awhile and bring her back later. Right now let's concentrate on this apprentice and finding my mother."

"I think we should re-visit Reed's room and the sphere chamber," said Henry.

"That's a good idea," Haley agreed. "Reed is a brownie," Haley explained. "Reed may have had the queen's confidence, but as her personal servant, he was something less than desired. I have always been suspicious of him, and since he disappeared right along with her, he has to be involved."

"I can't wait to visit the palace," said Carol.

"You'll love it," said Haley beaming. "That's where Valian and I will be married."

Carol sighed. "I'm having a hard time getting used to the idea." Haley looked at her mother worriedly.

Carol re-assured her. "Don't worry, honey. I couldn't have picked a better son-in-law, it's just… you've grown up so much, and what will I do without my Haley around?" she fretted.

"Oh, Mother," Haley said wrapping her arms around her. "We had to grow up eventually besides, you'll have me for three more years and you'll probably be glad to be finally rid of me."

"Never," said Carol with a tender smile.

"All right, you two," said Paul seeing the tears starting to well. "Enough with the water works."

"Is everybody ready to go?" Valian asked. Everyone put on their jackets, hoods and cloaks and left Hilda and Estelle sitting by the fire while Ike went back to his parent's apartment.

As they flew through the cold rain, everyone changed size, flitting from tree to tree, dodging the raindrops. Haley pointed out the little shops in the nooks and crannies of the forest. Carol was in seventh heaven and was just as delighted as Haley had been when she first visited. They landed in the courtyard and quickly went inside.

The guardians were at their usual posts and provided everyone with towels. The group went to the fires in the dining hall. As they warmed themselves Haley asked where Sersha was.

"She is on her way back," Valian answered. "She, Theodore and Troy were on the hunt for Violet, but I sent word she was on your side."

"I hope she gets here soon," said Haley.

Carol and Paul were impressed at the grandeur of the palace. Haley could tell it as they scanned the room. Carol's face was lit up like a Christmas tree. Valian led the way once again to Reed's quarters. It was the same sorry mess as when they last saw it. They searched high and low but found no new clues, and when they checked the sacred chamber, the results were the same.

Valian explained to Paul and Carol that the sacred sphere which was the source of all their knowledge, had been stolen right before the queen went missing.

"The sphere is a large glass ball full of moving color," Haley added. "It is just beautiful. The fairies can look into it and see the past and the future and… it is a time piece, able to go backward and forward in time. That's how we were able to save Sarah and the girls from the clutches of the swamp hag and prevent them from being taken hostage by the moss trolls."

"Sorry, we left out a few details when we first met," Valian apologized at the look on Carol's face. Valian was frustrated and called for a break. They went to the blue room to rest.

A new brownie came in with refreshments. Haley took a liking to him right away. She thought he was very cute. His head was shaped like a Hershey's kiss and he wore a pointed little hat. His brown ears were unusually large and stuck out from the sides of his head. They looked soft and velvety, like a deer's ears. He had a button nose, a very long skinny neck and his mouth was wide, taking up most of the lower half of his face.

His name was Jack and he stood tall and proud, only coming up to Haley's knees in height. He bowed to each person as he served them. He seemed honored to have been chosen for the job of serving the prince and wore a satisfied smile. Haley just wanted to pick him up and hug him but felt that would be inappropriate.

"Jack is Reed's little brother," said Valian, taking a tart from the tray.

"It is very nice to meet you, Jack," said Haley giving him a warm smile.

"Thank you, Milady, the pleasure is mine," he responded blushing, his face turning a darker shade of brown, if you could call that blushing.

"Tell me, Jack, when was the last time you saw Reed?" she asked nonchalantly.

"Not long, Milady."

Haley raised an eyebrow. "Do you know what he was doing; I mean was he acting strangely in any way?"

"No, Milady. He was preparing for an assignment by order of Queen Lilia. He was in a hurry and said it was an assignment of special significance. He was stressed he hadn't had more time to prepare. You know Reed; everything has to be planned out and just right. He didn't leave in the best of moods, I'm afraid."

Valian, Haley, and Henry exchanged surprised looks. "Where did he go, Jack?" Valian asked as calmly as he could.

Brownies had the tendency to break down in fear and clam up if they sensed they were in any way in the wrong or in trouble, and being questioned about anything had to be done delicately.

"He accompanied Queen Lilia on retreat, like you said."

"Y… yes, of course," said Valian with a positively speechless look. Haley quickly jumped in. "We know she was going on retreat," she said carefully choosing her words, "but we didn't actually meet up with her, we decided to go on separate retreats. She requested that she spend some time by herself, with Reed of course."

Jack didn't seem to catch her deception. "She went to the Palm realm by herself?" he asked. "That's odd isn't it?"

"Not really," Valian answered quickly. "She wanted time alone to reflect, without anyone to distract her from thinking and meditation. You know the queen; what she wants, she gets."

"As it should be," said Jack smiling proudly again.

Haley glanced at Valian.

"You know, she told us she was going to the Palm realm, but forgot to tell us where. Did she happen to mention it to you, or maybe you heard it in passing?"

"The Tempest Region," he answered, matter-of-factly, as if it was common knowledge.

"Wonderful," said Haley. "I hear it's a beautiful place. Julius Caesar sends his artists there for retreat."

"Ah, Julius, a fine fairy with square, purple spectacles. He is a great artist that does portraits for the fairies I'm told and has a wonderful sanctuary not far from here. I would like to go there someday," he said with a slight frown. "As soon as I've served long enough, maybe I will earn the opportunity and time to go."

"I'm sure you will," said Haley hardly able to contain her excitement.

She sat and fidgeted until Jack was finished and left the room. "Do you think it's true?" she asked as soon as he had gone.

"I don't know," Valian answered. "This is highly irregular. The queen has never done anything like this before. I know my mother, it just doesn't make sense. She always keeps us informed of her plans and schedule." Valian sat thinking quietly.

"This place is just marvelous," said Carol getting up and walking around the room, looking at the stunning décor. She gasped quietly when she spotted all the gem-filled glass bowls on the pedestal tables.

"So this is what all the fuss is about," she said. "I can understand Violet's interest and Ike's too, for that matter. This would be a temptation for anyone lacking in self restraint."

Haley looked toward her mother and at the gems. An idea began to form in her brain. Her smile grew and she looked at Valian. "I know how to catch Violet," she said triumphantly.

Valian turned toward her. "I know that look," he said smiling back. "What are you thinking?"

"Violet would love to get her hands on these gems," she said motioning to the glass bowls. "If we took a load of gems back to our side... like we plan on using them to gain riches like Ike did, it'll throw her into a tizzy. She'll be so jealous that we're doing it and not her..." Haley paused, running her plan through her mind.

"That's a dangerous idea," Valian replied. "How is she going to know about it if we don't know where she is?"

"I don't know, I haven't thought that far ahead yet."

"You keep thinking on that, in the meantime we must check out the Tempest Region. I've got to know if my mother is all right. We'll stay here tonight and set off first thing in the morning."

He reached into his tunic and pulled out one of those smooth stones and rapped it once on the table.

Jack entered moments later. "How may I be of service?" he asked bowing to the prince.

"Could you prepare a room for Haley's parents, and we are going to need fresh supplies. We will be leaving in the morning to check on the queen."

"If you don't mind my suggesting it sir, can't you just check the sacred sphere?"

"The sphere disappeared just before the queen left on retreat. Didn't you hear her tell everyone?"

"No sir, Prince Valian, not disappeared, the queen had it moved." The looks of shock on everyone's face made Jack take a step backward. "You mean she didn't tell you?" he almost wailed. As Valian shook his head, Jack became extremely upset.

"I wasn't supposed to tell you?" he cried burying his head in his arms, sobbing. His ears drooped as he chastised himself for making a mistake. Haley went to him and tried to console him but he wouldn't be comforted.

It wasn't until Valian spoke, that Jack looked up, a mixture of sorrow and fear on his face. Valian spoke softly but with authority. "There was no mistake Jack."

"Sir?" he half squeaked.

"The queen told you because she knew she could trust you."

"I don't understand, sir."

"You haven't told anyone else, right?"

"No sir."

"She knew that you would only tell me if I asked you about it. You passed the test."

Jack sniffed and wiped his little nose on the back of his hand. "Is that right sir, truly?"

"Absolutely."

"Yes, but you didn't ask me about it, I just blurted it out like a fool." Jacks eyes started to fill with tears again.

"Not exactly," said Haley, glancing at Valian. "We led you into mentioning the sphere." Jack looked at her confused. "We told you about checking on the queen, and you only did what you should have done, saving us from an unnecessary trip. You were only showing your loyalty."

"Oh," said Jack, his face lighting up. "I did, didn't I?"

"Yes, Jack," said Valian. "You are a humble and obedient servant, and you shall be rewarded."

Jack's eyes grew wide in surprise and anticipation.

"I hereby promote you to second in command, just under Reed." Valian pulled out his sword and laid it across each of Jacks shoulders. Jack bowed low, thanking the prince. He was beside himself.

Haley let out a quiet sigh, thankful they avoided another potential problem.

"Ok, Jack, as a token of our appreciation you will be assigned new quarters down the hall from the queen," said Valian.

Jack was all smiles and gave a couple joyous little hops.

"Your first order of business will be to take us to the new location of the sphere so we can look in on the queen. After that you are dismissed for the rest of the evening."

Jack was totally jazzed by this, but looked over at the dirty, half empty tray and mugs.

"Leave that for your replacement."

Jack bowed then held his head high as he led the group from the blue room. They followed him down the hall to the corridor full of doors. He went past the room the sphere used to be in and went to the last door on the left. He turned the knob and stepped aside for the prince. Valian pushed the door open and went inside.

Sure enough, there sat the sphere in all its exquisite glory; a six foot wide glass ball, alive with movement on the inside. Pale pastel colors swirled and tumbled over each other randomly. Carol and Paul stood mesmerized by its beauty.

Valian nodded and turned to Jack. "Did the queen tell anyone else that the sphere is here and in a new location?"

"Not that I'm aware of. I am the only one left to look after it until her return."

"Thank you, Sir Jack, you may leave us now," said Valian, turning back to the sphere.

Jack left the group for his new quarters with a spring in his step.

As soon as he was gone, Valian shut the door. "I can't believe this," he said exasperated. "Why would my mother do this, have it moved and not tell me or Sersha? And why would she just disappear like that? She would have had to have known how we would react."

Haley thought for a moment. "Maybe that was her purpose."

Valian turned to her. "Why would she do such a thing?"

"Maybe she wanted to see how you would react. Maybe it was a test on *you* and Sersha and the rest of us for that matter... to see how we would handle things. Perhaps she was seeing if we had problem solving skills and was testing how you would rule in her stead."

51

Valian's forehead creased in a frown. "My mother has never acted in such a manner. I can't see her conceiving such a plan."

"You're forgetting, my dear," said Haley taking his hand; "she is not wearing her given gem anymore. She is more than capable of hatching up a plan like that."

Valian's lip curled in a small smile. "I forgot about that."

Haley mouthed him a kiss.

He turned toward the sphere, waved his hand in front of it and spoke his mother's name. Immediately the swirling colors began to spin, faster and faster until they became a colorless blur. An image began to take shape, becoming clearer until Queen Lilia came into focus, young and beautiful.

A diamond crown sparkled upon her head. Her auburn hair was long and wavy. She looked very relaxed, sitting in a bowl shaped wicker chair which hung in the air by a long thick rope.

Great forest trees were visible through the large open window behind her. There was just a hint of breeze, softly blowing her hair.

It was dark and rainy. The glow of a lamp beside her cast enough light for them to see Sersha, and Reed and the other missing guardians Thorp, Dinora, and Finn.

"I don't believe it," Valian whispered shaking his head.

Everyone gathered around the sphere to look.

"It just amazes me my mother being so deceitful."

Haley smiled. "The wonders of emotion. Did we jump to conclusions or what?"

"Well what else were we supposed to think?" Valian asked looking at the sphere. "I wonder how she got the sphere into this room?"

"I know," Haley agreed.

"I still want to go see her," he said. "I want to know why she has done this."

Paul, Carol, and Henry stood quietly, watching the queen. "She is very beautiful," said Carol. "Sersha looks just like her."

Valian turned to the others. "We'll leave at first light. Get some sleep; it's a full day of traveling."

Everyone went to their rooms. Carol and Paul's room was next door to Haley's.

Haley gave her mother a hug. "If you take a bath you have to tell the water to turn on and off, and tell it hotter or colder. Ask for bubbles," she smiled walking into her room.

As she drifted off to sleep, she smiled to herself as she listened to Carol giggling next door.

Chapter 5
The Search For Lilia

Valian was up early the next morning giving Jack orders on what to pack. Jack couldn't understand the need for the trip but kept his questions to himself.

As Haley got dressed she wondered about the queens motives for disappearing the way she did and if it was as she thought. Her steward came to escort her and her parents to the dining hall for a quick breakfast. Henry was already there and was just finishing his meal.

Valian rose from his seat and kissed Haley's hand. "Good morning, my sweet, and Mrs. Miles you look lovely today."

Carol blushed and thanked him. Paul had an amused look on his face at his wife's delight at being treated like royalty. Haley grinned and Henry rolled his eyes as usual.

They discussed the trip to the Tempest region while they ate. "I've only been there a couple of times," said Valian, taking a drink of rainbow dew. "I remember the way, mostly. I recall the terrain is very wild and we'll have to walk part of the way. Everyone up to it?"

Haley raised her hand and Valian smiled as he gave her a high five. The rest of the group followed suit.

They leapt from the balcony and flew north. The skies were gray again, but the rain had let up. They passed over damp dark forests which smelled like quiet, silent age. Haley breathed the scent deeply. There was something about the smell that appealed to her. They flew at tree top level for miles, covering un-ending forests and streams that meandered in snakelike loops across the countryside. They stopped to rest at an outcropping of flat rocks half way up against the side of a tall cliff. From there, there was nothing but forest as far as the eye could see.

Everyone snacked on vimsom fruit, a delightful vegetable with arms like an octopus, which Carol was a little apprehensive in eating, but after her first bite she smiled with approval.

"A couple more miles," said Valian between mouthfuls, "we walk in. It's too dense for flying even if we change size."

They finished their break and took off again, flying single file until they reached the edge of one of the oldest woods Haley had ever seen. She felt excitement at the prospect of exploring as they landed and looked over at Henry. She could tell he felt the same.

They followed Valian through an opening in the thick underbrush surrounding the edge of the woods. It was very dark as they entered. Looking up at the canopy, Haley saw there were no breaks anywhere to let the sun in. The floor of the woods was silent as they walked, softened by the recent rains. Again the smell of decaying leaves and dirt appealed to her, a smell that brought back some distant childhood memory, although she couldn't put her finger on it.

They walked about two hundred yards and Valian stopped, turning to the others. "We'll have to be very quiet from here on in. Many strange creatures dwell in these woods. Some say it's haunted by wood trolls that you can't see until they are right on top of you, and they don't like strangers."

Haley felt the little prickles on the back of her neck as she looked around. Carol's eyes were wide and she fidgeted nervously. Nobody said a word.

"Stick close to me," Valian said, quietly.

They continued into the surrounding darkness. It was just light enough for Haley to see they were on a very old path, worn down by years of treading, by what, she could only imagine. The trees towered above them by hundreds of feet, their trunks covered in old dead moss. The branches were very low and thick. It was quiet, almost unearthly quiet, without a hint of a breeze. Water dripped all around them, hitting Haley on the back of the neck every once in awhile, causing her to flinch.

The group silently trudged on. It became darker as they went until Valian stopped. He picked up an old branch about two feet long, waved his hand and the end burst into flame, like a torch. He handed it to Henry. "Head up the rear."

He lit several more and passed them back until everyone had their own. Shadows danced in the firelight as they continued forward. The old pathway began to widen and Haley could see the floor of the woods was strangely bare of any kind of growth, not what she was used to seeing back home. Every once in awhile they could hear the creaking and groaning of an old tree. The hoot from an owl far off was quickly swallowed up by the thick darkness.

They walked for an hour, over small rises in the earth, up and down. The path curved and sometimes seemed to loop as if they were going in circles. Haley could have sworn they passed the same boulder more than once. Her feet were tired and her legs were sore. She tugged on Valian's arm. "I need to rest a bit," she whispered.

Valian looked at the others. They all nodded. Valian nodded his head in agreement although Haley thought he looked nervous. Everyone sat down on the path except for the prince, who stood at the head of the group, keeping a wary eye. They broke out some more vimsom which they ate hungrily.

As Haley finished one of the arms, she thought she heard something and paused, silently listening. She looked at the others. They didn't seem to have heard it as they continued eating.

There it was again. This time everyone else stopped and looked around, searching for the source.

The scratching would stop then start again. It reminded Haley of the sound a squirrel makes as it descends a tree, climbing a foot, pausing to check if the coast is clear, then continuing. She looked up and as she did, she dropped her torch, her mouth opened in a silent scream.

Valian, startled by her movement, lifted his torch and drew his sword. Ten feet above them was a horrific white face staring down upon them. It let out a high pitched scream the second it was discovered.

Everyone was frozen in fear where they sat.

"A banshee!" Valian yelled, pointing his sword toward her. Her face was grotesquely elongated and thin with a pointed chin, and her huge sunken eyes bulged outward as she screamed again. The bridge of her nose was very long and as thin as a pencil, but plastered against her face. Wide wrinkles spread across her forehead when she screamed. She moved extremely quick, running up and down the trunk of the tree, darting up and down and around the trunk as if deciding on whether to attack.

She stopped just out of sword reach and clung to the ancient moss with sharp claws. Her long bonelike arms and legs were covered in a thin, wispy, ragged garment. She began to sink into a crouch like position, making her look like a spindly four legged spider.

"Run!" Valian screamed.

Everyone scrambled to their feet and took off down the path. They could hear the banshee behind them screaming, and the crack of branches as she jumped from tree to tree as she gave chase.

"Her bite is poisonous! Don't let her touch you; use your torch!" Valian yelled. He slowed to let the others pass by.

Haley was terrified and kept looking back. "Valian, be careful!" she cried.

The adrenaline was pumping in everyone as they tore down the path. The banshee seemed like she was gaining on them. Haley could see the ghostly white face bobbing above her in the torchlight as the creature tried to get ahead of the group.

Quite suddenly it stopped and stared at them as they put ample distance between them and it.

Valian stopped. He bent over panting but with his head up, staring intently at the banshee. She stared right back. She would look away briefly as if she saw something more interesting then back at the group. She opened her mouth is if ready to scream again, stretching it in a long "O" shape, revealing one upper and one lower pointed tooth, but all that came out was what could only be described as a confused whimper.

She suddenly leapt to the tree behind her and disappeared into the darkness. They could hear her as she leapt from branch to branch until silence fell once again. Valian stood, waiting. When he was sure she wasn't coming back, he joined the members of his terrified party. They had stopped roughly thirty yards down the path and stood trying to catch their breath.

"What the hell was that?" Paul asked, holding a stitch in his side. Haley had never heard her father swear before or seen such fear in his face.

"A banshee," said Valian, taking deep breaths. "I heard she dwells in these woods, but I've never heard tell of her outright trying to attack anyone like this. The banshee stalks her prey quietly and sneaks up and bites them on the neck, usually while they're sleeping. Her poison works quickly and her prey never wakes up again."

"What does she do then, drink their blood?" Henry asked.

"Yes. What concerns me is why she stopped the attack. Banshees have no fear of anything except…" Valian was silent for a moment.

"We have to move on… quickly!" he urged, ushering everyone forward.

"What?" Haley asked alarmed.

"Wood trolls, tree trolls, whatever you want to call them. They will cast a spell on you and put you to sleep and leave you until the earth consumes your body… when they are done playing with you that is. They will eat the flesh of anything."

Sure enough as the group stood there resting, they began to sense movement among the trees just beyond the torchlight.

"Walk slowly and quietly," whispered Valian hoarsely. "Maybe they will let us pass if we keep moving."

The group made their way forward. "No sudden movements," he added. Everyone looked around as they went.

Glancing to her right, Haley let out a quiet gasp. There stood a troll. She could just make it out. It blended with the tree behind it so well she had to look again. It was the oddest looking thing she had seen yet. Not so scary but strange. It stood about four feet tall and wore a dark hood that was tied at the neck. The most noticeable thing was a huge, over sized nose that hung well past its chin. It looked very old as its face was careworn, covered in thick wrinkles. It had very large eyes and thick lips. It just stood there watching as they past.

Everyone was on edge, ready for something to happen. Paul and Carol, at the front of the group, stopped abruptly, causing the twins to bump into each other. Up ahead a troll stood in the middle of the path. It looked similar to the one Haley had seen.

Everyone froze.

Movement in the darkness around them caused Carol to let out a small squeak and she grabbed Paul's arm tightly. Valian slowly stepped forward and lifted his torch high into the air, revealing at least twenty others making their way toward the light.

Haley was right behind him, wide eyed with fright.

"We mean you no harm," stated Valian, trying to muster up as much authority as possible. "We are just passing through."

The trolls stepped aside as a larger one made its way forward. Haley assumed it was the leader. Its body looked just like it was made of tree bark, as if it was actually part of a tree, with thick short legs and arms and very large, hair covered hands and feet.

Valian stood ready, his sword in his hand, but not raised to strike. It walked right up to the prince without hesitation or fear. Valian towered over it as it stopped three feet in front of him.

It looked up at him, studying his face. This one wasn't wearing a hood and Haley saw its head was covered in short, stiff fur like a deer hide. Its eyes were dark and it wore a frown. "I don't know you," it said in a gruff voice.

It looked around at the others standing wide eyed behind Valian. When it laid eyes on Haley, it grunted loudly, startling everyone. It turned around to the other trolls and made a series of grunts. Several grunted in response as it turned back to Valian. "That is a rather fine looking specimen," it said, looking at Haley.

Haley stood behind the prince, clutching his arm. Valian looked from the troll and turned slightly toward Haley. "What, her?" he asked, motioning behind him.

The troll nodded as he looked at Haley hungrily. "She is not of this world, yes?"

"No…" Valian began.

"She would surely be a delight to the king." The trolls behind him began grunting again.

Haley, who was thoroughly petrified by now, started to shake. "You can't have her," said Valian, raising his voice and his sword an octave.

The troll remained unmoved by Valian's response. "Give her to us and you shall pass."

Valian stood silent. Haley could sense he was thinking hard on what to do. They were outnumbered, they couldn't fly, and Valian was the only one with a weapon.

"Agreed?" the troll demanded, staring at Haley with a covetous confidence.

Again, Valian was without an answer.

"He's afraid," Haley thought. "And desperate." Without thinking she stepped out from behind the prince. All the trolls began to grunt excitedly in rapid succession. The leader took a small step backward.

"Haley, what are you doing?" Carol whispered.

Valian grabbed Haley's arm as she stepped around him, but she put her hand back, holding Valian at bay. She had no idea what she was going to do. It began to rain softly and mists began to rise all around them.

"What do you want with me?" she asked, sounding braver than she felt.

"The king is in need of a new wife," the troll answered. "You could be queen of a vast empire."

Haley felt a warm sensation travel through her body with lightning speed and suddenly lost all her fear, which amazed her. "Ah ha! Really." she said, defiantly taking a step forward.

The troll took another step backward in surprise. A smile grew across his face, his thick lips in a rubbery grin.

"I am already betrothed to a prince," she continued, holding out her bejeweled hand.

His eyes were drawn to the rubies glittering in the torchlight. The troll scoffed. "That is pitiful," he said with an air of contempt. "We have hoards of jewels; better and larger than that sorry display."

Haley glared at the troll. Anger began to well up inside her.

Valian could sense this wasn't going well and touched her elbow, which she yanked away. He was alarmed at her reaction and knew she was headed for trouble. "Haley, my sweet…" he began, but his eyes were drawn past her and the trolls, to the pathway just as Haley turned around to look at him.

The look on his face as he stared ahead startled her. She turned back toward the trolls and saw emerging through the mists, an extremely beautiful woman. The trolls watched her approach and parted so that she could pass by if she so desired. They didn't seem to be surprised by her appearance in the least. She moved forward slowly. It didn't seem like her feet were on the ground but like she was gliding through the air.

She stopped at the edge of the torchlight, close enough for Haley could get a good look. Haley had never seen such beauty; not even Sersha could hold a candle to her. She had long black hair past her waist. It was wavy and shining. Her eyes were the bluest of blue with long thick, dark lashes. She had just a hint of color in her cheeks and her lips were full and a deep red. Her figure was, for lack of a better word, voluptuous. She wore a dark blue silk gown which hugged her body tightly, accentuating every curve as she moved.

She didn't stand still but seemed to move in place, almost like she was swaying, dancing for those present. Valian's eyes were glued to her. Her lips puckered slightly as if in a kiss and she slowly held out her arms toward him, beckoning him, enticing him. She continued to move her body in such a way as to draw him to her and she seemed to be singing in some far away voice. Valian's eyes narrowed as he began to grin.

Haley turned and looked up at him. Her mouth dropped open in shock. His pale blue eyes had become a dark gray.

"Valian," she said. It was as if he didn't hear her and as he took a step forward toward the woman, Haley saw with alarm, Paul and Henry had the same looks on their faces.

"Dad? Henry?" she yelled. They ignored her and began to follow Valian.

"Mom!" Haley cried. Carol could only stand there frozen in fear and watch her husband and son walk away.

Haley turned. "Valian! Valian!" she screamed. She began to go after them but the head troll blocked her path as the other trolls backed him up.

"You can't help them," he said, his voice sly and cunning.

"But... wait!" she yelled. "Valian!" She watched the woman lead them away, off the path and into the dark shadows of the woods.

"What is she?" Haley demanded. "Where is she taking them?"

The troll grinned at her. "She is a temptress, a huldra. There are very few left in existence. They roam in search of men. None can resist her charms."

Haley stood there as if numb, her anger growing as she tried to figure a way out of this. Carol stood behind her, unable to move. Her wings shuddered uncontrollably. Haley turned toward her and took her by the shoulders, whispering "It'll be all right, I have a plan."

She turned back to the troll who stood patiently. "What do you want?" she asked with determination.

"I shall present you to the king."

Haley was silent.

"She," he said, motioning to Carol, "can go."

"She stays with me," Haley answered. "I'll make a deal with you. You send some of your… group and set the others free from that temptress and I will go with you freely…" she paused again. "That's the deal, take it or leave it."

The troll thought about her offer a moment. "And if I decline?" he asked with an amused smirk.

"Then we will have no choice but to destroy you," she thundered in her most commanding voice.

The troll jerked his head back with a grunt and turned around, grunting at the others.

Haley had no idea what he said but it provoked a reaction from the group as they all began grunting, almost as if laughing. It gave her enough time to turn back to Carol who was still frozen in the same position, her wings shuddering madly. Haley whispered, "Can you fly?"

Carol couldn't speak but nodded ever so slightly.

"You'll have to change size, on my signal."

Carol swallowed hard.

Haley turned back toward the army of trolls who were still grunting. The leader turned back to her with a look of triumph. "There will be no bargain."

As he reached for Haley's hand, she screamed. "Change!" Grabbing Carol's hand, her wings sprung out of their veiled position. Together they shot straight up into the air.

The trolls grunted loudly and began throwing rocks at them and picked up sticks trying to bat at them, all the while yelling and grunting.

The branches of the trees were too thick for them to fly and they quickly landed on a branch behind the trunk of one the ancient trees. Carol was shaking badly and near tears. "What... what are we going to do?" she stuttered.

Haley was thinking hard. "I don't know," she answered, as a rock whizzed over their heads. "We can't stay here, but if we try and fly from branch to branch, we may run into the banshee."

Another rock hit the branch they were on and they nearly fell. Below, the trolls left the path and were traipsing into the woods, gathering around the tree.

"I wish I had one of those stones from Hilda," she said.

"It's no use!" yelled the head troll as the rocks stopped flying.

"Set Valian and the others free and I'll come quietly!" Haley yelled back.

"Come down and we'll discuss it!" came his reply.

She looked at her mother with concern. "It'll be all right," she said, taking Carol by the shoulders, giving her a reassuring shake. "Stay here."

"What? Where are you going?" Carol pleaded.

"Down there," she answered, pointing toward the ground. "I'll think of something, you just... don't budge until I come back."

Carol nodded.

Haley turned and yelled, "I'm coming down!"

She jumped from the branch and changed size, landing a couple yards from the troll. She was frustrated about the situation and grew angrier by the second. The troll walked toward her, looking confident and too sure of himself. Haley had a sudden urge to punch him in his big, fat honker of a nose.

He stopped in front of her, his head turned up, his fat lips curled in a smirk. "Wise decision," he said, mockingly.

"How dare you!" Haley scoffed loudly. "Who do you think you are? You have no right to make demands of me and my family!"

The other trolls began grunting excitedly at her outburst. She looked at them and smiled.

"You sound like a bunch of chattering monkeys!" she taunted and began to laugh. The head troll was taken aback at her boldness and the insult.

She bent down, her face inches from his. She wrinkled her nose at the disgusting smell emanating from him. "You stink. I have no intention of going anywhere with you or the rest of your smelly little monkeys, got that?"

The more insults she threw at him, the more confident she became. She stood up straight and tall and as she did, the witches' crest she wore around her neck fell out from under her garment.

A look of terror crossed the troll's face, and he let out a blood curdling scream. He stumbled backward and fell. Scrambling to his feet, grunting, he tore into the woods with his tail tucked between his legs, and the rest of his cohorts were right behind him.

Haley stood there in confusion as she watched them disappear in the dark. "What the…" She looked over toward the tree where her mother stood waiting. She smiled at Carol's tiny frame.

"What happened?" Carol called down.

"I have no idea," she replied. "Come down. Let's get out of here before they come back."

Carol flit down, landing beside her daughter and changed size.

They hugged then picked up the only torch that was still burning and started down the path. They went at a quick pace, walking then jogging. Haley could see that her mother was just as stressed as she was about the guys following the huldra into the woods. She could just about imagine what her mother was thinking.

"You know they were under a spell, right?" she asked.

Carol didn't respond right away. "Yes I know," she finally answered. "It just hurts, you know, the look of pleasure on their faces, and me, standing there scared out of my wits, frozen where I stood. I should have grabbed your father, shaken him to his senses…"

"It's not your fault," Haley interrupted. "You're in a different world. You had every reason to react the way you did, so would any other human if in the same situation."

"I know," said Carol, trying to come to grips with her feelings. "I should have been stronger."

"You will be. This is an entirely new experience for you. You can't expect to know how to process all this on your first day out."

Carol looked over at Haley with a little smile. "You are so smart. So much more mature than I was at your age. I'm so proud of you, Haley."

"Thank you, Mom," Haley smiled. "I learned from you."

The two continued their trek in silence. An hour later they were exhausted and had to stop to rest. Neither one knew where they were or how much longer they could endure, but neither would say it out loud.

"I wonder what time it is," said Carol.

"We've been in here for hours," Haley replied. "My guess is around ten, eleven maybe."

"I never would have believed a wood could be this dark in the middle of the morning," Carol said, as she stretched out the kinks in her back. She stopped abruptly, looking down the path ahead of them. "Did you hear something?" she whispered.

Haley turned her head and listened. They could barely hear it, singing way off in the distance. They looked at each other and took off at a light jog. Haley was grateful for the previous night's rain which silenced their steps as they went.

The singing became clearer with each step and they discovered with relief that it was growing lighter out.

They slowed as they grew closer to the huldra's voice. Haley stopped, looking toward the left. She could see the sun shining through the canopy in long dust filled beams, and she caught a whiff of pine. She sighed with pleasure at the smell.

The singing had stopped then began again.

"This way," Haley whispered, reluctantly leaving the comfort of the path.

They made their way quickly as the floor of the woods was clear of underbrush. Evergreens came into view and became more numerous. The ground was covered in wet pine needles, making their approach undetectable. The huldra continued to sing louder as they grew near.

Haley stopped and looked at her mother, raising her finger to her lips she began to creep forward, Carol right behind her. They made their way to a large pine and peeked around the edge. There through a gap in the pines ahead, they could see a quaint, little, ivy covered cottage made of very old gray stone. Smoke wafted from the chimney. The cottage door stood wide open, though it was quite dark inside. A lone round window was obscured, covered in years of moss.

They made their way forward, taking cover behind the pines. Haley crouched down to the ground and lay on her stomach to get a better view beneath the trees. She could see a very small yard, green with foliage, and strange looking toadstools with tall stems stretching in curved arcs, bearing extremely large heads in gray and brown with black splotches, bobbing in the light breeze as if nodding. They grew along the entire edge of the yard. Bright purple mushrooms grew in large patches and blanketed most of the yard.

The singing had stopped all together.

Carol stifled a squeal and pointed to a narrow path leading into the woods beyond. There was the huldra walking away from them, and she was alone. They watched as she got further and further away and disappeared around a bend.

"Come on," Haley said, bursting from her hiding spot and sprinting across the yard. She paused in the open doorway until her eyes adjusted to the dark. There sitting in three chairs against the wall were Valian, Paul, and Henry. Haley and Carol quickly hurried over to them.

At first they seemed to be asleep; then they realized their eyes were open, barely. They were all wearing those stupid little smiles, but they didn't seem to be conscious. Haley grabbed Valian by the arm and helped him to his feet as Carol followed suit with Paul. They each grabbed one of Henry's arms and quietly led them all outside. With a quick look around they led them back the way they had come, as quickly and quietly as they could. Haley kept stealing glances over her shoulder as they went.

Once they got back to the path in the woods, they hurried the guys as fast as they could. Haley kept looking up at Valian, but his demeanor was the same. They walked what must have been about thirty minutes when they heard a terrible scream from behind them. It was far away but it didn't matter. The girls hurried them on faster still. Finally they could see a break in the woods ahead.

Haley flashed a smile at Carol as they stepped into a bright green, sun filled meadow. Carol let out a big sigh of relief, but it quickly turned to a frown when she spotted another forest ahead. "We have to keep moving," said Haley with growing concern at the shape of the guys. Their eyes were still only open halfway and all three looked haggard.

"I have to rest," said Carol, "just for a bit."

Haley looked around. "Well… this is as good a place as any. At least we're out in the open and we'll be able to see anyone coming. Let's go to the middle of the meadow then we'll take a break."

They helped the guys along and came upon a very small stream where they let their charges sit down. Haley pulled out the last of her vimsom. Carol had eight arms left on hers and tried to get Paul and Henry to eat some. The guys slowly chewed their vimsom with blank expressions.

Suddenly a shadow passed overhead and something landed behind the group. Haley and Carol spun around in alarm and were totally shocked to see Dinora, one of the missing guardians standing there, tall and strong. Haley's mouth dropped open in surprise at how masculine and mad she looked. "Oh, my goodness," she exclaimed. "Am I glad to see you!"

Dinora was just as surprised and quickly went to Valian, then turned to Haley. "What's happened?" She looked extremely angry.

Haley quickly told her what happened.

"We must get them back to the fort immediately," Dinora said, looking frightened.

"What is it?" Haley asked in alarm, her heart pounding.

"They've been poisoned and will die if they are not treated soon."

"Poisoned?" Haley whispered.

"Get them to their feet and follow me," said Dinora.

They had difficulty getting them to stand and finally with much effort, followed Dinora toward the forest ahead. Haley was near tears as she struggled with the weight of Henry on her shoulder. Carol wasn't having much more luck with Paul. Dinora on the other hand didn't seem to have any trouble moving Valian along, although slowly.

They entered the forest and saw with relief it wasn't very far to the other side, and was down hill. Once they reached the break, Haley looked out and gazed upon a small fort. There were a half dozen cottages and a large pavilion. The entire compound was hidden by a canopy of extremely tall palm fronds. The fort was virtually invisible from the air.

Dinora went forward with Valian and the others followed her to a large cabin. She threw open the door and the group staggered in after her. Queen Lilia, Sersha, and Finn stood, startled.

"Dinora, what's happened…? Valian," gasped the queen, as Dinora steered him to a bed. Carol and Haley helped their guys toward beds and collapsed in a heap.

"They were captured by a huldra," said Dinora.

"A huldra!" Sersha hissed in fear.

"Quickly, Finn, get the St John's wort. They've lapsed into a depression," commanded Lilia urgently.

Finn rushed out the door and came back minutes later with a small cauldron and set it on an old fashioned stove in the corner of the room. He waved his hand and the wood underneath the burner burst into flame, like putting a lit match to gasoline. It wasn't long before purple steam began to emit from the cauldron along with a wretched smell.

Lilia paced the room as the contents began to bubble. Sersha opened the large window to let in some fresh air.

"There, it's ready," said Finn, just as nervous as everyone else in the room.

"Sersha…" said the queen.

They each took a spoonful of the mixture. Lilia held her spoon up to Valian's mouth, trying to force him to take it. Fear flashed behind the glazed look in his eyes and he tried to fight his way away from the spoon.

Finn jumped in and held the weakened prince down while Lilia shoved it into his mouth, holding his nose shut until he swallowed. Valian began to relax and sank back into his stupor.

Carol, Haley, Finn, and the queen treated Paul and Henry in the same manner. Lilia stepped back and observed them. "We need to get them covered to keep them warm. They have a rough night ahead of them." They got the group tucked in and stoked up the fire.

Just then, Thorp came in, his arms loaded down with firewood. The pleasant look on his face turned serious when he saw Haley's party tucked into bed. "What's going on?" he asked.

Lilia explained that they were captured by a huldra.

His face turned white. "Oh dear, are we in time?"

"I don't know," Lilia shook her head.

"I don't understand," said Haley.

"Come sit by the fire and I'll explain," said the queen. "Watch them, Thorp." Thorp nodded and pulled up a chair in front of the beds as Sersha sat beside Valian.

"The huldra are almost an extinct breed which means these are desperate times for them. Their main goal is to be married and become human. They have a weakness for mortal and immortal men." Lilia paused and sighed. "They used to band together and wipe out entire villages, leaving widows and their children weeping and having to fend for themselves."

"Wiped out? I thought you said their goal was to be married," said Haley.

"I was just getting to that. Once a mortal man is captured, if the huldra are not satisfied with the one they've ensnared, they will suck the life out of him and move onto the next."

"Geez Louise," said Haley helplessly. "Is that what's happening to them?"

"It looks like she had just started. The huldra's appetite for the human soul is strong, but seeing as she had three to choose from, she probably couldn't make up her mind. She obviously took a sample of each and got filled up. That's what saved them so far I hope."

Haley sat quietly for a moment. "I don't understand what happened to them in the woods. Valian got this look on his face..." she paused, "like he was totally enamored and his eyes became almost cloudy. They weren't even near each other. How did she do it?"

"Was the huldra singing?" Lilia asked.

"Yes, if you could call it singing."

"That's what did it. The huldra's voice has a powerful effect on men, especially human men. Valian may have been more fortunate than Henry and your father since he is fairy kind, but he is without the protection of his given gem... well, you understand."

Haley shook her head. "Singing..."

Lilia nodded. "Huldra's are temptresses, seductresses. They can cast a spell on the strongest if taken by surprise. Not many can resist their charms."

Again Haley shook her head in disbelief. "So now what, we wait to see if our men die?" she asked, her eyes welling up.

The queen didn't answer.

Haley looked over at Carol. Her face was white. She seemed at a loss for words.

Lilia looked at them with compassion. "It will take some time to tell," she said sadly. "If they develop fevers as I hope, that means the St John's wort is working. Then they will begin to sweat, at which time we will need to keep them as warm as possible. We will have to give them a mixture of herbs in various amounts and at regular intervals. That will pull them through."

Haley couldn't stop shaking her head in disbelief.

"Why don't you rest," said the queen. "There are beds in the next cottage."

"I don't think I could sleep," said Haley, in a far off voice.

"Go lay down for awhile. Take your mother and I'll have something sent in to relax you."

Haley looked at Carol and nodded.

"We'll wake you if anything changes, but that won't be for some time."

Haley took Carol's hand and led her next door. "I don't like it here," said Carol, with a mournful look.

Haley put her arms around her. "It'll be all right, Mom. You're not exactly seeing Wisen at its best. Estelle once warned Henry and I that Wisen is full of dangers. I never realized the truth of her words until Valian and Sersha were ambushed in the Spicewood Realm. You definitely have to be on your guard in unfamiliar places, but don't worry, they're in good hands, you'll see."

They each took a bed and sat down.

Finn knocked on the door and brought in what looked like tea. "Drink this, it'll help calm you," he said, as he left the cottage.

They sat quietly sipping their drinks. It wasn't long before Carol set her tea down and fell asleep. Haley's eyes became heavy as she watched her mother, and she was soon in a dreamless sleep herself.

Chapter 6
Rest and Recuperation

haley slept soundly. When she woke she looked over at Carol sawing logs next to her. She tiptoed to the door and saw it was still light out. She stood in the doorway for several minutes. The sun was warm on her face and she felt calm and peaceful, not wanting to spoil the mood.

With a sigh she walked next door.

Queen Lilia and Sersha were sitting by the fire. It was extremely warm in the room, almost uncomfortably warm.

"How are they?" she asked.

"No change yet," said Lilia. "Hopefully it won't be too much longer. I've sent Finn and Reed to fetch the ingredients for their medicine."

Haley walked over to her family. She looked down at them, sleeping peacefully. They didn't look well. All three were pale and quivered slightly under their blankets.

"This is all my fault," she said, shaking her head.

"What do you mean?" Lilia asked.

"I should have talked Valian out of coming here. We saw that you were safe when we looked in the sphere. I should have talked him out of it," she repeated.

"This wasn't anyone's fault," said the queen. "You had no way of knowing this would happen."

Haley smiled, sadly. "Can I ask you something?"

Lilia nodded.

"Why did you hide the sphere and disappear?"

Lilia sighed. "I thought I was doing the right thing. I wanted to see how things would be handled without me there."

"I thought that's what it might be," said Haley. "I just don't understand why now? Especially when all the fairies had removed their given gems. The entire city was in chaos. They couldn't handle the onslaught of emotions they were experiencing. I take full responsibility for my suggestion in having them remove their gems."

Lilia was quiet for a moment. "I'm not going to be around forever. I'd like to retire someday and let Valian become king. It's time that you and Valian, and Sersha, take control in running the kingdom. Unfortunately I was a bit hasty in my decision. I should have waited. Now look where we are. No, Haley, if anyone is to blame it is I."

The door opened behind them. Reed and Finn came in, their arms loaded down with various plants.

"Good," said the queen. "Let's get working on the medicine. Haley we can use your help."

"Of course," Haley answered. She went over to the kitchenette and watched Reed and Finn separate each plant species into piles.

Lilia took two large cauldrons from the cabinet next to the sink, filled them half way with water, and set them on the stove. "All right, Haley, as soon as they begin to boil, I want you to add this blue gum to the pot, stirring occasionally. Once it has boiled for twenty minutes or so we'll remove half of it and put it in this bowl to cool. The other half we will leave to simmer."

"What is it?" Haley asked.

"Blue gum has healing properties. The men will have to inhale it, and we'll sponge the cooled blue gum on their chests. It will help them from developing any respiratory problems. We'll repeat the process every thirty minutes."

"Ok," Haley sighed.

"Now, the lions tooth is for eating as soon as they are conscious. It's been used to protect the body's organs for thousands of years. As for the rest of these herbs, we will make them into a tea, that's what the other cauldron is for. As soon as the water boils, we'll remove it from heat, add the rest of the ingredients, and let them steep."

"Ok," Haley said again, with a small smile. "So what are these?" she asked, picking up a handful of herbs with little flowers on them.

"That's horehound. That has also been used for thousands of years to prevent respiratory problems. This is yarrow. It has healing properties, helping the digestive system and keeping them calm and relaxed. And finally we have maidenhair tree. It keeps the blood circulation strong, especially to the brain. Combine these three herbs into a tea which they'll need to drink every couple of hours."

"Gee," said Haley, "how do you know all this?"

"We've known about these cures for thousands of years as I said. They are used regularly at the infirmary to treat a variety of conditions."

"I am so glad you're here," said Haley. "I shudder to think what would have happened if Dinora hadn't discovered us. I hope it's not too late."

"I think we were in time," said Lilia. "Judging by the looks of it, they are definitely on the mend. It will just take some time."

The water in the cauldrons began to bubble and soon came to a rolling boil. Haley added her blue gum to the pot and began stirring as Lilia removed her cauldron from the stove and began to add her herbs a little at a time.

The door opened and Carol entered, looking pretty rough. "Hi, Mom," said Haley as Carol walked over to Paul's bed.

"How are they?" she asked, as she sat on the edge of the bed.

"I think they are out of the woods," the queen replied. "This will be a slow recovery. They would have been in a lot worse shape had much more time passed."

Carol took a deep breath and began to cry with relief.

Lilia took over for Haley as she went to her mother. She sat next to her and put her arm around her shoulder. She could find no words of comfort other than what she'd already said.

"I was so scared," she said, looking up at Haley.

"I know, so was I. You know what they say; that which does not kill us makes us stronger."

Carol gave her a small smile.

"They'll be fine," she said, giving her mother a reassuring squeeze.

"Is there anything I can do?" Carol asked.

"Yes," Lilia answered. "In about twenty minutes you can start sponging this onto Paul's chest, like a sponge bath."

When Haley's cauldron was ready, she poured half into the bowl to cool. As they began to sponge it on, the men began to sweat and shiver.

Finn added more wood to the fire and the temperature rose at least ten degrees. Reed brought steaming cups of blue gum to Carol and Haley so the men could inhale the fumes. Queen Lilia tended to Valian while Finn continued to stir the tea. An hour later, Henry opened his eyes. They were still cloudy, but there was a tiny spark of recognition. Haley called attention to it and everyone gathered around him.

Lilia smiled. "Thank heavens! This is a very good sign."

Haley held the tea for him and he took several sips. Encouraged, everyone continued their rounds of sponging and holding steaming cups of blue gum to their loved ones noses.

As afternoon became evening, Valian and Paul showed signs of improvement. They both opened their eyes and were served cups of healing tea. They were still shivering however, so Reed and Finn kept the fire burning hot.

Around midnight, Paul's fever broke and he managed to give Carol a little smile. Carol was elated and doubled her efforts at sponging even though she was extremely tired.

It was long after that Henry and Valian were semi awake. Their eyes would open and they'd look around, slightly confused, take some tea and drift back to sleep.

Haley sat on the edge of Valian's bed and looked down at him with loving but anxious eyes. She had been so scared that she would lose him.

She gently sponged his neck and chest and caressed his golden locks. Tears welled up in her eyes as she realized how close she had come to losing them all, the three men she loved so dearly: her father; her twin brother; her Fiancé. How careless they had been, taking this journey without weapons.

Lilia and Sersha left Reed, Finn, and Thorp to watch after the group while they went to rest. Carol lay down next to her husband and fell asleep.

By morning all three patients were able to sit up a bit. They were still extremely weak and drifted in and out. Finn took advantage of the opportunity to give them lion's tooth to chew.

Several days passed and everyone was settled into a routine. Sponging and serving tea. Thorp and Dinora had to go out for fresh herbs regularly so they could brew up fresh batches.

Sunrise on the fourth day, as Haley was getting ready to sponge Valian, he spoke. "My sweet," he whispered.

Haley broke out in a huge smile. "Hello my darling. How do you feel?"

"Like I was ambushed by a hundred boar trolls."

Lilia, Sersha, and Carol came over, all smiles. "How do you feel?" Lilia asked.

"Like I was telling Haley, like I was ambushed by a hundred boar trolls. What happened?" he asked, looking over at Paul and Henry sleeping across the room.

"It was a huldra," the queen answered, "by the sound of it, it was Iris."

"Iris?" Haley asked.

"Iris," Valian whispered with a serious face.

"She is the queen of the huldra's and one of the most powerful," she said, turning to Haley. "I'll bet you she was furious to find the guys missing."

"We heard her screaming in the distance, right before we left the woods," said Haley. "She wasn't happy. Thank goodness Dinora happened to come across us resting in a meadow."

Valian squeezed Haley's hand. "It's a good thing you kept your wits about you. How did you ever get away from the tree trolls?"

"I don't know," she answered. "One minute I was bent forward, staring him right in the face and the next minute he let out a shriek, tucked tail, and ran. Neither mom nor myself knew what it was that scared him off and we weren't going to stick around to find out. Luckily, if it hadn't been for her singing, we would never have found you," she said, her voice trailing off.

"I don't remember much," said Valian. "I remember everything about the tree trolls, then nothing until sometime last night."

"It's just as well," said Lilia.

Haley bent over and kissed Valian on the forehead.

"What's that?" the queen asked.

"What?"

"Around your neck."

"Oh that, it's a medallion Estelle gave me of the witches crest."

"Let me see," said Lilia, lifting up the medallion. "This is what scared the trolls. It's made of iron."

"Huh?" asked Haley

"It is widely believed that trolls are deathly afraid of iron and steel. I don't know why, but they fear it."

Haley looked at her medallion curiously.

"What a strange land this is. I could spend the rest of my life here and never learn it all or understand it."

"Indeed," Lilia agreed. "I still learn new things every day and I've been here thousands of years."

"I'm pretty hungry," said Valian. "Is there anything to eat other than lion's tooth?" he grinned.

Haley and Sersha grinned at each other.

"We'll fix you some breakfast," said Sersha.

She and Haley busied themselves in the little kitchenette and soon the smell of sausages filled the cottage. It wasn't long before Henry's nose woke him up. Haley went over and gave him a big hug. "Welcome back, Henry. I missed you."

"Where are we?" came Paul's voice behind her. Carol was sitting on the edge of his bed, smiling brightly.

The whole room was full of smiling faces and everyone began talking at once. Haley filled them in on the trolls and they became very quiet when she told them about Iris the huldra and the effect she had on them. Paul and Valian looked rather embarrassed.

Haley could see they were a little uncomfortable about it, so she reaffirmed the fact that they were under a spell. Haley and Carol exchanged a quick glance at each other. "Can I help with anything?" Carol asked, changing the subject.

"Sure," said Sersha. "Tell the dishes to come to the table."

"What?" Carol asked.

"The cottage is charmed," Sersha explained. "They'll do what you tell them."

Carol looked doubtfully at the cupboard. "Plates… come to the table."

The delight on her face brought Haley some relief. She was worried about Carol's comment of not liking it here. She didn't want anything to affect her chances of marrying Prince Valian in three years, and she wanted to show her mother all the wonderful things in Wisen.

"Forks…" Carol continued, thoroughly enjoying herself as Haley and Sersha brought eggs, sausage, and fruit to the table.

They made up plates for the guys and watched them gobble the food down. They each received large helpings of lion's tooth to boot.

"You know this is pretty tasty," said Henry, popping a leaf in his mouth. "What is it?"

"Its lion's tooth," said Sersha, bringing him a fresh cup of tea. "I believe it's called dandelion in your world."

"Dandelion?" he said, turning up his nose. Sersha nodded. Henry looked at her with a warm smile. She smiled right back and watched him eat.

Haley and Valian exchanged surprised looks as they sat together. Haley looked over at the queen. She also noticed her daughter's attentiveness and displayed just a hint of a smile as she looked away.

The guys each had three helpings and lay back in their beds like fat satisfied cats. "You three need some fresh air and sunshine," said Lilia, waving her hand. "All right girls, let's get them tucked in good and we'll wheel them to the pavilion."

Haley hadn't noticed the beds were on wheels and found she could easily push the bed. She, Carol, and Sersha followed Lilia out the door, into the warm sunshine. The temperature was perfect.

Haley looked up and was amazed that the canopy that hid the fort so well was gone. The sky was bright blue with puffy little popcorn clouds floating lazily by.

"Thank goodness the storms have finally passed," said Lilia, opening the French doors to the pavilion.

Haley was pleasantly surprised to see the wooden walls and ceiling had been replaced by glass. Sunshine poured into the room as they steered the beds inside. Reed and Finn came in with the fresh tea and blue gum they had been brewing in their cottage.

"We must continue their treatment," said Lilia. "They may seem better but they are still very weak and need to continue resting. Haley, would you mind taking care of Valian? I have some things to tend to." Haley flashed a smile at her.

Carol and Sersha took blue gum and went to their charges.

"What a beautiful room," Carol remarked.

The very top part of the ceiling was open to the sky. The ceiling fans pushed in the warm fresh air in gentle waves. It smelled sweet like the scent of roses.

Tall palms surrounded the room, their giant leaves casting bouncing shadows in the light breeze. Flowering vines crept up the supporting beams on the outside of the structure.

Haley felt like she was in a greenhouse. There were plants everywhere she looked, plants on stands and tabletops, in pots of varying sizes, and hanging from large hooks. There were odd looking, exotic flowers she'd never seen before and she sighed, contented. She was in a beautiful place, surrounded by her family and friends and the man she loved. It didn't get much better than this she thought to herself.

Valian began to drift off as she dipped her cloth in blue gum and sponged him gently. He wore a soft smile of contentment himself as he tried to keep his eyes open. The warmth of the sun won, and he was asleep in minutes. She looked at the others. It seemed the sweet fragrance and surroundings did its magic on them and they rested in peaceful slumber.

Haley woke an hour later, surprised she had fallen asleep. Valian was awake and lay there watching her. "Hello, My Sweet," he smiled, as he struggled to sit up.

"You relax now darling," she said. "Don't overdo it. You need your rest."

"I'm sorry to have been such trouble," Valian said sadly.

"Not at all," she replied, puffing up his pillow. "I love you."

"Where is everyone?" he asked.

She looked around the room, startled to see the others gone.

"I don't know. I'll check next door."

She quickly went to the next cottage and found everyone there.

Paul and Henry were awake and were actually out of bed, sitting up on the loungers, though still covered in blankets.

"Hi, Hale," said Henry weakly. "Where's Valian?"

"I left him in the pavilion," she replied. "What are you doing back in here?"

"We woke up hungry," he answered. "We didn't want to wake you."

"Here," said Carol, handing Haley a plate. "Why don't you take him a snack. Crackers… cheese, fruit…" she commanded, delighted, as they came flying to the table. "This is such fun," she added. The others smiled as they watched Carol entertain herself.

Haley took the plate back to the pavilion with a spring in her step. Her heart was filled with joy to be able to tend to Valian as if they were already married. They sat quietly together, eating, enjoying each other's company. Colorful birds flocked around a feeder just outside one of the windows. They tweeted harmoniously as they dropped from the feeder to the ground and back again. Little spats broke out as they argued over the seed.

"Now that I'm on the mend, we should think about what we're going to do about Violet," said Valian.

"Why don't we just let her stew like you said?" Haley asked.

"Yes, tempting isn't it? She needs to be held accountable for her actions. Theodore and Troy were hurt, not to mention embarrassed, and if we find out that she had anything to do with Ike and the swamp hag…"

Haley gave him a look of disapproval. "You mean Heime."

"Yes, I'm sorry, Heime. If she had anything to do with Ike and Heime, she has committed an atrocity. She has broken a sacred law; interfering with humans is forbidden."

"We've got to find her first," said Haley. "And how are we going to do that?"

"I know!" said Valian, excitedly, "we'll use Ike!"

"She may have tried to kill him," Haley answered.

"I know, but since she's been stuck on your side she's probably discovering what a mistake she's made. She's probably been frantically trying to find a portal to get back to Wisen, but she can't see them and she doesn't dare try and use the one she knows about in the swamp."

"Yeah," Haley agreed. "She thinks Ike was killed by Heime and wouldn't take the chance entering there. She's probably getting pretty desperate by now."

"Yes, and if Ike returns, she may try and get back into good graces with him. You know how devious she's become. She'll lie and make up some story about how she slipped and missed the portal or something like that..." Valian trailed off.

They sat quietly, thinking about the possibilities. "Ike would be more than happy to help especially after what happened to him. He said that as soon as he was well enough he would be going back," said Haley.

Suddenly her face lit up as a new idea popped into her head. "Oh, my goodness, I have just thought of something!"

"What?" Valian asked in anticipation.

"The festival, the autumn festival."

"What about it?"

"It's the perfect place to lay a trap. Remember when you and Sersha showed up at the party in the park last year? Nobody realized you were real fairies, it was Halloween. We can all go. The Bonners are planning on going. We'll get a bunch of guardians Violet doesn't know and won't recognize to be there for her capture. Ike will be there with his family, and she'll be so distracted at him being alive and with all the crowds, we won't be noticed."

"Excellent idea, my sweet!" said Valian. "You're so smart."

"Nah, just read a lot of mystery novels," Haley replied, giving him a loving smile.

His eyes were beginning to droop. "Have a nap and I'll be back shortly," she said, kissing him on the forehead. Valian dozed off after a couple minutes and she tiptoed out the door.

She stood outside in the warm breeze, enjoying the sunshine and the serenity of the fort. It was so lush and green and had a park like feel about it.

She thought about their plan to ensnare Violet. If successful, they would have only one other problem to solve and that would be the biggest challenge; figuring out how to defeat Molock the Merciless. That evil presence in the land of Wisen kept the fairies on their guard, as it constantly tried to use its powers to influence any creature it could to take over and rule.

Sersha once told her that Molock was so evil that those that looked upon it went mad and most never survived. They had been extremely lucky that Zeb pulled through unscathed after they rescued him, and Ike; she had no idea how Ike escaped without any residual effects. "How do you track down and defeat something that could cause you to lose your mind and reason?" she asked herself.

It reminded her of Medusa and her head full of snakes. One direct look at her and you'd turn to stone. She wondered as she looked back at Valian sleeping peacefully, if all the fairy tales she'd been told as a child were real, then, could Medusa be real too? She half hoped it wasn't true, but if it was…?

Chapter 7
The Bonners Return

The party kept watch over the guys and saw improvement with each new day. Queen Lilia would wave her hand every evening and the canopy would spread over the fort, concealing it from aerial view, and then opened it back up in the morning.

Haley woke up the next day with a genuine feeling of joy. She looked over at her mother sleeping in the next bed. She had a smile on her face, and Haley wondered what she was dreaming about.

She showered and dressed quietly and went outside. The sun was shining bright and the forest was alive with sounds of birds. The air was crisp and the dew sparkled on the grass like diamonds.

She took a deep breath, taking in the fresh air. Smoke rose high in the sky from next door, shaped like a cyclone. There was barely a whisper of wind. She heard the door open next door as Valian came out. "Look at you!" she exclaimed. "You look so much better today!"

"Thank you, I feel great. The guys and I are going to try flying today. If all goes well we'll leave for Roan in a day or two. We want to be sure we're well enough for the trip."

"Wonderful," Haley smiled.

After breakfast, Valian, Henry, and Paul spent a good share of the day flying and changing size. They did pretty well considering all they'd been through, but by mid afternoon they were tuckered out. They got a good night's sleep and picked up where they left off.

The queen was satisfied the three were ready and made preparations to leave the following morning. By sun up she had everyone's knapsack stocked and was busy straightening up and locking up the cottages.

They gathered together in front of the pavilion after a last minute check and rose into the air. They hovered as the queen waved her hand at the fort below. The canopy of palms stretched out their leaves and covered the fort completely.

The group moved forward, flying in pairs. The trip back to Roan was free of incident. Everyone flew at an even pace only stopping for a brief rest every once in awhile. The entire journey was only a few hours.

When they landed on the palace balcony, several guardians were there to greet them, especially welcoming Queen Lilia. The group went to their rooms to get cleaned up and met back in the dining hall for an early lunch. Lilia sent messengers to call for an assembly for the following morning.

After lunch everyone but Valian and Haley went out to the balcony to sit and relax. Sersha and Henry took Paul and Carol on a little sail through Roan while Lilia was fawned over by a host of guardians.

Valian and Haley went to the blue room to talk some more about the upcoming autumn festival in Bonners Ferry. They picked out a handful of guardians that would go including Finn, Thorp, and Dinora. Troy and Theodore unfortunately would be recognized and were still recovering from their ordeal. They made plans to have the queen bestow shrouds for everyone involved and Haley's ideas of disguising them excited her.

As they discussed how they would proceed, again the thought about Medusa came back to her. "Valian, have you ever heard of Medusa?"

"Yes," he answered, looking at her curiously. "She lived in the Desert Mountains in the Desolation Realm over ten thousand years ago. It's been told that the rift shifted the weather patterns and the mountains were frozen in a great ice storm that lasted one hundred years."

"So she's dead?" Haley asked.

"One can only assume; why do you ask?"

"I don't know how true any of this is, but in our world, stories are told that she could turn you to stone with one look upon her face and she had a head full of snakes instead of hair," Haley stated.

"That is the general belief," Valian replied, still looking at her curiously.

"Before you say anything, hear me out, ok?" she said hesitantly.

"Ok," Valian agreed.

"Well I was thinking about how Molock could possibly be defeated. From what I can remember, some stories said she could turn any being to stone, whether in physical form or not, alive or dead."

Valian nodded.

"Well… if we could find her and bring back her head…"

Valian gave her a horrified look as the implication of her words began to dawn on him. He let out a heavy sigh. "We'll have to think on this… a lot. Your idea would probably work, but it would be the most dangerous undertaking. Not only would we need to consult the council, but also get the support of almost every creature in the land."

He sighed again as he pondered the idea. "We'll discuss this at another time. Right now we have other matters that need attention."

Haley nodded.

"Let's go out and join mother and get some fresh air and relax, and we'll tell her our plan for the autumn festival."

They joined the queen and enjoyed a quiet afternoon, drinking rainbow dew and watching some of the fairy children playing in the flower gardens below.

Lilia agreed to shroud the wings of all who would be going to the festival.

Sersha, Henry, Paul, and Carol came flying up and landed on the balcony beside them. Carol and Paul were loaded down with packages.

"We went shopping," Carol exclaimed excitedly. "Haley wait until you see the seeds I bought, and look," she said, pulling several silk gowns from one of the bags. "Aren't they beautiful?"

Henry and Paul rolled their eyes lovingly at her as she held each one up for Haley to see.

"Bought?" Haley asked.

"Well, bartered, that's what they do here, so I arranged to do some paintings for them when we get home."

Haley smiled at her mother's excitement and enthusiasm. "They're gorgeous," she agreed, picking up one of the gowns. "Oh! I love this one," she said, holding it up. It was a dark red color, covered in shimmering sequins.

"I'm so glad you like it because I bought it for you," said Carol, with a big smile.

"Thank you, Mom," Haley said excitedly. "I can't wait to try it on!"

"Here, I got these satin slippers to go with it."

Haley gasped. They were exquisite. Red satin with diamond studs across the toe.

"I'd love to see you wear that at the engagement gala," said Valian. "You'll look stunning."

She flashed him a smile.

"So what did we miss?" Sersha asked.

"Well," Haley began; "the autumn festival and Halloween party is coming up."

"We've been discussing the plan to hopefully capture Violet," Valian added. "Haley has some great costume ideas for us. We'll arrive a few days before the festival begins and get a good look at the park. Tomorrow Haley and I are going to visit with Ike and his parents. We have an idea that we will try and get Ike's help. Maybe use him as a decoy to distract her, if she shows up that is."

"I just hope she hasn't been roaming through the estate," said Haley.

Carol nodded in agreement.

"Well I think I will go freshen up before dinner," said the queen, rising from her seat.

Just then, Ruena walked onto the balcony. Lilia stood there looking at her as if trying to figure out who she was.

"Ruena," Haley greeted her, "you look great."

"Thank you Milady…" she began.

"Ruena!" snapped the queen, looking over at Valian with an almost angry look.

Ruena took a step back, fearful. "Your Majesty…" she began.

"What is the meaning of this?" Lilia demanded, looking from Ruena to Valian.

"I'm sorry, Mother, I completely forgot to tell you," said Valian. "With everything that's happened, it slipped my mind. Ruena was instrumental in capturing Ike."

"What are you talking about?" Lilia asked, slightly confused.

"My apologies, Mother. I can't believe we haven't told you. So much has happened since you disappeared."

Haley sighed. This was going to take some explaining.

"We had to make some decisions while you were away. Ruena here was one of them."

He explained how Ruena showed up at the Miles estate, offering her assistance in finding Princess Sersha, the fact that they split up into two teams to search for her, how Violet and Ike hooked up together, and how Ruena showed up and captured Ike.

"So you see, Mother, we all voted in favor of setting Ruena free, and I personally believe in her innocence."

"And so do I," said Haley.

"And I," said Sersha.

"Ditto," Henry agreed with a grin.

"Well… it seems I have been overruled," said Lilia. "Normally I would have my doubts, but I trust your judgment," she said to the group. "Ruena, I apologize. It is possible that my anger clouded my judgment and I accused you falsely."

"Thank you, your Highness, truly. I would have done the same, had I been in your shoes and I apologize myself on behalf of my late sister Heime."

"Late?" said the queen.

Ruena nodded. "She was taken by the earth recently. Somehow she sustained injury she couldn't heal from."

Valian and Haley glanced at each other knowing full well how Heime was injured. It was Ike's handiwork, and the sight of Heime's caved in face flashed through her mind. It was a secret neither of them would ever tell.

"I am sorry for your loss Ruena, sincerely. It sounds like you had quite an adventure," she continued. "I am proud of the effort you put forth to find me, and it seems you performed admirably under the circumstances, without my assistance or guidance. You are well on your way to kingship my son, and you couldn't have anyone better by your side than Haley."

"Thank you, your Majesty," said Haley.

Valian grinned at her, his eyes sparkling.

"Well, now that that's settled, I am going to freshen up," said the queen. "I'll see you all at dinner."

The steward came to escort Haley to the dining hall and when they arrived, the room was teaming with fairies, chattering excitedly because Queen Lilia had returned from retreat.

Valian and Sersha were already seated. Valian rose as Haley approached. "Milady, you look lovely as usual," he said with a smile.

"Thank you, Sir Valian," she replied with a glow on her cheeks, as he pulled out her chair. She sat beside him, her heart content. She wished this feeling would never go away.

Valian rose from his seat as Henry, Paul, and Carol were escorted to their table. Most of the room watched Haley's parents curiously and looked around to see if anyone else recognized them. Paul and Carol looked around the room in wonder.

Haley could see the excitement in her mother's eyes and hoped the fear and apprehension she displayed at the fort was gone from her mind, being in the safety of the palace. Henry plopped down across the table and grinned at her, rubbing his stomach. She was amused to see her betrothed was doing the same thing. "You two are like two peas in a pod," she said, laughing.

The gong sounded and everyone stood as Queen Lilia entered. Carol and Haley's eyes were wide as she neared. The queen's gown was cream colored lace. It looked so soft, Haley had the urge to reach out and touch it. Lilia wore a silver crown, inlaid with bright emeralds that complimented her beautiful auburn hair. She walked with grace and poise, worth and nobility, a true queen.

The entire room bowed.

"Please be seated," she said.

Her gentle and confident voice impressed Haley and she wondered if she would ever be able to present herself in such a way before the court.

She didn't have nearly the confidence as the queen displayed each time she appeared. Haley being such a tomboy had serious doubts that she could pass as a princess.

Still, she sighed happily and decided she would study the queen, her movements and mannerisms; perhaps the queen would give her lessons on how to act more like a princess.

"Good evening," said Lilia. The room exploded in cheers and applause. "Thank you for such a warm reception." Again, more applause.

"It is good to be back from my retreat. We are well rested and rejuvenated. I must apologize for the mayhem that was caused by my order for you to all remove your given gems. I should have exercised more foresight of the consequences of such a move. Fortunately, Prince Valian and his betrothed," she smiled at Haley, "had the sense to have you put them back on for the time being. I understand you have all been given the choice in deciding whether you wish to wear them, and I agree. The prince and princess will be hosting a new academy next year, and hopefully Haley and Henry Miles will join our staff. They have a great deal to offer, especially in the field of emotion. All those that are interested in attending, I encourage to take advantage of the benefits that will be afforded you in removing your given gems. I believe it will be our best academy to date, and an exceptional graduating class. Those of you already serving as guardians, I highly recommend you consider it as well. All those who elect to take the challenge will do so under the princes' authority, in other words, don't do it on your own. You will be under strict supervision."

She paused for a moment and observed her audience. The room was quiet.

"If you have any questions, kindly see the prince after dinner. Thank you," the queen finished, taking her seat.

The crowd applauded as the brownies emerged with the usual platters of food. Wonderful smells filled the room as everyone got busy talking and smiling as they loaded their plates and toasted the queen and the meal.

It was an unusually long dinner. It seemed no one wanted to leave. Everyone was involved in conversation and small talk. Laughter rose up from different clusters of fairies as jokes were told and old stories were re-told.

Valian and Haley held hands as Carol decided to tell everyone at the table about some of Haley's embarrassing moments of childhood. Valian chuckled and looked at her lovingly. Henry roared with laughter right along with everyone else as the memories came alive once more, and he looked at his sister affectionately. Sersha giggled, but could see Haley's embarrassment and shot her a compassionate look.

Finally the queen stood and tinked her glass. "One other thing, anyone who would like to volunteer their time and services for the upcoming engagement gala, please see me in the morning. I will be in the throne room promptly after breakfast." There was more clapping as the queen said good night and was escorted from the hall.

Paul and Carol also said goodnight as the foursome retired to the blue room for after dinner refreshments and more in depth discussion about the Bonners Ferry autumn festival.

The following morning after breakfast, Lilia went to the throne room as Valian, Haley, Sersha, and Henry left for the Seers' apartment.

Paul and Carol stayed behind as the Bonner family was coming for a visit.

It was a beautiful morning. The sun was shining brightly; the skies were exceptionally blue with puffy white clouds. There was a slight nip in the air Haley felt was refreshing as they flit through the canopy toward the outskirts. They changed size as they crested the forest and looked down on the sprawling city below.

Haley was surprised to see the leaves had started turning. The outskirts were dotted in brilliant groves of red and yellow, and the smell of burning wood brought a feeling of ease and relaxation. They landed on the main street just up from the pub. A large, dirty, closed sign hung on the door.

Norman and Mable were pleased to see them and quickly had them seated, teacups in hand. The group was surprised to find Ike was not there. "He's been getting up early to go for a run every morning," Mable shared proudly. "I am so pleased he's looking so much better and getting fit."

The fact that Ike was out on his own, made Haley a bit nervous and she could see by the look on Valian's face, he felt the same.

"He should be back shortly," Mable continued as she came in from the kitchen with a plate of cookies. "Here he comes now."

They could hear pounding on the stairs and looked toward the door as Ike came in. Haley's mouth dropped open as he came down the hall. He looked completely different. She was amazed at such a significant change in such a short amount of time. He was dripping in sweat and his cheeks were rosy red. He was no longer the skinny man she had met at the Bonners Ferry post office. He was lean and toned, with muscles on his chest and arms. She actually found him rather attractive.

He smiled wide when he saw them sitting there. "Hi!" he gasped, out of breath. "Beautiful day."

"Ike, I am amazed at the change in you," Haley smiled.

"Thank you. I feel so alive and energetic here," he said, grabbing a towel. "It's so nice to see you are back. I hope you had a pleasant trip."

Valian looked at Haley and smiled.

"It was, shall I say… interesting," he replied.

"So what's up?" Ike asked, plopping down on the sofa.

"Yes," said Valian. "We've been discussing the autumn festival coming up in Bonners Ferry."

Ike looked at the prince, nodding. "Yes, it will be good to get back… I think. I really don't recall much of the past except bits and pieces. I know I am married to Judy and have two sons, but there's so much that is missing."

"We'll work through it," Haley said, smiling encouragingly.

Valian took a deep breath, ready to continue. Ike looked at the prince. "But?" he asked.

Valian looked at Haley for support. She picked up his hand and looked over at Ike. "Part of our plan is to capture Violet."

Ike's face changed. He frowned and didn't say anything for a moment.

"We'd like your help," said Valian.

"She tried to kill me," Ike said quietly. "Of course I'll help you. Whatever you want me to do."

"She must be caught and brought back to stand before the Lords and Ladies of the court for her crimes against you, Sersha, and Henry."

Ike thought for a moment. "What about my crimes?" he asked.

"The only crime you committed was your actions under the influence of the obsidian stone. You cannot be held responsible for that.

The first time you left Wisen with your pockets full of our gems, was granted. We only asked one thing from you in return, and that was your silence about our world.

You kept your promise to us; therefore no crime was knowingly committed. Violet, on the other hand, has no excuse. Her actions were exercised freely."

"All right," said Ike, "what will you have me do?"

Preparations were made for the return to Bonners Ferry. The famous young foursome, the Bonner family, Haley's parents, and the Seers family, along with the guardians, met together in the outskirts. They set out for the portal that would lead them right out at the Miles estate inside their courtyard, surrounded by a two story stone wall that kept prying eyes from seeing the goings on inside was as expected.

They arrived one at a time, waiting for the next one to enter. Henry was the last to come through.

Zeb and Sarah stood wide eyed and silent, looking around at the outer walls. Zeb spotted the old cistern he constructed almost two hundred years earlier.

Haley watched the Bonners walk over to the giant oak tree that had stood watch over Zeb's labor, in the center of the courtyard.

"Remember when I planted this tree?" he asked Sarah, softly. She nodded at him, unable to speak.

Zeb's eyes rested on the trap door in the ground and all the memories of the past came flooding back. His sorrow and despair at the certain loss of his beloved wife and daughters, drowned in the Kootenai River overwhelmed him anew. His eyes welled up with tears. "This is where I buried you," he said to Sarah, pointing at the ground.

"I want to see it," she whispered.

Zeb nodded.

"Let's go inside shall we," Paul said to the others. Everyone understood and followed Paul through the arched doors and into the foyer.

Zeb and Sarah stood over the trap door almost as if afraid to go any further. Zeb sighed and grabbed the brass handle and lifted the heavy door. The sun shined into the dark stairs leading down to the crypt. Just as Zeb was about to take the first step, Henry came out of the estate.

"You'll need this," he said, handing Zeb a flashlight and then turned back toward the house.

Zeb looked at Sarah. "Are you sure you want to?" he asked, a tear rolling down his cheek.

Sarah smiled softly and nodded.

They descended the dusty stairs and went to the old wooden door. A very old, tarnished lantern hung just where he left it. Tears flowed from his eyes as he opened the door and went inside. There before them were three coffins. Zeb stood rooted to the spot, unable to take another step.

Sarah took the flashlight and approached the first of two small coffins. She lifted the lid and looked inside, and stared silently at the empty box. She followed suit at the other coffin, and when she lifted the lid of her own coffin, she began to cry.

Zeb went to her. They held each other, silently. "That was the worst day of my life," he whispered into her hair as he cradled her head to his face.

"I'm sorry, Zebulan," she whispered back. "It must have been so devastating for you to go through the agony of losing us, especially the children."

They continued to hold each other. Sarah was trembling with her own grief. "I'm so glad you're here," she said. "I feel so safe in your arms."

"You know, as much as I despised the swamp hag, I am grateful she pulled you through. You and the girls would have surely drowned. I often wonder if Valian and the others hadn't traveled back in time to rescue you, would we have ever found each other? It was only because of the swamp hag, that I found out you were still alive, and then I somehow became ensnared by Molock in my search for you. Thank the good Lord for the others. If it hadn't been for them…" his voice trailed off.

"We owe them a lot," Sarah agreed.

They ascended the stairs and walked out into the morning sun; thankful to be alive. They walked through the courtyard totally amazed at their old homestead. "I would never have recognized this place had it not been for this old oak and the cistern. That is all that remains from our past."

They sighed happily and walked through the stone archway into the estate. When they entered the foyer, they stood, overwhelmed at the sight before them. Sarah's eyes were immediately drawn to the grand marble staircase with the polished oak rails and the led crystal chandelier hanging from the center of the room. The black marble floor gleamed as she walked into the room, stopping to admire the beautiful tapestries. "My goodness," she whispered. "I've never seen anything like this. I didn't know they could build such things."

Zeb looked around the room in awe. "This is unbelievable," he said, running his hand across one of the oak rails.

"And look at the furniture in here," Sarah exclaimed as she walked into the dining room. The carpet was dark crimson in color and a large mahogany table shined, surrounded by matching chairs. "This just takes my breath away." Her eyes were wide as she walked into the living room and looked around.

"Things certainly have changed," said Zeb, a little sad. "It really isn't our home anymore."

"That's all right, darling," Sarah replied. "We have a home in the outskirts I wouldn't change for anything."

Zeb put his arms around her. "I love you so much, Sarah, and I thank you for our home and all you've made it."

She stood on her tiptoes and gave Zeb a kiss. "I love you too."

The door to the kitchen swung open and Valian came out with a grin. "What do you think of your old place?"

"It's beautiful," Sarah answered, "but it's really not the same."

"I guess we're just two old fashioned folks that like things plain and simple," Zeb added.

"I do wish we could have brought the girls to see this though," said Sarah. "They would have been fascinated."

"Maybe next time," said Zeb.

Ike came out of the kitchen, followed by Norman and Mable, who were just thrilled with the décor. "Paul is going to let me borrow his car to take mom and dad to my place," he said, excitedly. "I can't wait for them to meet Judy and the boys."

Haley came hurrying out of the kitchen. "Ike, could I see you for a minute?" she asked.

Ike walked over and she led him down the hall to the library. He looked at her curiously.

"Have a seat for a minute," she said, apprehensively. "Ike I'm so glad you're back and you are so much better, but I have to tell you something you probably don't remember."

"Is it something bad?" he asked, quietly.

"Well, I don't know for sure, I wasn't there but… well, Sersha and Henry overheard you telling some stranger that Judy had moved out with your sons, Ike Jr. and Ernie, and that you were talking about how she was going to get half."

A shocked look crossed Ike's face like he just had gotten slapped.

"But," Haley continued quickly, "after you disappeared into Wisen, she moved back in. Now I don't know what that means. If she had second thoughts or she was worried about what happened to you…"

Ike hung his head. "I don't blame her," he said, softly. "I haven't been much of a husband, let alone a father."

"Now don't you talk that way," said Haley. "Most of what happened to you wasn't your fault. You've changed. Judy will see it the minute she lays eyes on you."

"I hope so, I've messed things up so badly."

"She'll forgive you, I'm sure she will. You'll see. You two will start a whole new beginning together as a family, just like you did with your parents."

"We'll see I guess," said Ike. "Unfortunately, Judy was somewhat of a snob when I met her I'm sorry to say, but it's true. She only married me because of my money, money that really wasn't mine. The fairies let me keep the gems I found only because it meant so much to me and so little to them."

"You do have a good heart," said Haley, patting his hand.

Ike smiled. "You know, I've never felt so free, not in a very long time. I just hope it isn't too late."

Haley smiled back and gave him a thumbs up.

"It'll be fine, once they get over the shock," she said softly.

"You're an amazing kid, Haley, thank you," he said. "This room hasn't changed a bit," he said, looking around. "When I was a kid, old man Johnson owned this place and he used to let me come in here and read sometimes, until…"

"I know," said Haley. "I've heard the legend, and I know Mr. Johnson was found dead on the banks of the Kootenai River. I expect it was Heime the swamp hag that got hold of him. He must have fought with her half in and half out of the portal and escaped back on our side, but died of his injuries."

Ike sat silently for a moment. "Their world has turned ours upside down, you know?"

"To put it mildly," Haley agreed.

"Well, wish me luck," Ike grinned, walking to the door.

"Keep your chin up," she smiled.

"Are you two ready?" Ike asked his parents, as he entered the foyer.

"I can't wait," said Mable, her eyes shining with anticipation.

Haley waved goodbye as they piled into the minivan. As they closed the door, she sighed deeply. "I hope everything goes well," she said to Valian, standing behind her.

He put his hands on her shoulders. "I have a feeling there's going to be a lot of excitement across the valley, very shortly," he smiled.

"I'd love to be a fly on their wall," Haley giggled.

They turned and went into the living room where Sarah and Zeb were looking around, still in awe. "Come into the kitchen," Haley invited, leading them through the swinging door.

Sarah drew in a breath as she entered. She was simply delighted at all the modern conveniences and marveled at the appliances.

Paul and Carol were busy at the counter with Estelle who had come back to the estate via her postern. Sersha and the group of guardians were gathered at the table, having tea. It was mostly small talk during a late breakfast, mostly about the Miles estate and all the changes.

Haley stood up and cleared her throat for attention when she finished eating. "When everyone is through, Henry and I will show you to your rooms, then you are free to just relax and get to know the place. You two," she said, looking at Zeb and Sarah, "we have a room I think you're really going to like. Several of the bedrooms were furnished when we moved in and I believe it is with furniture from your era."

"Wonderful," said Sarah.

"It's in pretty good shape," Haley continued. "I think the owners throughout the years wanted to preserve some of Bonners Ferry history." She took Zeb and Sarah up the grand staircase and led them down the west hall. She opened the door on the right and turned on the light as Sarah gasped.

"Oh, Zeb, look!" All the bedroom furniture Zeb had made filled the room. Sarah rushed over to the bed where the quilt she made all those years ago still looked great, and was folded neatly at the foot of the bed. She gently picked it up and held it to her heart. The pair looked around the room, lost in memory. Sarah tilted her head slightly as she looked at the old chest of drawers sitting under the window. Her eyes were wide as she approached and picked up a small carved wooden box and lovingly caressed the top.

"My mother gave this to me," she smiled, softly. She lifted the lid and found it empty. She turned to Zeb. "How I miss her." Zeb went over and put his arms around her. Haley backed out the door, closing it quietly behind her, leaving the displaced couple content in their loving memories.

Chapter 8
Breakdowns and Revelations

Ike climbed behind the wheel of the Miles minivan and shut the door. Norman sat beside him in the passenger seat. He turned to face his mother. He looked at them both very seriously.

"By now you know I haven't been the best family man, but thanks to Haley, her family, and the fairies, they have shown me the error of my ways and how wonderful life could be. I just want to let you know before we get there, Judy…" he paused, looking for the right words, "Judy married me for my money, plain and simple. But I have always loved her from the day I met her in school, and I truly believe she has grown to love me. Still our relationship is rather formal, like I said; I haven't been the best family man. The affection she has shown me, I have ignored, in pursuit of my own agenda and in the process, I pushed her and the boys away. There's a lot I don't remember, but what I do, isn't very good. I think we've just gone through the motions of being a family."

Norman and Mable sat and listened without comment. Mable looked a little uncomfortable but seemed to understand.

"I want you to know, my whole outlook on life has changed. I want a strong bond with my family and I am so grateful to have you back in my life."

Mable reached forward and gave Ike's shoulder a squeeze. "Whatever we can do to help, you have our support."

"Absolutely," Norman agreed.

Ike smiled wide and started the van. The trip to the Seers house was only about fifteen minutes, but to Ike it felt like forever. Excitement was written all over his face, but his parents could feel his anxiousness.

By now the sun was high overhead and took the chill out of the air. He pulled onto the long driveway. His parents really enjoyed the scenery, commenting on the beautiful foliage. As the house came into view, Ike breathed deeply at the sight of Judy's Cadillac sitting next to the house. He parked and as they got out, Judy came out the door. Her eyes were wide with surprise.

"Ike," she exclaimed as they approached each other. Her mouth hung open as she looked at her husband. "What's happened to you? Where have you been?" she asked, looking at Norman and Mable.

Ike grabbed her and picked her up, swinging her around. "Judy something wonderful has happened," he said, setting her down.

Judy stood there in shock as she continued to stare at the two strangers standing there with huge smiles on their faces. "Who…?" she began.

"Judy you're not going to believe this, but…" he said, turning toward his parents. "This is my mother Mable and my father Norman. They are alive!"

Judy stood staring at them, unable to comprehend his words. "What…?"

"They are alive. They escaped the fire!"

"Your parents?" she whispered.

Ike grinned and nodded.

Mable stepped forward and startled Judy with a big hug.

"It's nice to meet you, Judy," she said with a motherly smile. Judy stood silent, still in a state of shock.

Norman smiled. "Ike, you have a beautiful wife," he said, taking Judy's hand in his own.

Ike began to chuckle. "Honey, I know this must be a total shock to you, it was for me too."

Judy finally found her voice. "Where have they been all these years?" she asked. "It's nice to meet you both, too," she added.

"That's a long story," said Ike, as he put his arm around her shoulder. "Let's go inside and I'll tell you all about it."

He had to lead her as her legs had become locked in place from shock. They went into the very posh living room which was sparkling clean, and sat down together. "Judy, you remember years ago I was raised by my grandparents and how we were very poor?" Judy nodded. "Then you remember that I told everyone how I had an invention that I sold for a lot of money? Well that isn't exactly what happened."

Judy sat quietly as if she didn't know what to ask first, so Ike continued. "Honey, I actually found a treasure of gemstones that I sold for a huge amount of money. That's how I was able to afford to build this house."

She shook her head. "So what's that got to do with your parents being alive?"

"Well," Ike hesitated, "I found those gems… in another realm."

She looked at Ike as though he'd lost his mind.

"This is going to be difficult for you to believe, but the day of the fire at my parents', they were transported through an invisible portal and had no memory of what happened. They have been living there all these years without a clue to their past until just recently."

Judy stood up with an angry look on her face. "You're crazy!" she said, loudly, backing away from the couch.

"I know it sounds crazy," Ike said, desperately, "but it's the truth."

"Why would you tell such a story and bring these people here, pretending to be your parents? Are you insane?" she screeched, storming out of the room into the kitchen. Ike followed her while Norman and Mable looked at each other helplessly.

"Honey, please listen," said Ike, as Judy got a glass of water.

"I'm not listening!" she yelled. "I get it; you wanted a divorce, now you've concocted this crazy story! Why? You're afraid you'll never see the boys again, is that it? And you think I am gullible enough to fall for it? Who are those people?" she demanded. "I don't understand you. You never cared anything for me! Look at our marriage. We've never been close…" she began to sob and shake and sat down as if defeated, putting her head in her hands.

Ike went to her and laid his hand on her shoulder, speaking gently. "I know. Judy honey, I know I haven't been a good husband to you, and for that I am truly sorry."

She looked up at him, her eyes brimming with tears, confused by his tenderness. "What's happened to you?" she whispered.

"Something wonderful," he smiled softly. "I love you Judy, I always have, and that's the truth. I have had an earth shattering, mind bending experience that has given me a whole new perspective. I don't think I could even begin to explain it in words you could understand or believe. I will have to show you," he said, taking her by the hand. "I have been so blind, but I now realize how beautiful and wonderful you are. What a wonderful wife and mother you have been, and how much time I've wasted on my own interests. Come with me and I'll show you what has turned my world upside down."

Judy stood, hesitantly; as if unsure she could trust this man that was so different than the man she was used to.

"Where are the boys?" he asked with a sparkle in his eyes she had never seen before.

"Upstairs playing video games, they don't know you are here, they're wearing their headphones."

Ike nodded and led her back to the living room where Norman and Mable sat, looking very uncomfortable.

"Please sit," said Ike, "and hear me out, all right?"

Judy nodded.

"This portal I mentioned, it leads into another realm, another world, filled with creatures that most of us don't believe in. Things we stopped believing in as we grew up." He paused, looking for the easiest way to explain. "There are fairies Judy, real live fairies."

Judy again looked at him as if he was out of his mind, but she kept silent as he continued.

"I can prove it to you, we can prove it. This is important and it's real."

"How?" Judy asked, determined to see through his charade.

"I have invited two of these fairies to lunch because I knew you would have a hard time believing this."

"Really," Judy responded, sarcastically.

"Yes," said Ike.

"Ok fine. I'll make some lunch. Will they be flying in?" she asked, in the same sarcastic tone.

"As a matter of fact, yes," he replied. "They are across the valley at the Miles estate."

"The Miles estate?" she said in disgust. "Those people? Are you kidding me? How can you consort with such people?"

Ike sighed. "I've spent some time with them. They are fine people."

Judy looked at him almost in distaste. "Ha!"

Ike looked at her tenderly and smiled softly.

"I don't understand you. They are so much lower than us, honestly. Our situation I can handle, but this…" she said, frowning.

"Judy, forgive me… but you are a snob. All you care about it seems is being wealthy and above everyone else."

Judy's mouth dropped open in surprise. "How dare you call me a snob, especially since you're one yourself?"

Norman and Mable sat fidgeting nervously. "Son," said Norman, "maybe we should go."

"That won't be necessary…"

"Son?" Judy asked sarcastically. "You actually have these people believing that they are your parents?" She seemed fit to be tied, rolling her eyes. "I'll go make lunch. When are these *fairies* supposed to arrive?"

"Noon," Ike replied softly.

She stomped back into the kitchen.

Ike shrugged his shoulders at his parents. "I'm sorry. This is going to be a lot harder than I thought."

"It's going to take time, Ike. You can't expect her to believe something this outrageous without proof," said Norman, rubbing his chin.

"I know. I could hardly believe it myself and I was there. I can just imagine what she's thinking. I wish I had a picture of you from all those years ago."

"Well for what it's worth, I think Judy is beautiful, and with time I think she'll come around," Mable said, with a smile.

"Thanks Mom, I appreciate that."

"Your home is beautiful," Mable added, getting up to look around. "Where are my grandsons?" she asked.

"They're upstairs, but I think it would be best to wait a bit, at least until Valian and Sersha arrive so Judy has a chance to… adjust," he answered, with a slight grin.

Mable smiled. "This will be, what's the word, interesting to see."

Ike checked the clock on the mantle above the fireplace. Eleven: Fifty a.m. He sighed deeply and went to the window and looked out at the sky. Nothing.

Judy came out of the kitchen five minutes later.

"Well?" she asked.

"They should be here any minute," said Ike. "Why don't we go out onto the porch and wait?"

"This I gotta see," she said in that same sarcastic tone.

They stood on the porch as the minutes ticked by. Ike checked his watch. Eleven: Fifty Nine a.m. He looked toward the sky again, and a slight smile crossed his face. He looked at Judy. "Here they come."

Judy looked to the sky and saw two small dots approaching quickly. Her skepticism began to fade as the figures grew nearer. Her eyes got bigger and bigger and her skin began to pale a bit.

Valian landed first, ten feet from the porch, larger than life, his wings extended out fully, a smile on his face and a twinkle in his eye.

"Ike," he began, "I hope we are not late."

"Right on time," Ike smiled.

Judy stumbled backward a couple steps as she stared at the magnificent figure before her.

Sersha lit quietly beside him.

"Hello, Ike, Mable, Norman," she smiled.

Her aurora permeated the air around her in gentle waves. Everyone could feel it, even Judy.

"This must be your lovely wife," said Valian as he approached Judy.

Judy was taken aback in total shock.

Valian wore only a tunic, revealing bulging muscles and a strong, confident face. He took Judy's hand gently and kissed her fingertips.

"Milady, it is a great pleasure to meet you at last."

It was too much for her and she fell to the floor in a heap.

"I expected as much," Ike chuckled, walking over to his wife.

Valian and Sersha shrouded their wings as Valian helped Ike carry Judy into the house. They laid her on the couch and looked at each other grinning.

"That went well," said Valian with a small laugh. "How did she take the news?"

"Not good," Ike replied. "Thank you for coming. I'm sure she thinks I'm totally nuts."

A couple minutes later Judy's eyes fluttered and she looked up at Ike and the others. Her mouth fell open but no sound came out.

"Honey, I think this is the first time you've ever been at a loss for words," Ike smiled.

She looked at him, shaking her head in disbelief.

"Judy, this is Prince Valian and his sister, Princess Sersha of the Woodland Realm."

She sat there with a blank expression. "It's... nice to meet you," she whispered, her eyes wide.

"Ike thought you may have a hard time with his news so he asked Sersha and I to come," said Valian.

Judy nodded though still speechless.

"You should be very proud of your husband," Valian began, "he has gone through a great struggle, and I am so pleased to tell you that he has come out of it so much stronger than he has ever been."

For the next hour Valian, Sersha, and Ike told Judy the story of the land of Wisen, how Ike discovered a portal to their world when he was seventeen years old, and the powerful influence of Molock the Merciless. They left a lot of the details of Ike's involvement out, out of respect and just touched on the major highlights. They explained how Haley and Henry were insurmountable in Ike's transformation. Norman and Mable told their story.

Judy sat quietly the entire time as if frozen to her seat. They could tell she was overwhelmed and tried to put her at ease, speaking softly and smiling a lot. She finally took a deep breath and sighed.

"I would have thought you were a bunch of lunatics had I not seen with my own eyes. It's the most incredible thing I have ever heard," she said, standing. "Do you mind if I have moment?"

"Not at all," said Valian, as Judy turned and went back to the kitchen.

Ike looked at the others and gave them a thumbs up and went after her.

She was standing at the counter, pouring herself a drink. She drank it in one gulp and let out a long sigh. Turning she saw Ike and gave him a half hearted smile.

"You all right?" Ike smiled back.

"I will be once I get over the shock," Judy answered. "That's the craziest story I have ever heard but… it's real."

"Yes," said Ike as he walked up and put his arms around her.

"And this change in you…" Judy began, "you are so… fit and your personality, it's so different, I don't know what to say."

"Is it good?" Ike asked.

"Yes, I never knew what I was missing until now. I'm having feelings I haven't felt since I was a little girl. My parents didn't show me the kind of love most kids experienced. They were always too busy with their parties and their social engagements… it was a lonely way to grow up. They were never physical with me; you know, like kisses and hugs, we barely ever talked…" she trailed off without finishing her sentence.

"Judy, do you realize this is the first time you've ever spoken about your past with me?"

"I was embarrassed and I didn't think you cared."

"Oh, Honey, I'm so sorry. I've wasted so much precious time," he said, his eyes beginning to well up. "Things are going to change, I promise."

He held his wife in his arms and felt her stiff and ridged form start to relax. They stood there for several minutes then the kitchen door flew open and Ike Jr. and Ernie screeched to a halt in the doorway as if shell shocked. They had never seen their parents hug before.

"Dad?" said Ike Jr. as if he couldn't believe his eyes. "Is that you?"

"It's me," said Ike, walking over to his sons, hugging them both. "It's good to be home."

The boys looked over at Judy, and she smiled and nodded her head.

"Your dad's been away at… a spa, getting in shape and healthy. Doesn't he look great?"

Ike Jr. didn't answer but stared at his father curiously.

"Did you know there are a bunch of strangers in the living room?" he asked.

"Jeez," said Ike, "I almost forgot about them. Come in boys and meet your grandparents."

"I thought they were dead," said Ike Jr., as he and Ernie followed him into the living room.

Ike introduced the boys to his parents and watched as Mable wrapped her arms around each of them.

"My land," she said, standing back for a good look. "You both look so much like your father."

She wore a huge smile and kept hugging them.

Judy stood in the kitchen doorway watching.

For the first time since Ike knew her, she looked relaxed and content and actually happy as if she didn't have to worry any more.

He introduced Valian and Sersha as Norman's and Mable's friends as he motioned Judy to join him on the couch.

Ike Jr. was captivated by Sersha. Her compassion and gentle confidence with herself seemed to confuse him, as if he'd never seen such a thing. He stared at her with an embarrassed grin on his face and watched her every move.

Sersha glanced at Valian as he tried to hide the smirk on his face.

"I'll go get lunch on the table," said Judy, getting up and walking toward the kitchen.

"Let me help you," said Ike, getting up from his chair.

Judy, surprised, smiled to herself as they left the room.

Ike Jr. continued to stare at Sersha while his parents set the table and brought out the food. He rushed over to pull out Sersha's chair and took a seat beside her.

After lunch he was glued to her wherever she went, even out on the front porch when she went to check out the old carousel.

She sat down and Ike Jr. began to spin it gently for her and finally managed enough courage to ask her out.

"Do you... would you like to go to the festival with me?"

Sersha gave him that wondrous smile as the carousel slowed to a stop in front of him.

"Are you asking me on a date?" she asked.

He nodded shyly as he turned an off pink color.

"Ike, I think you are very bright and it would be a pleasure to go to the festival with you, however I've already made plans to attend with someone else, but I will see you there. I must be honest with you, my heart belongs to another."

Ike's reaction was typical of a teenage boy, disappointed at the rejection, but hopeful at the idea of being at the same event she would be at. He was very much like his mother; used to getting his way.

"Thank you for asking me, you've made me feel special. I'll see you at the festival," she said walking back to the house.

"I'll make her want me," he said to himself with determination as he watched her go.

Valian and Sersha said their goodbyes and walked down the driveway until they were out of sight then quickly took to the air.

"My goodness," said Valian, as they crossed the valley. "That boy's got it bad for you."

"I know," she responded. "I see possible trouble down the road with him. He asked me to go to the festival with him."

"And what did you say?" Valian chuckled.

"I told him my heart belonged to another, but that I would see him there."

"I knew it," said Valian. "I could tell the day we found you in Ike's basement. It's Henry isn't it?"

Sersha blushed and didn't answer.

"Wait until Mother finds out!" he laughed with pleasure.

"Don't you dare tell her," she said, flashing him a look of warning. "I want to enjoy our secret for awhile. She'll find out soon enough."

Valian grinned as they flew up the bluff to the Miles' kitchen door.

Haley was on pins and needles with worry the entire time they were gone, and when Valian's frame filled the kitchen doorway, she rushed over and hugged him like he'd been gone a week.

"What happened?" she asked nervously.

"It went well," Valian answered. "It didn't start out that way. We could tell they had been arguing. When we arrived the place was thick with tension. Mrs. Seers thought the whole lot of them were crazy until she saw us fly in. I've got to give Ike credit. He was as cool as a cucumber and very patient."

"I was so worried it would go badly for Ike," Haley sighed with relief. "How did the Seers boys take it?"

"The only thing they know is that their grandparents are alive and that their parents are acting peculiar," Valian answered.

"They don't know who you are?"

"No, we thought it best."

"Thank goodness. They don't need to know," Haley laughed. "Come with me," she said, taking Valian by the hand. "Estelle is putting the finishing touches on your costume but she wanted to get another measurement before she finished."

They headed for Estelle's room and spotted Henry entertaining the Bonners with television.

Zeb and Sarah were perched on the edge of their seats, staring wide eyed at an episode of The Beverly Hillbillies.

Haley grinned as they passed through foyer to Estelle's bedroom door. She knocked and went in to find Estelle busy placing Valian's costume on a manikin. Dozens of stick pins hovered in front of her as she plucked them one by one from the air.

"Valian, good, come here. I need a measurement of your chest," she said, pointing to a tape measure.

It flew through the air and wrapped itself around his body.

Haley laughed as Valian's arms were pinned to his sides as a look of embarrassment crossed his face.

"You have to lift up your arms," Estelle giggled, re-directing the tape.

Valian rolled his eyes, slightly amused at all their fussing.

"Ah ha, forty five, I'll have to let this out a bit," she said, hurrying back to the manikin. "Send Sersha in, in about a half an hour will you?" she threw over her shoulder as they left the room.

They went to join the others in the living room, but Valian stopped her half way into the foyer and motioned her to follow him down the hall, past Paul's office and into the study. As he closed the door behind them he looked at Haley with a gleam in his eye and whispered. "Sersha is in love with your brother."

Haley's mouth fell open. "Are you kidding me?" she responded in excitement.

"Shh," Valian whispered. "She doesn't want anyone else to know yet."

Haley's wings popped out and she did a little air dance in celebration. Valian grinned up at her as she twirled around with joy.

"I just knew it," she said, quietly. "I had a feeling about those two when we found them in Ike's basement."

"So did I!" Valian replied in surprise.

"That's because we're so in tune to each other," Haley lovingly smiled at him.

"We may have a more serious problem though," he continued. "Ike Jr. has eyes for her as well."

"Ike Jr.? For goodness sakes, he needn't bother wasting his time. Sersha could never entertain the idea of any kind of relationship with that creep."

"Haley, I'm surprised at you. You've never spoken unkindly toward anyone since I met you, not even Violet with all her meddling."

"You don't know the Seers boys like I do," Haley replied. "Henry and I have had to endure their bullying since we moved here. They are Ike Sr. and Judy rolled up into one. Ernie never talks, I don't even know if he can talk."

"You needn't worry your beautiful little head about it," said Valian. "Ike Jr. doesn't stand a chance with Sersha, and I think Ike and Judy will straighten their sons out with time."

"I doubt it," Haley snorted sarcastically. "That's a miracle I'd love to see."

Valian looked at her, compassion and gentleness flowing from him. Haley felt like she was absorbing it, right into her heart. He put his strong arms around her and held her tight.

"You are truly my sunshine," he said. "You have made my life so much better. I look forward to each new day that I can spend loving you."

"That is the most wonderful thing anyone has ever said to me," she said, looking into his eyes.

As they kissed, Haley felt like she was floating, just her and Valian, floating off into the future. As they drew apart she saw they were about a foot off the floor and she giggled.

She sighed happily as they sank to the floor and they held hands as they went down the hall to the living room.

The next couple of days were enjoyable. The morning sun warmed things up nicely, melting the snow, and the group relaxed as they hung about the estate, learning how the other half lived.

The twin's Labrador, Casey, had somehow escaped the confines of the courtyard. When? They weren't sure, but she was about to give birth.

Later, the fairies were fascinated and delighted by the four new puppies, and spent as much time as they could, watching them and holding them, when Casey would allow it.

Haley enjoyed watching the guardians as they prepared to play a game called 'Jungo' in the courtyard. It was kind of like soccer, except it was played in the air, and instead of a soccer ball they used what was called a wiggett.

Haley watched fascinated as one of the guardians pointed into the air and two smoke rings about three feet in diameter appeared. He pointed at one of the rings and directed it nearly one hundred yards away. The two rings hung stationary in the air.

"What they have to do is get the wiggett into the other team's ring, but they can't use their hands. If one team scores, their own ring moves ten yards closer to the other team's ring and they receive a point. The other team gets a demerit, like minus a point. The object of the game is to get your team's ring to merge with the other team's ring. Then you win."

Haley looked confused.

"Oh, and another thing, when your own team scores a point, your own ring gets smaller, while the other team's ring grows bigger, making it harder for the opposing team to score, and easier for you to score, get it?"

"I think so," she hesitated with a slight frown.

"A couple other things…"

"There's more?" Haley grinned at him.

"When you take a shot and the wiggett hits the ring instead of going through it, the ring will grab the wiggett and spit it to the other team. To top it all off, the teams have to avoid cupid's arrows."

"Cupid's arrows?" Haley asked.

Valian smiled. "Each team also gets a cupid whose main job is to shoot an arrow at whoever has the wiggett. If they get hit, they lose temporary control of themselves in fits of laughter giving the other team a chance to steal. If cupid misses, the arrow will harmlessly drift to the ground.

The game began with the wiggett being thrown into the air by a referee. Valian and Haley's guardians, Celio and Lonato, were captains of each team and took off like a shot after the wiggett, batting it with their wings and feet. Haley watched mesmerized as they battled it out, totally amazed at their skills. They were very competitive. Lonato had the wiggett, kicking it like a hacky sack, heading for Celio's ring. With a strong slap of his wing he knocked it through Celio's ring, and Haley squealed as the ring shot out a burst of fireworks high into the air. Lonato's team ring grew smaller and moved closer to Celio's now larger ring.

The wiggett was thrown to the referee and he tossed it high into the air to Lonato. Arrows flew through the air missing their targets as the two cupids scrambled to make contact. The team members were busy protecting their captains, batting the arrows with what looked like ping pong paddles called scullers. By fifteen minutes after the game started, the guardian's scullers were loaded with arrows and it was becoming more and more difficult to repel them.

Haley laughed and squealed every time a team scored, sending fireworks into the sky. Lonato let out a yelp as an arrow made contact with his behind, and he began to laugh as if being tickled relentlessly holding his sides as Celio zipped below him, kicking the wiggett toward the goal. She didn't know how he did it but Celio managed to swat the wiggett into Lonato's ring, moving the two rings one score short of merging.

Lonato finally composed himself and accepted the wiggett gratefully from the referee and sent it flying with the bat of his wing, straight into Celio's ring.

The fireworks roared as the two rings became one with a giant burst of sparks and stars.

Haley laughed and clapped as Valian sat beside her with a huge grin. "It reminds me of the fourth of July!" she cried out.

"Yes, I've seen your fourth of July celebrations," said Valian, "very impressive."

"How often do the fairies visit our side?" Haley asked.

"Pretty regularly, Cupid visits a lot more often than we do."

"I thought it was forbidden for you to interfere with us."

"That is a hard thing to explain," Valian began. "We are not allowed to interfere as far as using our magic to make a human do something they would normally not do, unless the innocent are in great peril. There's a fine line between assisting and bestowing our gifts and acting in a manner that could cause more harm than good."

"I'm not quite sure I understand," Haley replied, shaking her head.

"Take Violet for instance," said Valian. "She not only appeared to the human side, which is not wrong in itself, but she acted on achieving her own desire. She collaborated with a human and she plotted against other humans, Henry and Ike, and sought to harm. We are never to use our powers to gain for ourselves, do you understand?"

"I think I do," Haley answered, scratching her eyebrow.

They sat silently holding hands as the fireworks continued to burst forth and finally began to burn out.

"Oooh," Haley sighed, "how pretty."

"You're so cute," Valian laughed.

"Haley, come try on your costume!" Estelle yelled, poking her head out the door.

Haley jumped up from her seat. "See ya in a little bit," she threw over her shoulder.

Chapter 9
Violet Revealed

Clara Owens was a heavy set woman, how old, nobody knew. Her thinning, silver gray hair was pulled into a severe, small bun on the back of her head. Clara stood in the window of the Owens Country store in Bonners Ferry looking toward the west. She had seen the bursts of sparks in the sky and stood watching, a suspicious look on her face.

She had met Haley and Carol right after they moved onto the estate on a cold rainy day one year ago. She told them of the legend of Bonners Ferry, how children went missing, and about the mournful wailing that could be heard up and down the valley every year around the time of the autumn festival. However her memory had been wiped clean of that meeting. Now she knew a family had moved in, but had no recollection of ever meeting them.

The country store had been passed down from one generation to the next; in fact it used to be a thriving place, two hundred years ago when Bonners Ferry was heavily populated with couples and families who had headed west. Not much had changed at the store in all those years except the owners, but the gold rush had people move on in search of the almighty nugget. A good share of the countryside's old cabins stood empty and silent. The laughter of children could not be heard anymore.

People became suspicious of each other with the wailing and disappearances, and the deaths, especially when old man Johnson was found at the river. Most of the town was already gone by his time, but the rumors clung to those left behind, Clara being one of them. When Ike Seers disappeared, she seriously considered closing up the old store and moving to Spokane to be with her granddaughter, but she couldn't bring herself to let go of one of the last businesses still open in town. Even the tiny post office across the road was only open on Mondays and Fridays.

She drummed her fingers on the window sill. She was tired. The town had dried up and she was tired. Tired of sitting at the store day after day, hoping a customer would pull into her lot, wishing something exciting would happen so she would have some juicy new gossip to spread with the few families still left. Even Judy Seers stopped coming as often as she used to.

She sighed heavily and went to the wood stove. The tinkling of the bells that hung on the door caused her to turn and look.

There before her was a pretty little thing weighed down with a heavy jacket. She had the most intense purple eyes Clara had ever seen. Her long blonde hair was unkempt and dirty. She was a pitiful sight, like she'd been wandering for days.

She hurried over to the stove to warm herself and kept looking around as though frightened.

Clara's heart went out to her. She looked completely lost.

"You all right, honey?" Clara asked. "Ya lost?"

The young girl didn't answer and continued to rub her hands together and hold them in front of the stove.

Clara watched her for a moment. She reminded her of her own daughter, Tara who was young and beautiful when she passed away. She lost as Tara as Tara gave birth to her granddaughter.

"Ya hungry?" she asked.

The girl turned toward Clara and nodded.

"How 'bout I heat up some soup?"

The girl didn't respond, but her eyes said yes, and Clara hurried over to the small kitchen in the back. By the time she returned, the girl's face was a little rosier and she seemed just a little more relaxed.

Clara put the soup on the counter and the girl hurried over and began to devour it. She had brought out a half loaf of home baked bread and a tray of butter as well. The girl tore off large chunks, stuffing her mouth as if she hadn't had a meal for a long time.

"Slow down, honey," Clara said smiling. "There's plenny' more."

The girl ignored her and kept eating like a wild animal. She finally stepped back, looking around the store as if in search of something.

"Thirsty," she whispered.

Clara hurried over to the refrigerated section and pulled out a quart of milk, which the girl gulped down quickly.

She looked up at Clara with a half smile.

Clara smiled back. "Ya'll by yerself?"

The girl nodded.

"Wha's yer name?"

"Violet," the girl whispered.

"Where ya from?"

The girl shook her head.

"Don' know?"

Violet shook her head again.

"Can't 'member?"

Again, the same response.

"Well, I got me a room upstairs if ya wan' ta stay for a spell, 'till ya git yer memory back."

Violet nodded.

Clara cocked her head and stared at the black stone hanging on the girl's necklace. "Say, I seed that stone before. Ike Seers got one jus' like it."

Violet raised an eyebrow as she recognized Ike's name.

Clara watched Violets reaction curiously.

"Ya know him?"

Violet shook her head.

"He's one of the richest men in the county," Clara offered. "No matter."

Violet reached into her jacket pocket and pulled out a black stone just like the one she wore, only smaller, and held it out to Clara.

"Thank you," she whispered.

Clara's eyes lit up.

"Thank ya kindly, but ya don' need ta pay me."

Violet shook her head and pushed the stone closer.

"O.k., if ya insist."

Clara took the stone and put it in her pocket. Just a hint of a frown crossed her face as she led Violet out the back door and up a steep set of stairs.

"It ain't much, but it's home," she said, leading her guest inside the dark apartment and turning on the lights, setting her keys and the stone on the table.

It was a small place, kind of shabby looking with a lot of old and worn furniture, but it was clean and neat. There were about a dozen crocheted blankets laid across the sofa and chairs and faded white doilies covered every table in the room.

"Only got one bedroom, but the couch is pretty comfy," said Clara. "Bathroom's through there," she pointed.

Violet glanced inside.

There was no shower, but a very old claw foot tub sat along the far wall with a permanent dull ring around the inside. The commode looked as though it was ready to fall through the floor from years of slow leaking. The tank cover had a large, dirt filled crack across the top.

Violet wrinkled her nose.

"Been meanin' ta fix that," Clara said from behind.

Violet jerked, startled at how close Clara was standing.

"Let's git ya cleaned up," she said, turning on the water.

Violet backed away nervously and went back toward the table. She picked up the black stone and held it out toward Clara again.

"Wear?" she whispered, pulling a chain from her pocket.

"Clara smiled and took the chain. When she took the stone into her hand another frown began to form. Her brow creased almost nervously and she seemed slightly annoyed as she fastened the stone and put the chain around her neck. She looked at her purple-eyed guest and made an attempt at a smile.

Violet smiled widely which pleased Clara.

"Let's check yer bath," she said, going back to the bathroom. She checked the water. "Jus' right," she said.

Violet walked in and shut the door and began to disrobe. Had she known about door locks she would have made sure it was secure, and ten minutes after she climbed in, Clara was knocking at the door.

"I got some clothes that might fit ya," she yelled through the door. "Belonged to my daughter."

Violet froze a moment. She sat with her wings tucked behind her as best she could.

"Thank you," she said, loudly.

Clara turned the knob and just as she was about to open the door, the little bells downstairs rang.

"I gotta run downstairs, be back in a minute," she called as she left the apartment.

Violet rushed through her bath as fast as she could, and tiptoed into the other room, dripping water everywhere as she looked for the clothes. She quickly retreated back to the bathroom and got dressed.

She'd never worn jeans before and couldn't figure out how to fasten them. The shirt was a little large for her but she somehow managed to pull it over her laid back wings, and looked in the mirror, frowning at her appearance.

"I look like hell," she muttered to herself.

The bulge in the back of her shirt was surely to give her away, so she put her jacket back on. It was the same jacket she had stolen from Ike's house after she had tricked him into Heime's swamp portal.

By the time Clara returned, Violet was sitting on the couch, fully dressed.

"Are ya cold?" she asked, eyeing Violet's jacket.

Violet nodded.

"I'll stoke up the stove," she said, starting a fire.

Soon the room was almost stifling and beads of sweat began to form on Violet's forehead. She began to pace the room.

"Sure are a nervous little thing," said Clara. "Take off yer coat and sit a spell."

Violet hesitated a moment, faced Clara and removed her coat.

The first thing Clara noticed was that Violet didn't have her pants zipped.

"Come here, Honey; let me help ya with that."

Violet reluctantly went to her and let her fasten her jeans.

Clara looked up and noticed the bulges sticking out the sides of Violet's back.

"Land sakes," she said, reaching out to touch her. "Are ya injured?"

Violet jerked away from her and went back to the couch.

Clara studied her face. "Born with it?" she asked.

Violet didn't seem to understand, but nodded.

"Humpbacked?" Clara asked further.

Violet nodded again.

"Nothin' ta be ashamed of," Clara replied. "Had a cousin once, born with six fingers on each hand." she began to laugh. "Fastest poker player in town. Disappeared 'bout ten years ago."

Violet just sat and listened to Clara ramble.

"Bin pretty quiet round here las' few years… least we got the festival comin' up. Hey, ya wan' ta go?"

Clara's face lit up at the thought.

Violet cocked her head and nodded.

"Sure don' talk much, do ya?"

Violet just smiled.

"I gotta stock of costumes downstairs. Wan' ta go pick one out?" Clara asked. Violet followed her down to the store and went to a small section in the hardware aisle. She browsed through the few costumes Clara had ordered.

"Not much ta pick from. Sorry, jus' no call to git many anymore…"

Violet picked out the only witch costume. It was several sizes too large.

"Kinda' big for ya ain't it?"

But Violet held it to her chest as if she'd made up her mind.

"Kay, think I can fix it up so it'll fit better," Clara smiled.

Violet wandered through the store, looking at the merchandise. In the hygiene aisle she stopped and stared. She picked up a box of black hair coloring and smiled to herself. She continued visiting all the aisles, picking up whatever she pleased and then went out the back door.

On her way up the stairs, she heard the sound of small explosions and stopped to look for the source. She had heard that sound about an hour ago, and it frightened her.

She looked toward the west as another blast went off. Her eyes grew wide as a small burst of sparkle rose above the tree line and disappeared.

"The fairies are back," she said to herself.

"Whas' sat?" Clara said behind her, causing her to jump.

She flashed Clara an annoyed look.

"Sorry 'bout that," Clara apologized. "Whatcha got there?" she asked, looking at all the stuff in Violet's arms.

She spotted the box of hair coloring and frowned.

"Yer not gonna use that are ya? Not on that beautiful hair of yers?"

Violet ignored her and continued up the steps, flashing a look toward the west as she went inside. She promptly went to the bathroom and shut the door. Forty five minutes later she came out smiling as she showed Clara her long black locks.

"It's different," said Clara. "It'll go good with yer costume."

"When is the festival?" Violet asked.

"That's the mos' you've said since I met ya. It's on Saturday."

Violet frowned.

"Two days from now," Clara said. "Yer not from 'round here, are ya?"

Violet shook her head.

"Where 'bouts?" Clara asked.

Violet didn't answer and went over to her costume. She held it up and smiled.

"You will help me?" she asked.

"Course," Clara answered.

Violet put the outfit down.

"I'm going out for awhile. I'll be back later," she said, going to the door.

"Where ya goin'?" Clara asked a little alarmed. "There's nowhere ta go. Ya'll git lost."

Violet ignored her and went down the stairs and walked into the forest behind the store.

Clara watched with a frown as Violet disappeared into the trees.

118

As soon as she was out of sight, Violet removed her shirt and extended her wings with a sigh of relief. She flapped her stiff wings with the speed of a humming bird to work out the kinks and took flight.

She flew directly toward the place where she had seen the fireworks. Half way there she came upon the Seers property and suddenly stopped and stared.

Ike Sr. and Judy were outside sitting on the faded carousel with their arms around each other, giggling in the sun.

Violet grew pale and sunk below the tree line before she was spotted. She sat at the top of a tree, hidden in the leaves and watched the couple. She couldn't put her finger on it but Ike looked different somehow. She could hardly get over the shock of seeing him alive, let alone the physical change in him.

"How can this be?" she asked herself.

She heard a noise and turned to see a minivan coming down the drive. She sank a little lower into the leaves, drawing in a quick breath as Haley, Valian, Sersha, and Henry got out and walked over to Ike and Judy. She leaned forward to hear what they were saying, but she was too far away.

Ike and Judy laughed and went into the house and came out a couple minutes later and piled into the vehicle with everyone else and drove off.

She scowled as she watched them go and decided to follow them.

The Miles minivan pulled into the gravel parking lot of Owens Country store and everyone got out.

Haley opened the door and everyone walked inside.

Clara had just come in from the back. She wore a small frown as she hurried up the isle to the front.

"Hi, Clara," Haley said cheerfully

"Do I know ya?" Clara frowned even more.

Haley had forgotten almost everyone's memories had been wiped clean.

"I…"

"Howdy, Ike, Judy," she grumbled, going behind the counter.

Everyone exchanged looks, puzzled by her tone.

"Howdy to you," said Ike. "We thought we'd do a little shopping before the festival. Judy's got a lot of cooking planned."

"What happened to yer cook?" Clara asked.

"Oh… on vacation," Judy said, quickly.

"I would like some pipe tobacco while we're here," said Ike.

"Since when did ya start smokin a pipe?" Clara asked.

"Oh, I like a pipe every once in awhile," Ike responded, walking up to the counter while the others looked around the store.

Clara bent down and grabbed a package of tobacco, and as she did, her necklace was clearly visible.

Ike stared at it as if trying to remember something.

"Where'd you get that necklace?" he asked, almost accusingly.

"Was a gift," Clara answered.

"From who?"

"A little girl that wandered in a few hours ago."

Haley had just come around the corner and caught the tail end of the conversation. She spotted the necklace and the stone Clara was holding in her fingers.

"What did this little girl look like?" she asked.

"I'm sorry, didn't git yer name."

"I am Haley Miles. What did you say she looked like?"

"Where ya from?" Clara asked.

Haley was getting annoyed at being interrupted.

"We've moved onto the Johnson estate. Please, about the girl…"

"Pretty little thing. Pitch black hair, small in stature, why'd ya ask?"

Haley was disappointed and her heart sank.

"I just thought it was someone we're looking for."

"Got the purplest eyes I ever seed," Clara continued.

Haley and Ike exchanged glances.

"She's got black hair?" Haley asked.

"Well, was blonde when she came in, but she dyed it. What in tar nation she did that fer, I'll never know…"

"Where is she?" Haley asked, excitedly. "Is she here?"

"Left bout twenty minutes ago, didn't say where she was goin'."

"Valian!" Haley yelled. "That is a beautiful necklace," she continued, "mind if I have a closer look?"

Clara bent forward, over the counter.

Haley reached up and took the stone in her fingers then suddenly ripped it from Clara's neck.

"What the…" Clara's demeanor changed quickly as Valian tore around the corner of the last aisle, a mixture of fear and concern on his face.

"What…?"

Haley held the necklace out to him as Sersha and Judy hurried up to the counter.

"Can you please restore her memory?" she said, under her breath to Sersha.

"Violet's been here," she said to Valian.

Valian took the stone, looking at it with distaste.

Sersha waved her hand in front of Clara nonchalantly as Valian pocketed the stone.

Clara shook her head, slightly confused.

"Wha's goin' on here?" she asked.

"The girl that gave you the necklace, which way did she go?" Haley asked.

"Girl?" Clara asked, with a frown. "Oh, yeah, she went out back inta the forest."

"Clara says she dyed her hair black," Haley stated.

"Huh?" said Valian, "she did what?"

"Never mind, I'll explain it to you later. Clara, tell us everything you know about this girl," prompted Haley.

Clara told them about the way the girl gobbled down her food, the fact that she was a humpback, and about her picking out a witch costume for the festival.

The four looked at each other in contemplation. Valian motioned the others to follow him and they walked over to the stove.

"What should we do?" Sersha asked.

"Let's get the stuff we came here for and act like nothing's wrong," said Valian. "We'll let her think we don't know anything; that way she'll still go to the festival and we can carry out our plan."

"Good idea," said Haley, "but what are we going to do about Clara? She is bound to mention we were asking about Violet."

"I'll wipe her memory of that conversation," said Sersha, grinning. "As far as she'll know we just came here to shop."

"You're just too bad," Haley grinned, giving her a high five, and walked back over to Clara and made small talk while the others did their shopping.

As they left the store, Sersha waved her hand again and they glanced at Clara standing in the window, shaking her head in confusion as they pulled away.

Violet watched from the park across the road as the minivan drove away. She flew quickly to the forest behind the store and retrieved her shirt and went in the back door, hurrying up to the counter.

"There ya are," Clara smiled, as Violet approached. "Where'd ya go?"

"What did those people want?" Violet demanded

"Jus' came in to do some shoppin'," Clara answered.

"Did they ask about me?" she asked.

"No, jus' bought a bunch of groceries an' left. You in some kinda trouble or somfin'?"

Violet ignored the question and frowned as she stood deep in thought for a minute. She looked at Clara and gave her a forced smile.

"No," she answered. "Everything is fine…"

Chapter 10
The Autumn Festival

The next two days couldn't have gone slower for Haley and the others. Haley was on pins and needles, worried that something would happen and Violet would disappear.

The group busied themselves with costume preparation, helping Estelle with minor little details.

Haley had planned to go to the festival dressed as a fairy but thought she might be recognized by Violet so she decided to go as cat woman.

She was delighted at the great job Estelle did putting it all together, complete with a very long tail that hung to the ground, a black body suit, black mask and great pointed ears and whiskers.

Valian was going as Zorro, also dressed in black, with a long black cape and mask. "Nobody will recognize us," he commented, as he modeled his mask for her.

"I'd know those dimples anywhere," Haley giggled.

Henry and Sersha were dressed in genuine Native American attire you would typically see at a powwow, bright and beautiful, complete with feather headdresses, elaborate jewelry and moccasins.

"You two look great," Haley said, as they showed off their outfits. "I love the Native American culture," she remarked, as she straightened Henry's headdress.

Blue, red, and yellow feathers fanned out above his head and the blue and red beaded headband shined. Around his neck he wore a beaded necklace in like colors and his shirt and pants complimented the headdress.

Sersha's outfit was not as bold, but in softer tones of light pink. Her feathers were white and hung down the back of her hair. Her shirt was pale pink, made from soft suede with white beads intertwined in the stitching. Her long skirt was similar with white beading down the front, and she wore a simple beaded necklace.

Everyone smiled at each other as they paraded in front of the full length mirror in Estelle's room.

"I wouldn't doubt that you and Henry wind up winning first prize," said Haley.

Paul and Carol walked in and Haley burst into laughter. Everyone looked at the couple, dressed as Jethro and Ellie Mae from The Beverly Hillbillies.

"Well?" Carol blushed. "How do we look?"

Carol was wearing a braided blonde wig, a flannel shirt and blue jeans with a rope for a belt, and had painted little black freckles on her cheeks.

"You look great, Mom," Haley giggled.

Paul was quite comical in his outfit. A couple pieces of straw stuck out of his hair. He also had on a flannel shirt and blue jeans with legs that came up past his ankles.

"You expecting a flood?" Henry grinned.

"Your mother insisted," Paul replied, turning red.

His black combat boots really tied it all together.

Estelle sat on the bed, watching the entire time, pleased with her work.

"You all look terrific," she said. "Have you gotten a look at the guardians costumes?"

"No," Haley answered. "Where are they?"

"They're in the study, helping each other get dressed," Estelle answered.

Everyone headed for the study.

"I'll get dinner started," Estelle called after them.

Henry opened the study door and stood there with his mouth open.

There before him stood tin soldiers.

"Wow," said Haley, as she pushed past him. "I don't believe it!"

The guardians stood at attention, dressed in black and red uniforms. All wore high black boots and helmets that partially covered their eyes.

"Soldiers from the Nutcracker! They look like the real thing!" Carol marveled.

"Estelle said we needed to learn how to march as one," said Lonato. "What did she mean?"

"Let's show em Henry," Haley smiled.

"Left, left, left right left," Henry chanted, as the two of them began to march across the room, single file.

The guardians glanced at each other.

"All right, you guys try it," said Henry.

The guardians began to march totally out of step.

The twins laughed and stepped in to try and make some sense out of it all.

"I feel rather silly," said Celio, as he tried to match the others.

"It'll be all right," Haley giggled. "You can practice some more after dinner if you want."

Paul and Carol watched for a bit then decided to go change back into their clothes.

"I'm going to help Estelle with dinner, then it's right to bed soon after that. We have a big day tomorrow, and I want everyone to be well rested."

Haley, Valian, Sersha, and Henry watched the guardians continue their feeble attempts at marching. They finally gave up hope they'd ever get it right and left to change.

Carol and Estelle stayed in the kitchen after dinner, cooking up a storm for the festival. Carol made one of the kids' favorites; tater tot casserole, along with a couple apple pies, and also marinated a big pot of ribs.

The rest of the group went to the living room to watch a little TV before bed. The fairies were all gathered around the set, watching old re-runs of Bewitched, shrieking with laughter.

Haley really enjoyed it and thought it more fun to watch their reactions than watching the show.

Estelle came out of the kitchen with ember potions for all, but only gave them half a cup.

"A full cup will have you all sleeping in," she said, as she handed them out.

Soon everyone's eyes began to droop and they went to bed.

Haley woke the next morning, excited before she even got out of bed. The sun was shining brightly through her tower walls, which were mostly all glass. She and Sersha shared her room and she looked over to find Sersha still asleep.

She looked out the windows at the valley below. Most of the snow from the freakish storm was completely gone as the last few days had been so warm.

The leaves had begun to turn, causing her heart to feel joyous and light. She loved autumn. It was her favorite time of year, when the trees turned; the temperatures were mild during the day, and the nights nippy.

"Sersha, wake up," she said, walking over and giving her a nudge.

Sersha turned over burying her head under her pillow and moaning. "It's too early," she mumbled.

"Come on," Haley smiled, "today is the festival. We have to get dressed and get there early." Sersha looked up at her, her pillow still on top of her head, and sighed. "You're still not much of a morning person are you?" Haley laughed.

Sersha's beautiful auburn hair was all askew and her deep green, brown speckled eyes were only half open. "Oh darn," she said. "I was having a dreamy dream."

"What about?" Haley asked.

"Henry," she blushed.

"Henry?" Haley asked, acting surprised. "And what about Henry?" she said playfully.

"You promise not to say anything?" Sersha asked with a slight frown.

"Of course I promise."

"I think he's cute," Sersha whispered.

"Do you mean…" Haley began, grinning.

Sersha nodded.

"I had a feeling about you two," Haley said, plopping down on the bed.

"We were holding hands in my dream and we kissed." Sersha's face turned red and she sighed again. "Do you think he likes me?" she asked.

"Well of course he likes you, can't you tell?"

"I guess so," Sersha replied.

Haley thought for a moment. "You know; guys seem to have a harder time showing their feelings than girls do."

"How come?"

"I don't know, it's in their genes maybe. You can help draw it out of him you know."

"Really?" Sersha asked, giving Haley her complete attention. "How?"

"You could come right out and tell him," Haley suggested.

"I could never do that, I'd be too nervous."

"You'll have to be more subtle then," said Haley.

"What does that mean?"

"You know, like drop him a hint occasionally. Sit by him at meal times, hang out with him, smile at him and bat those beautiful eyes. Like today at the festival, you could tell him you're glad he's there and since your both dressed in the same kind of costume; you're a couple, so link arms and arrive like a couple, you know what I mean, flirt with him."

"You mean like laugh at his jokes?" Sersha grinned.

"Yes. Go for a walk with him through the park. Talk about the beautiful day, confide in him, tell him your dreams."

Sersha sighed again. "It's so complicated."

"It doesn't have to be," Haley replied. "Just act natural; your heart will do the rest."

"You're a good friend, Haley," Sersha smiled.

"Come on; let's get into our costumes and go down for breakfast," said Haley.

"I can't wait," Sersha exclaimed.

Haley was pleased with Sersha's excitement, and pleased about the match with Henry.

The girls spent the next hour getting showered and dressed, primping in front of the mirror and giggling like a couple of school girls.

Haley took delight in curling Sersha's hair and adding a little lipstick. She was already stunning and had no need for makeup. Haley remarked at how perfect Sersha's skin was.

She had long thick lashes and her cheeks had a natural glow and she had a pretty figure to boot.

"You could be a model," said Haley.

"Thank you," said Sersha. "I've often wished I could be a model."

"You know what that is?" Haley asked, surprised.

"Sure," Sersha replied. "Every five years we have the fabled fairy pageant. I wouldn't dream I could enter such a contest."

"Why not?" Haley demanded. "You're gorgeous."

"You really think so?" Sersha asked, blushing.

"Yes!"

"I don't know. You should see those fairies," Sersha said doubtfully.

"I can't imagine any of them being more beautiful than you," Haley stated.

Sersha turned red and grinned. Haley smiled and rolled her eyes and grabbed Sersha's arm as they headed down the tower stairs where they ran into Henry and Valian coming out of Henry's room.

"Well good morning, my sweet," said Valian, kissing Haley's hand. "You look like a feisty feline this morning," he grinned.

Haley giggled.

"And you look dashing and mysterious," she replied.

Henry looked at Sersha with a boyish smile.

"You look... pretty."

"Thank you, Sir Henry. You look like a respected chief," said Sersha, returning the compliment.

Valian and Haley exchanged smiles and led the way down the stairs.

Carol and Estelle were up to their elbows getting everything ready for the festival besides getting breakfast on the table for so many people.

The Nutcracker guardians were gathered in the dining room at the table, which the cooks had set up like a buffet, filling their plates and taking them to the TV trays in the living room.

Zeb and Sarah sat at the butcher block table in the kitchen, finishing their breakfast when the foursome walked in.

"I'm starved," Henry and Valian said in unison, which made Haley giggle.

The Bonners stared at their costumes in awe. They had not seen them the night before, being used to going to bed when the sun went down and rising before dawn.

"What are you two wearing?" Sarah asked, looking at Henry and Sersha.

"We're Native Americans," Henry smiled.

"Native Americans, what's that?" she asked.

"We're Indians," Henry explained.

"I've never seen an Indian dressed that way," Sarah replied.

"Well they don't. usually. This is what they might wear at a powwow."

"Powwow?" Zeb asked.

"It's when they meet together and perform hunting or healing rituals in dance," Henry smiled.

"It's like a celebration," Haley added. "They dance traditional dances and rejoice in their culture. It's a fascinating and wonderful thing to be a part of."

"Our world sure has changed since we've been gone," said Sarah.

"Yes," said Zeb nodding in agreement. "I can hardly believe the progress. The motorcars, the kitchen aid's and your... what did you call it, TV. What kind of minds must have thought all this up, this... progress."

Sarah had that melancholy look on her face again.

Haley looked at her kindly, almost motherly.

"It must be difficult for you to see such change, never being a part of it."

Sarah smiled. It was like looking in a mirror for her, only to see a reflection from far away in an uncertain future.

"It'll be fine," Haley smiled back. "Which reminds me, Sersha did you get a chance to restore everyone's memory? People will think you are me," she said to Sarah, grinning.

"No, I haven't," Sarah replied. "I'll do it now."

She waved her hand as they grabbed a quick bite then helped carry all the food to the van.

"We're gonna have to make two trips," said Paul, as he handed Henry an armful. "I think we're also gonna have to buy another vehicle."

Zeb came out with his hands full.

"Why aren't you dressed up?" Haley asked, as she took the plates from him.

"Sarah and I are coming as ourselves," he answered, proudly. "No one will recognize us so we'll dress in clothes from our time."

"I like it," Haley replied.

Paul climbed behind the wheel as the famous foursome and the Bonner's piled into the van.

The drive to Bonners Ferry was filled with excited chatter and anticipation. There were only a couple families already there, setting up the fire pits and moving picnic tables around.

Decorations had already begun. A group of seniors from the Moyie Springs High School had volunteered for the job and soon the park was full of witches and ghosts hanging from the trees.

Black and orange crepe paper streamers were strung. Spider webs hung from the doors of the post office and outhouses.

As the group climbed out of the van and began unloading, a truck filled with hay bales and pumpkins backed in and two hefty men began to set them up.

The trail to the old deserted house at the other end of the park was lined with pumpkins, scarecrows and small paper bags with candles in them, and two of the seniors began to fill one tree with big, black bats.

Valian and Henry lay claim to one of the picnic tables and dragged it to the back of the park, next to the post office so no one could set up next to them except on their left.

Sersha and Haley laid a tablecloth on and began setting up the dishes as Paul backed out and headed back to the estate.

Zeb and Sarah unfolded the lounge chairs they brought and set them in small groups around the site, then sat and watched, wide-eyed at all the activity.

Valian and Henry got their fire pit lit and stood talking.

The Bonners decided to take a walk through the park. They were mere shadows of days long gone, and Haley imagined what it must have been like all those years ago. Women dressed in long skirts and wide brimmed hats walking through the town with their parasols' open, the horses and buggies lining the dusty streets, and the sound of the blacksmiths hammer.

She was enjoying the daydream and the warmth of the sun on her face when Henry called out to her.

He motioned to Zeb and Sarah as they stood in front of the bronze statue of Zeb. They stood there for several minutes, their arms around each other, staring and reading the words. Finally they ambled over to the post office.

The four quickly followed and caught the tail end of the Bonner's conversation.

"...don't remember this building being here," Sarah was saying when she stopped suddenly and gasped at the portrait hanging on the wall. "Zebulan," she whispered. "This is... I can't find the words, it's... spooky."

"It's overwhelming," Zeb agreed, giving his wife a squeeze.

"I feel strange, like we shouldn't be here," said Sarah, gripping Zeb's arm. "I want to go home, back to the other side."

"Yes," Zeb nodded. "It doesn't feel right."

"We'll take you back tonight after the festival," Valian offered.

"I'd rather go now if that's all right," said Sarah. "I'm very uncomfortable here. It was nice to visit... but... this new world frightens me."

"I really should take them now," said Valian, looking at the others. "I'll only be gone a short time. Sersha, you and the others keep your eye on things and I'll be back as soon as I can."

They turned to leave the post office as Paul and Carol pulled in with the guardians and began to unload what was left.

Valian went to have a word with Paul in private. Minutes later Paul left with the Bonners and Valian while the rest of the group got settled.

"What's going on?" Carol asked as she set out the condiments.

Haley explained what happened.

"Poor thing," said Carol. "I know exactly how she feels. Visiting Roan was a scary thing; a bit fun, but scary. There really is no place like home and familiar surroundings."

Just then they heard a beep as a pretty red Cadillac pulled up. Ike and Judy waved when they saw Henry, Sersha and the two legged black cat.

The group waved back and walked over to the car as Norman and the Seers boys climbed out of the back. Ike Jr. took one look at the Miles twins and promptly took off looking for their friends. Ike Jr., however, kept a close eye on the group, especially Sersha and Henry, his jealousy totally apparent as he stole glances at them.

Ike began to unload the Caddy as Judy and Mable walked over, congratulating them on such splendid costumes, explaining that she and Ike decided not to dress up this year.

"I don't like the looks of that," said Henry as Ike Jr. joined his hoodlum friends with Ernie tagging along behind.

Ike Jr. and Ernie were both dressed like pirates, Ike's costume being the better of the two. He wore a black pirate hat, a black, long sleeved shirt with a red vest, black eye patch, and black pants and boots with silver buckles.

He stood with his friends, laughing it up, and watching the horseplay, all the while glaring at Henry.

"Let me go talk to him. I can smooth things over," said Sersha, heading in Ike Jr.'s direction.

Henry didn't know what he should do, let her go over or try to stop her, then decided to wait and see what would happen.

Ike Jr.'s group suddenly got quiet as they watched Sersha approach. Ike Jr. said something quietly to them and they all laughed as they looked in Henry's direction. Henry grew red in the face, though it was hard to tell with all the face paint he had on.

"Steady there," Haley said quietly.

"Good morning, Ike," Sersha said, softly. "It's nice to see you."

The effect her voice had on the group was nothing short of miraculous, and the boys stood behind Ike Jr. with blank expressions, they were so taken by her beauty. Ike Jr. grew red around the ears.

"Good morning, Sersha, nice costume."

"Thank you, Ike, yours is nice as well. I thought you might join us at our table."

Ike Jr.'s ears grew so red they matched his vest.

"Ah… ah… I don't think so, but thanks. I'm just hanging with the guys today," he stuttered, his face beginning to warm.

"Very well," Sersha replied, turning to go.

Ike Jr.'s friends began to jab and nudge him to accept her offer, giving him a push forward, which prompted him to speak.

"I'll take a rain check though," he called out, blushing immensely.

"Rain check?" Sersha repeated, turning around.

"Yeah, like maybe some other time?"

"I'll consider it," she replied and walked back toward Henry.

Ike Jr. turned around with a triumphant grin and slugged one of his friends on the arm as his group hooted and laughed, congratulating him.

"What did you say to him?" Henry asked when she got back.

"I invited him to join us."

Henry's mouth fell open.

"He refused of course. He seemed to want to accept, but I think he was embarrassed."

"I'm sure," said Henry. "He wouldn't want to be seen hanging around with us," he continued, motioning toward Haley.

"That was amazing," said Haley. "He was like putty in your hands. See how emotions can make you act, say silly things you would never expect yourself to say?"

"Yes," Sersha smiled. "I'm beginning to see how powerful emotion can be. I felt like I could have led him right off a cliff without any objection."

"That's a thought," Haley grinned.

Henry chuckled at the implication.

Carol sat in a lounge chair listening. "How did you get so smart, you two?" she asked proudly. The twins just smiled and went to join her.

Haley sat quietly while the others made small talk and puttered around their site. She was worried about Valian and concerned about the Bonners, and disappointed that they had to leave, but she couldn't blame them for how they felt.

Paul and Valian returned a half an hour later as more and more people arrived. Soon the park was teeming with families in a host of costumes.

Haley gave Valian a big hug, and he filled her in on the Bonners. "We got back to the estate and Sarah wanted to take some of her belongings back with her. That's what took so long. I took them through the portal and left them in the outskirts."

"How were they?" Haley asked.

"Relieved," Valian replied. "They said to tell your family thank you for your hospitality. So anything going on?"

"Not yet," Haley replied. "No sign of any black haired witches yet, but we had a few tense moments when Ike Jr. arrived," she continued, filling him in.

"Isn't love grand?" he smiled.

"Yes it is," Haley agreed.

Ike Sr. and Judy came strolling over after greeting some of their friends, which weren't many, but word spread like wild fire about Ike's physical and personality change. Judy was even mentioned in conversation as looking so much cheerier than usual.

As the noon hour approached, folks gathered at a very long table in the middle of the park where everyone brought their dishes to pass. The sun was shining bright and warm.

Cat woman and Zorro began to sweat, all dressed in black. Haley had to roll up her sleeves and Valian removed his cape with a sigh. There was just a hint of a breeze to cool them.

As they walked back to their site with their plates, they reminisced about the first time they saw each other at last year's autumn festival, and how they finally met at the old pub in the outskirts, and how so much had happened since then.

The horseshoe tournament was just beginning as they finished eating. Henry had Sersha talked into signing up. Valian and Haley sat in the shade and watched with amusement as Sersha tried her hand at it.

Ike, Judy, Paul, and Carol also joined in the fun as Norman and Mable enjoyed the game in the comfort of lounge chairs while sipping cool drinks. Haley was almost doubled over with laughter at Judy and Carol's attempts at hitting the pole.

As the tournament wound down, couples dragged blankets and loungers to the side of the road for the annual parade.

Valian kept watch from the shadows of the woods with Haley while the rest of the group joined in the fun. As the floats and fire engines lumbered past, Haley gasped.

"What?" Valian asked.

"I thought I saw a witch."

"Where?"

She pointed at the Owens Country Store across the road.

"I was almost positive I saw a witch with black hair."

Just then they both did a double take at the float about to go past. It was a haunted house full of black haired witches with their heads sticking out from every window, all waving at the crowds.

They exchanged looks of concern.

"She could be any one of them," cried Haley, exasperated.

"Great!" Valian snorted in disgust. "How are we going to figure out which one?"

Haley shook her head.

"I know! Nobody I've ever met has violet eyes like she does!" exclaimed Valian, with a proud smile at thinking it up himself.

"Let's keep our eyes peeled," said Haley.

"Eyes peeled?" Valian frowned. "How can you peel…?"

"That's something else I'll explain to you later," Haley giggled.

They left their site and went to mingle with the others.

Chapter 11
The Kidnapping

The Bonners Ferry autumn festival was in full swing by early afternoon. There were almost twice the number of people in attendance than usual, and the park could barely contain them.

Half the adults were gathered together in groups enjoying beverages and playing in poker tournaments. Music was blaring from a dozen different radios.

Local vendors from Moyie Springs had set up panel trucks that opened up into smaller versions of kitchens at the far end of the park where they sold popcorn, cotton candy, beverages and all kinds of goodies for the kids.

Frisbees and footballs were thrown while the smaller children played that age old, ever popular, game of tag.

Ike Jr. and his pack of bullies had disappeared into the forest much to Henry's relief and the group sat back and relaxed and watched.

The Nutcracker soldiers were fascinated by all the activity, costumes and games, spending most of the afternoon roaming the park and observing with amusement.

Lounge chairs had to be moved regularly to keep up with the sun's movement so people wouldn't be baked.

Though it seemed most of the Miles' party were engrossed in the goings on, they kept a watchful eye on everything.

Paul and Carol came hurrying over excitedly and told them some investors were there scoping out the area to build a ski resort.

"That would really boost our economy!" Paul was telling Ike Sr. "Our property values will sky rocket, our town will start to grow. Maybe it will become a vacation destination, not just in the winter; there's some really great hiking to be had."

Haley had never seen her father so excited. Though she didn't know much about business, she thought it would be a good thing too.

"Not only that," Paul went on, "but we could really capitalize on the Bonners Ferry legend. I think it would be a great attraction, don't you? I'm an architect. We could restore some of the old buildings of the past…"

It looked like his mind was spinning with ideas.

"Not only would it be good business for us, but for all the neighboring towns," he added as though trying to convince everyone listening.

"I agree," said Judy, surprising everyone with her input. "Really, I think it's a marvelous idea. You know, like some towns have attractions of houses that are supposedly haunted, that kind of thing. Look at all the old deserted properties that are scattered throughout our mountain, the possibilities are endless."

Paul grinned at her gratefully.

They all sat for the rest of the afternoon discussing their ideas while the foursome and guardians kept a look out.

As the sun began to sink and the bonfires were lit, Haley grew more and more tense.

"Maybe she's not coming," she said.

"She'll come," Valian said, quietly. "She won't be able to resist. Her curiosity will get the better of her and she'll try and get to Ike. If there's any possibility he knows where the portals are hidden, she'll come. She can't live out her life here as a humpback," he chuckled, his eyes filled with humor.

Haley smiled and sighed.

The guardians kept a continuous rotation around the park, checking the eyes of every black haired witch that walked by.

As it grew darker, the candles in the bags and the pumpkins lining the path to the old deserted house were lit as the children chanted, "Haunted house, haunted house!"

The adults gathered up their little ones and headed in that direction. The screams of young girls rang out as goblins and ghosts jumped out at them as they made their way, filled with excitement at what lie ahead.

Haley got up and began to pace nervously on edge.

The bonfires cast flickering shadows throughout the park making faces hard to recognize.

Haley stopped abruptly as she saw a pirate and a dark haired witch with a pointed hat, standing just past the edge of the forest, in the trees. It was Ike Jr., she was sure of it. She grabbed Valian's wing and pointed at them, whispering.

"Look, there's a witch over there with Ike Jr."

Valian's eyes narrowed as he stared.

The two disappeared into the forest.

"That couldn't have been her," said Valian. "What would she want with Ike Jr., and how would she even know who he is?"

"I don't know. I just have a feeling something isn't right," Haley frowned.

They stood silently staring at all the activity, which was hard to distinguish until the clouds overhead passed, and a huge beautiful full moon lit up the countryside.

"Wow," Haley remarked. "How fitting for Halloween," she added, gazing up at it. "Perfect."

"I don't think I've ever seen it so big," said Valian, following her gaze.

Laughter and screams filled the park. Owens Country store and the gas station across the road were lit up with strings of glowing pumpkin lights, and jack-o-lanterns grinned through hideous grimaces and evil smiles. Candles lit up every window at Clara's.

As she gazed across the road, she noticed Ike Sr. and Judy come out holding hands and giggling.

Haley smiled. It felt so good to see the two of them so happy together.

Movement around the side of the store drew her attention. It was the same pirate and witch she had seen disappear in the forest. They were standing together just beyond the light.

As she was about to tell Valian, the pirate disappeared before her very eyes. She gasped as the witch stepped into the light, grabbed Ike Sr.

by the arm taking him by surprise, and yanked him around the corner of the building.

Judy let out a scream, but no one paid any attention as there were shrieks and screams ringing out from all over the park. Judy continued to scream as Haley grabbed Valian by the arm.

"Valian, look!"

They could see a struggle in the shadows. Valian yelled loudly.

"Guardians!"

As Judy continued to scream, people in the park began to turn their attention toward the store as they realized they weren't hearing screams of delight but of sheer terror.

The guardians' response was immediate as they all came running over along with Sersha and Henry.

"There!" Valian yelled, pointing to the store.

As they started running toward the struggle in the shadows almost the entire park was quiet as they stared.

Suddenly two black figures shot over the tree line and flew over the park toward Clara's.

There were gasps from everyone there as they watched another dark figure burst around the side of the building and shoot across the sky as the others shot after it. Their figures were plainly clear in dark cloaks, pointed hats, riding on broomsticks with their cloaks flapping behind them.

"Go after them!" Valian commanded.

The tin men dropped their costumes, unveiling large wings and took off in pursuit, while Valian and the rest went rushing over to the store where they found Ike Sr. sitting on the ground, a large gash on his forehead.

"It was Violet," he panted. "She's got Ike Jr."

Everyone stood there shocked at the news.

"She's done something to him... he's only an inch tall..."

The four exchanged worried looks.

"Who were they?" Henry asked. "Where did they come from and what were they doing here?" he continued pressing for information.

"It's obvious they were witches," said Valian, glancing back at the park as families were hastily gathering up protesting children, ushering them into their cars.

"This is not good," he remarked, as he watched the confusion spreading across the road.

Ike recovered his bearings enough to stand up as Judy clung to him shaking like a leaf. "Where are the boys?" she sobbed looking around the dark park across the road. "Where are the boys?" she asked again desperately when she spotted Ernie up the street heading straight for her.

"She changed Ike Jr. into such a tiny person and she held him up like a bug, threatening to kill him if I didn't tell her where the gateway was. I tried to tell her I didn't know what she was talking about, but she wouldn't hear it. Then she heard you," he said, looking at Valian, "and those witches blasting out of nowhere... she saw them coming and took off like a bat out of you know where."

"Oh my God," said Sersha. "This is terrible. Not only has she threatened a human life, but she's kidnapped him and exposed our world to half the county, and it seems we've solved the mystery of who stole the dwindle drops."

"Dwindle drops?" Ike asked. "They sound familiar."

"I'll explain later," Sersha replied.

"Well, can't you wipe their memories like you did before?" asked Henry.

"Not all of them. When we did it before, we knew who they were after observing them over the years, and we only modified those we knew would be affected by your absence. We have several towns here tonight and don't know who they are!" Sersha exclaimed. "Have you been watching? Half of everyone in that park were on their cell phones the minute the guardians flew after them. The news has probably already spread across your world!"

"What a mess," said Haley. "What are we going to do?"

"All right, listen," said Valian. "Let's regroup at your house, Haley. Hopefully the guardians will know to go there."

The group disbursed and went to their cars.

Paul and Carol were waiting, and Haley explained what happened as they pulled away. She glanced back at a deserted park.

The bonfires were still burning, the pathway to the haunted house was still lit up, and people had abandoned their belongings.

The park was eerily silent and still, but for the dancing shadows of the flickering candles and the bats fluttering slightly on their strings in the bright moonlight.

Night mists rose in the meadows and fog began to form on the roads, obscuring their vision as the Miles' family drove toward the estate.

Ike Sr., Judy, and Ernie, who seemed to be in a daze, sat in the front seat of their car. Norman and Mable were in the back as a shadow crossed the moon. No one saw it, as they turned onto Blue Bell Glen.

The slamming of car doors brought Estelle to the outer arched doors of the courtyard.

"Come in! Come in quickly," she urged them. She closed the door and marched hurriedly through the stone archway, through the foyer, into the kitchen and over to the stove. Everyone gathered in a group around a large table Estelle had magically conjured, and sat silently, waiting for her to speak.

She continued at the stove for several minutes then turned and walked to the table with a large teapot, waved her hand and nine cups materialized in front of them as she began pouring. When she was finished she gave them all a serious look.

"Queen Lilia was just here..."

Everyone exchanged worried looks.

"And she was very upset," Estelle continued. "It seems that Molock's new apprentice... is Violet!"

Everyone's mouth dropped open.

"Violet..." Haley began.

"Let me finish," Estelle interrupted. "Maximillion and Tilly paid her a visit. They told her a wayward witch returned to the head sorcerers after serving his sentence for some kind of infraction, which they didn't elaborate on, but the witch had seen firsthand, Violet enter the cave of the dead mountain and come out wearing an amulet made from obsidian stone. She flew from there very quickly. They said the witch would have reported it sooner, but he was forbidden to return to the witches' council until he was done serving his time."

"This is most disturbing," said Valian. "Ike Jr. is in serious danger."

Estelle looked at him questioningly.

He quickly filled her in about what happened in the park. Estelle's eyes grew wide.

"Land sakes," she said, softly. "She has caused the exposure of your world."

"Yeah but who would believe it?" said Henry. "Nobody believes in witches and fairies."

"Except those that saw what happened tonight," Valian replied.

"Well… that's something about humans," Haley interjected. "They can see it with their eyes, but still won't believe it. They'll explain it away with some excuse like they all dreamed it or something they drank caused them to hallucinate. The most this will do is put more stock in the legend of Bonners Ferry."

"It gets better," Estelle said, sounding a bit annoyed. "After Maximillion and Tilly left the palace, the queen had Reed and Jack move the sacred sphere into a new secret chamber, and it did something very odd, something it's never done before. It acted without a command from the queen and showed her where Violet was. She didn't tell me where she saw her, but whatever she saw alarmed her and she immediately summoned the witches' council and they sent out a garrison to intercept Violet. Now we know where Violet was and what she was doing."

Everyone was quiet, deep in thought.

"Unbelievable," said Haley, shaking her head. "I knew Violet was capable of great mischief but this… Molock must surely have her under his control." She thought for a moment and frowned. "Ike, in all the commotion I didn't quite catch what she wanted from you. Did you say gateway?"

Valian cocked his head, a very serious look forming on his face. "Gateway," he whispered, looking at Ike intently. "Did you say gateway?"

The others around the table looked confused at the question, except Sersha.

Ike nodded and repeated what Violet said. "She said she would kill Ike Jr. if I didn't tell her where the gateway was. I didn't know what she was talking about," Ike groaned. Clutching his arm tightly, Judy sat beside him with the most fearful look.

"What are we gonna do? What is this gateway?" Haley asked.

Valian, Sersha, and Estelle exchanged looks.

142

"What?" Haley demanded.

"The gateway is where the rift began as it tore our worlds apart," said Valian. "After the rift the Lords and Ladies and the reigning King and Queen ordered the gateway to be concealed so that it could never be used as an entrance or doorway. It's been told they feared it, and ordered that it should never be seen again."

Haley's eyes grew wide as realization dawned on her.

"What's wrong?" Valian asked, as Haley turned pale.

"He wants to enter our world," she whispered, looking around at everyone. "That's been his goal all along. He can't use the portals for some reason, and has been using those beings he has managed to ensnare to do his bidding and locate this gateway."

Sersha grew pale herself as fear crept into her mind.

Haley saw it immediately and went to her.

"I can see what you're feeling. You need to focus, Sersha. Don't think about what might happen, focus on the facts and the present. Letting your imagination run wild will not help."

She gave Sersha a stern look as if trying to push her logic into Sersha's brain.

Sersha nodded and took a deep breath.

Just then they heard a loud bang at the back door of the kitchen. It startled everyone.

"The guardians?" Sersha whispered.

Valian went to the door and opened it.

"Come in," he said urgently as the guardians entered, tired and out of breath and alone.

"She got away my Lord," said Celio.

Valian's face sank as did everyone else's.

Estelle went over and took Celio by the arm and steered him to a chair, and the other guardians followed.

"We were hot on her trail. She was fast, somehow faster than we. The witches couldn't even keep up with her. It was like she had super fairy strength. Then she swooped around the edge of the forest and she was gone, just gone. We searched the entire area but found nothing but an old empty building. The witches were ahead of us and they were gone too. Prince Sorcerer Maximillion and Tilly were yelling back and forth to each other the entire time, barking out orders to all the others."

143

Haley sighed deeply.

"I need to take a break and stop thinking about all this for awhile. It helps to get your mind off it and come back later with a clearer head," she continued, at the questioning looks by the fairies.

She went into the living room and Valian, Henry, and Sersha joined her minutes later.

They sat on the sofa and recliners quietly.

Haley grabbed the remote control for the TV and switched it on.

Everyone's eyes were drawn to the set.

Haley sighed at the dishwasher detergent commercial, claiming to get your dishes as spotless and clean as a whistle.

Paul, Carol, Ike, and Judy came in as the nightly news came on.

The newscaster reported about an ongoing investigation of a mysterious death and a body found in the forest, three miles outside Spokane.

"In other news, there have been numerous reports of witches and fairies flying in the night sky over the city," he chuckled. "Some are claiming they are UFO's, others swear they saw pointed hats and flowing cloaks as at least six witches flew past the moon on broomsticks. It has also been reported that witches were spotted leaving the scene of a scuffle at the Owens Country Store in Bonners Ferry where it has also been reported a teenager has disappeared. Authorities on the scene have released little information as yet, and are withholding the identity of the missing teen until the parents are located. Reliable sources say this could be a hoax hatched up by the locals to revive the old Bonners Ferry legend."

The news caster smiled again. "And a happy Halloween to you all," he chuckled, turning to his co-host who was also chuckling.

"Anything to bring the spooks out, eh?" the co-host laughed.

Haley turned the TV off. The group sat stunned.

"This is not good," she said.

Valian had stood up at the start of the story and now began pacing the floor.

"What are we going to do?" he asked in frustration.

"They said authorities were on the scene," said Henry. "That means the police are probably looking for you two right now," he continued, looking at Ike and Judy.

Ike stood up and began pacing as well.

"What are we gonna tell them?" said Ike. "That a fairy from another world shrank my son and flew off with him?"

"Don't worry about all that," said Sersha. "I'll wipe their memories. They can't help us and they would just be in the way. So what if the story is all over the news, no one's going to believe it, and you heard what they said, everyone thinks it's a prank. Our main concern right now is to rally together with the witches and Mother and figure out what to do."

Valian nodded in agreement.

"If Violet really is Molock's apprentice, Ike Jr. could be a goner if we don't intervene."

Judy let out a sob.

Ike went to her and put his arms around her.

"Don't worry darling, we'll figure out what to do," he said, trying to comfort her. "Everyone here is familiar with Violet, we'll get him back."

The sound of crunching gravel could be heard as several cars pulled up outside. Car doors slammed and there was pounding at the courtyard door.

Paul hurried out while the others waited with bated breath.

Moments later Paul came back followed by six officers.

"Ike Seers?" the one in the front asked, looking at Ike.

Ike stepped forward.

"We'd like to ask you some questions."

Ike looked at Sersha as he cleared his throat to answer.

Sersha waved her hand in a wide arc and all six looked around the room confused.

"Ah… what was I saying?" said the officer. "What…?"

He turned to look at the other officers for answers as to what they were doing there, but they only returned blank looks.

"I… I seem to have forgotten…" he paused, turning red in the face. "Well, thank you for your time," he said, scratching his head. "You folks have a nice evening. Sorry to have bothered you," he hurried out the door with the other officer's bumbling behind him with frowns on their faces.

"Whew!" said Henry. "That's some neat trick you got there," he said to Sersha, grinning broadly.

"All right," said Valian. "Let's get back to the palace."

"And soon," said Sersha. "That won't hold them for long. When they get back they're going to have to explain to their superiors why they have no answers and will soon be back. Perhaps you should lock up everything before we go. Valian maybe you should shroud the estate to be doubly sure."

"You can do that?" Henry exclaimed.

"Valian can. I'm not learned enough or strong enough to do it myself yet."

"That's a great idea," said Valian. "I'll do it now."

"I'm coming with you," said Haley.

"Me too," said Henry. "This I gotta see."

"All right, we'll be back shortly," said Valian.

The twins followed Valian through the courtyard and out the arched doors. The skies were clear and the moon cast the mountains in a ghostly bath of lackluster light. The night mists made it feel colder than it really was, causing Haley's nose to run.

"Maybe we should change size," Haley suggested, "just in case anyone might be snooping around. We'll be almost impossible to see."

All three shrank with a snap and Haley began to giggle.

"What's funny?" Valian asked.

"Snap, crackle, and pop," she continued to laugh.

"I don't get it," said Valian as Henry laughed.

"I'll explain…"

"I know, you'll explain later," Valian smirked. "Follow me."

They flew down the long curving driveway just below the tree line all the way to the main road where Valian changed size again.

The twins followed suit and looked around. There wasn't a sound but for the occasional, sporadic zephyr shaking what leaves remained on the trees. Everything was damp and cold, muffling any noise.

Haley could see her breath and smell the sweet scent of the earth at the beginning stages of its magnificent transformation.

She breathed in deeply and let it out slowly. The smell gave her a feeling of familiar comfort, reminding her of all the Halloweens gone by.

The excitement of her first Halloween where she and Henry were given permission to go out on their own after dark, walking the streets, going door to door trick or treating, seeing scary costumed kids darting across the street in front of them, hearing screams echoing into the night, and smelling that sweet scent of decaying leaves and vegetation.

"I love this time of year," she whispered.

Valian looked over at her, reached out and ran his hand across her wing causing it to shudder involuntarily.

Henry raised an eyebrow.

"How did you do that?" he whispered.

"I don't know," she whispered back.

She reached over and ran her hand across Henry's wing in the same manner and giggled quietly as his wing began to twitch very fast.

"It's like when we scratch Casey in that certain spot, her leg thumps uncontrollably," Henry grinned.

The twins continued to caress each other's wings and giggle.

"All right you two," said Valian, with amusement. "We're gonna have to get rid of the road sign too."

He snapped his finger and the Blue Bell Glen sign faded from sight.

"Wow," Henry whispered.

"Now we have to start walking backward," Valian said, quietly.

They began to walk backward as Valian passed his hand from left to right, drawing an invisible arch.

Their eyes grew wide as the branches and leaves of the trees on both sides of the drive began to grow, stretching out and meeting in the middle, intertwining and winding their way around each other.

New trees began sprouting up in the driveway here and there, causing the dirt road to buckle in spots.

Valian continued to draw arches as he walked. The forest grew back together as it once was. The gap in the trees was no more.

It took fifteen minutes to undo what probably took weeks to clear. The road was gone and the forest, impossible to navigate through.

Valian stood back admiring his handiwork when they heard the approach of a car engine.

They stood silently; listening as the vehicle came to a stop, paused for a moment then pulled ahead and paused again. For several minutes they listened to a number of cars stopping and starting and stopping again, finally driving away, the hum of the motors fading in the distance.

The trio grinned at each other and turned toward the estate.

Haley marveled at what a picturesque view it was. The grounds were absent of any man made light. The glow of the moon stripped it of color as it stood silently, nestled in the trees as if it grew there right along with the rest of the forest.

The willow swayed gently, the rock wall stood out like a dark gray snake winding its way around the property. The birch grove on the left stood out, stark white like tall dried up bleached bones giving it a spooky feel.

"How are you going to…?" Henry began, just as Valian rose in the air a couple of feet and traced another large arch in the air.

Before their eyes, the estate began to fade then was gone. The twins were at a loss for words. It was completely gone like it had never been there.

They could still see the great oak tree that grew in the courtyard and all the trees that surrounded the estate, but nothing else.

"How are we going to find our way back inside?" Henry asked.

"Take my hand," Valian said to Haley, "and take Henry's hand too."

She reached out and took her brother's hand.

"Step forward," Valian continued.

They took several steps.

Haley felt a change in temperature. It was like walking into a fog. She looked around and saw nothing but a thick haze as they took the next step. The outer perimeter suddenly was right in front of them.

"Geez Louise!" Henry exclaimed. "That was cool."

"Not bad, if I do say so myself," Valian grinned.

148

The guardians were pacing as Valian opened the door. Relief instantly flooded the foyer.

Paul and Carol came out of the kitchen and went to Haley.

"Your dad and I are staying here."

Haley looked at her in disbelief.

"But…"

"No, we've made up our minds," said Carol. "I've had enough adventure for a while, besides someone has got to keep an eye on things here. Who knows what may develop because of what's happened here tonight? Also, we really can't leave Casey and her puppies alone."

Haley smiled half heartedly and nodded.

"I agree," said Valian. "We really do need someone to keep an eye out and report any goings on. You have Estelle's postern if you need it and here…"

He handed Paul a smooth, round, blue stone.

Haley recognized it immediately.

"If you get into trouble, rap this on any surface three times. It will alert us and we'll come straight away."

Paul took the stone and put it in his pocket.

"Shall we go?" Valian asked everyone.

"Wait, wait just a minute," said Haley. "I'm going to change first. I'm not going back to Wisen dressed as a cat."

Everyone laughed.

"I'd almost forgotten," said Valian, chuckling.

"I really don't want you to go," Carol said, looking at the twins. "It scares me to think what might happen to you."

Haley opened her mouth to protest.

"But, I know you have to go. They need you," Carol said, as her eyes began to well up.

Haley frowned at her mother's worried look.

"What is it?" she asked, taking Carol by the hand.

"We missed your birthday. We just realized it this morning."

"What?" Haley exclaimed, surprised.

Carol nodded.

"An entire year has passed and we missed it."

"You know, you're right. I didn't even realize… this time difference is enough to drive me crazy," said Haley, shaking her head.

"Me too," said Henry, obviously distressed at missing their birthday. "Has it really been a whole year?"

"We'll have a big party for you when this is all over," Carol smiled.

The travelers went to their rooms and changed out of their costumes, then met back at Estelle's bedroom door.

Ike and Judy stood there ready to follow.

"What about Ernie?" Haley asked, looking over at the skinny, pimply faced boy sitting on the recliner with a blank stare.

"Oh! Goodness sakes, I almost forgot," said Judy, frowning. "Is he all right?" she asked, concerned at the paleness of his face.

"He's all right," Sersha answered. "I zapped him at the park."

"Zapped him?" said Judy.

"Well, yes. He'd seen everything, the witches and the guardians unveiling their wings. We couldn't very well have him walking around with that information in his head, what if he talked?"

"How long will he be that way?" Judy asked, concerned.

"Until I restore his mind. For now he'll just go through the motions."

"I don't like it," said Judy, shaking her head.

"He'll be fine, honey," said Ike, reassuringly. "The princess wouldn't do anything that would hurt him."

"What are we going to do with him?" Judy asked. "We can't leave him…"

"We'll watch him," Carol volunteered.

"Absolutely," Paul agreed. "You go and do what needs to be done and get back safe."

Judy was reluctant but agreed to go. Ike Jr.'s welfare was at stake.

"Ok, but if there's any problem, any problem…"

"We'll get a hold of you immediately," said Carol.

The group proceeded into Estelle's room ready to go.

The postern was bright and sunny as each one entered.

"It's just like walking into another world," Judy was saying as they came out next to the old waterwheel.

"We are in another world," Ike smiled as he enjoyed Judy's reaction to the outskirts.

Valian led them down the main street and stopped at the narrow stairs leading up to Norman and Mable's.

"Ike, you and the rest stay here for a bit. Haley and I will be right back with the elixir."

"Elixir?" said Ike, as he saw everyone smiling at him.

"Explain it to them," Valian said to the others as he rose into the air.

They watched Valian and Haley fly to the canopy and disappear, then went into the apartment where it was explained to them what the elixir was for.

Valian and Haley returned with the elixir a short time later. Haley handed Judy a backless gown to put on.

She came out from the bathroom beaming.

"I've never worn anything so beautiful," she said softly, as Ike raised an eyebrow, a small smile spreading on his face as he stood there shirtless.

Valian handed them each a small stein.

"Drink it all," he instructed.

Judy wrinkled her nose at the smell.

"Cheers," said Ike, clinking his stein against Judy's.

Judy held her nose and went for it.

Valian stood behind Ike as Sersha took her place behind Judy.

Haley watched the couple wobble unsteadily on their feet as Valian instructed them to bend forward and take deep breaths.

After a minute or so, the familiar sight of humps appeared on their backs, soft and wet, as rubbery protrusions emerged and took shape.

Ike and Judy were looking at each other the entire time with looks of surprise, fear, and pleasure.

"Ooh," Judy cooed, as her wings began to unfold.

Haley brought out a mirror so they could see them better.

Judy's wings were a blue-green color like on a peacock's feathers, brilliant in vibrant color.

"Wow," said Sersha. "I'm jealous."

"How beautiful," Haley agreed.

Judy's wings were outlined in wisps of the deepest plum.

Her face lit up as she looked in the mirror.

Valian instructed her to stay still as they dried and hardened.

Ike's wings took a little longer to open but when they did, everyone was speechless as they stared. His wings were black like dark charcoal with hayseed colored stripes like a zebra.

Valian and Sersha exchanged looks. It was obvious neither one had ever seen wings like these.

Haley and Henry's wings were glittery and in soft pastel colors. They were beautiful, but nothing like this.

"Is there something wrong?" Ike asked, at the looks on their faces.

"No, your wings are in fine shape from what I can see," Valian answered. "We've just never seen such unusual coloring."

The coloring didn't seem to bother either one of them.

Judy fanned her wings slowly, in sheer ecstasy.

"Your wings match your eyes," said Ike, giving her the eye as she blushed with embarrassment.

As soon as their wings were hard, Valian handed them each what looked like frozen droplets of water.

"Eat these and you'll be able to shrink, like this," he said, as he popped to about seven inches with a snap and back again. "It's called a dwindle drop."

Judy let out a squeal of surprise and quickly ate hers. She immediately shrank to about four inches, laughing with joy.

Ike stood there looking at his itty bitty wife with his mouth open.

Her tiny wings buzzed, lifting her up to his astounded face and she hovered in front of his nose, laughing and twirling in circles.

Everyone stood grinning at her merriment.

Ike put out his finger to touch her and she landed on it. Her cheeks were rosy and she was holding her stomach from laughing so much.

"She's a natural!" Sersha remarked. "We haven't even explained how to fly."

"It's easy," Judy called out in her small voice, taking flight and zipping around the room yelling, "weee!"

Ike quickly ate his dwindle drop and with a burst of spark joined his wife and flit around the room, elated.

"This is wonderful!" he cried, landing on the sofa cushion and popped back to his regular size.

Judy followed suit and sat beside her husband, grinning from ear to ear.

"That was so enjoyable," said Ike. "So why have you bestowed such a gift upon us?"

"You can't very well join us at the palace without wings and the ability to change. You need to be able to go where we go," Valian replied.

Ike and Judy practiced shrinking and flying for awhile, zipping back and forth and up and down. Finally Valian decided it was time to go.

They said their goodbyes with much encouragement from Norman and Mable and took flight.

Ike and Judy were thrilled as they followed Valian and Haley through the canopy, their eyes were filled with wonder at the little shops and houses tucked away in the trees, and they marveled at how large everything grew.

"Are these sequoias?" Ike called out.

"Some are," came Sersha's answer. "The smaller trees are redwoods and there are oaks, maples, elder, hickory, and elms. I believe there is just about every variety in this part of the forest."

Ike breathed in deeply, catching the scent of pine heating up in the sunshine.

Judy looked down at the forest floor far below. It was quiet and still. The sunbeams dancing all around were pleasing to the eye and cried out the magic of the land, mysterious and venturesome.

She gasped as they rose above the canopy and she got her first glimpse of the palace, shining in the morning sun.

The great white columns stood majestic and true over the castle courtyards like sentinels. The flower gardens and grounds were impeccable and stood out in brilliant color, sparkling in morning dew.

The cobblestone terraces were strangely absent from the usual morning assembly of fairies, chattering and celebrating the new day with breakfast, alfresco style.

The group landed and went through the great stone archway, into the dining hall. A guardian emerged from the hallway leading to the private living quarters and hurried over.

"Welcome, Prince Valian, Princess Sersha," he greeted them, bowing. "Sir Henry, Milady Haley, Queen Lilia sends word for you to report to the blue room as soon as you've arrived."

Valian nodded and led the group down the corridor to the door made of colorful cut glass.

Chapter 12
Ransom Demands

The queen stood at one of the many windows, gazing out at her kingdom. Much to Haley's surprise, Maximillion and Tilly were sitting on one of the sofas along with two other sorcerers

Lilia turned as they entered. She was stunning as usual in an off red gown, a crown of rubies on her head, but she looked upset and weary. Her cheeks were flushed and matched her gown.

"Mother, are you all right?" Valian asked hurrying over to her.

"I am appalled!" she replied. "Violet better pray I never get my hands on her. This is outrageous! She has exposed herself to the human world!" she continued as she went to the sofa and sat down in a huff.

"Your Majesty," Maximillion began, "rest assured; with our help she will be caught."

"Excuse me?" said Valian. "Your help? You didn't lift a finger to help find her Majesty, what makes you think we need or want your..."

"Calm down, Valian," the queen interrupted. "Sit down. This is far bigger than trying to find me. I have asked Prince Maximillion and Tilly to come here. You know how important and urgent this is. We will need all the help we can get. That boy is in terrible danger!"

"I know Mother. Forgive my outburst," said Valian throwing a cold stare at the smirk on Maximillion's face.

The queen cast a stern look of warning at Valian.

Valian stood and walked over to the sorcerer. "Can we call a truce long enough to capture Violet and save Ike's son?" He held out his hand.

Maximillion stood. "No hard feelings," he replied. "You won fair and square." He shook Valian's hand for just a second and then sat down.

Valian hesitated then turned and took a seat, but didn't take his eyes off of the sorcerer. The two glared at each other. Everyone could feel the tension in the room.

Haley rolled her eyes as Ike and Judy sat down and looked around, shifting in their seats uncomfortably. Haley walked over to the sofas. All eyes were on her. "May I say something before we get started?" she asked in a calm, cool tone.

"Please do," answered the queen.

Haley turned her attention to Valian and Maximillion. "For goodness sake, you two, knock it off!" They looked at her innocently.

"Prince Maximillion, I have no interest in you or any intention of letting myself be drawn into this little conquest of yours. I am in love with Prince Valian, and I plan on marrying him, not you," she continued, flashing an impatient look at Valian as his mouth dropped open in surprise. "I am disappointed with you. Did you not hear me when I told you I couldn't be interested in such a man?"

"I'm sorry, darling, I…"

"Don't you, "darling" me. I've had about enough of your jealousy, and yours," she said glaring at both men equally. "Get it through your heads, you're acting like a couple of babies, and I've had just about enough of it!"

The queen and Tilly looked impressed, displaying small smirks on their faces as Haley continued.

"Now get your acts together!" she demanded, slamming herself into a chair in a huff.

The room was quiet for a moment as Valian and Maximillion squirmed in their seats. Both were red in the face.

"You'll make a fine princess," said Lilia rising from her seat.

Tilly looked at Haley curiously and nodded her approval. Her emerald green eyes seemed to bore into Haley's as if trying to read her, to figure her out. Haley curled her lip in a tiny grin. "I think I would quite like to get to know you better when this is over," Tilly said quietly, surprising Haley.

Haley had never really heard her speak before. Her voice was as deep and mysterious as Maximillion's. "I would like that," Haley replied softly. "Let's do lunch sometime."

Tilly gave her a smile as they turned their attention to the queen.

The meeting lasted well into the afternoon, and by the time they were done, Haley's stomach was keeping tune with Henry's.

Maximillion and Tilly left, and Reed showed up with Jack to serve them a late lunch while Lilia retired to her quarters.

"She looks tired," said Haley as Lilia walked out.

"I know," said Valian.

"Do you think she's sick?" Haley asked.

Valian shook his head.

"This is the first time Judy and I have seen the queen," Ike commented, "and we agree she looks, sort of worn out."

"Maybe we should have Dr. Gretta come and check her out," Haley suggested.

"Mother wouldn't stand for that. She's very stubborn. I can hear her now."

"I'm fine, I don't need a doctor," mimicked Valian.

Haley looked at him in surprise. "You mean this has happened before?"

"A couple of times, but she always manages to be herself in a few days," Sersha replied.

"Hmm," Haley murmured.

They finished lunch and went to one of the balconies.

"For such a long meeting, we sure didn't make much headway devising a plan," Haley said discouraged.

"Well there's not a whole lot we can do right now," said Henry, "other than what we did in alerting all the guardians to be on the lookout. We haven't any idea where Violet is."

"I know, I just feel helpless sitting here, enjoying this beautiful sunny day, knowing Ike Jr. is out there somewhere in a whole lot of trouble."

Judy and Ike Sr. sat quietly listening. Their faces said it all.

"Don't forget all the witches are on alert as well, and all the other fairy bands, at least the friendly ones," Sersha added.

"How many are there?" Henry asked, moving closer to Sersha.

Sersha's eyes were bright as she glanced at him.

"There are thousands of species. I don't think anyone knows how many. Thank goodness we have the sphere. Mother can communicate with most of the bands. She's gotten the word out for sure."

"Well, I can't just sit here and wait for something to happen," said Haley getting to her feet. "Anyone up for a sail?"

Ike and Judy looked at each other uncertainly.

"Sure, I'll go," said Sersha, batting her eyes at Henry.

"Valian?" Haley asked.

Valian sighed, but got to his feet. "Why not?" he answered.

Everyone looked at Ike and Judy.

"We're going flying," said Haley. "Come see the sights and the lay of the land."

"Maybe we'll get lucky," said Henry with a grin.

Sersha blushed and grabbed Henry by the hand. "Come on, let's lead the way."

They jumped from the balcony as the others followed behind them into the canopy.

"Let's show Judy some of the shops," said Sersha veering to the left.

They bobbed up and down with every beat of their wings like birds in flight, weaving in and out, dodging branches when Haley called out. "Bella's! I want to stop there!"

The girls landed while the guys continued down a ways to Anah's Armory.

Haley, Sersha, and Judy thoroughly enjoyed their visit, walking down the aisles, examining the rows and rows of greenery and the fantastic blooms. Haley was drawn to the corner in the front of the store by the window.

There were tiny pots lined against the wall, full of delicate little flowers that shuddered slightly. Their heads were bell shaped with the most unusual designs on their petals, much like the dark spots you would see on a monarch butterfly, shaped like eyes, and they had long feather-like leaves.

What really caught Haley's eye was that as she neared, they lifted their leaves and held them together as if praying, and as she stood before them, they raised their heads to gaze up at her.

She was startled to see that the dark spots that looked like eyes really were eyes, and they batted them at her. It was like looking at a dog in a pet shop, begging to be adopted.

Her heart went out to them. She reached over to touch one of the flowers with beautiful blood red coloring, and it began to sing. Its tiny voice was soft and sweet, and as she put out her hand, it wrapped its little praying leaves around her finger and purred like a cat.

All the other flowers looked up at her, stretching out their leaves, trying to touch her.

Haley giggled. She felt such delight toward them as she looked around for assistance.

A petite little fairy, wearing a dirt covered apron came rushing toward her as if she had been just waiting for someone to help. It was the same fairy who had tried to sell her bulwarks the last time she visited the shop.

"Can I help you?" she asked excitedly.

"Yes," Haley smiled. "What are these delightful flowers?"

"Those are of the pansy variety."

"Pansies? I've never seen pansies like these."

"Yes, they are an unusual type. They are born every three years…"

"Did you say born?" Haley interrupted.

The fairy nodded. "The male and female can only produce young every three years. We just got them in this morning. They sell very quickly, so… if you're interested, you'll have to decide soon. Once word gets out, we'll be packed in here."

"What do they do? I mean what are they for?" Haley asked.

"Each one is uniquely different. They all have special gifts. Some will whisper compliments in your ear, others like to nuzzle. Some can warn you of approaching danger, and some will tell you the secrets of the universe. That's not all of course, but you get the idea. So, have you made up your mind?"

Haley gave the fairy an amused look. "I'll take the red one here," she replied.

The fairy's eyes lit up. "Wonderful!" she exclaimed. "Now, they only eat sugar, and here are some containers for you to carry it in your lapel. You have to be sure to give it lots of love and attention. They are very sensitive. Water weekly, and change the soil once a month, otherwise it gets a little smelly," she whispered.

Haley looked at her, speechless.

Judy and Sersha wandered over as the fairy got together all the supplies Haley would need, and began to coo and fuss over the pansies.

"Oh, how sweet," Judy cried, picking up one of the pots. It contained a banana yellow flower that immediately began stroking Judy's hand with its long pea green leaves.

"These are special pansies," said Sersha. "They only come in every few years."

"That's what the clerk was telling me," Haley replied.

"They never grow any bigger, and they shed their petals monthly and grow back a different color," Sersha added.

Judy couldn't get over the fact that her particular flower kept kissing her hand. "I've got to get me one of these!" she remarked, holding it up to her cheek.

"Looks like you have a very affectionate flower there," said Sersha. "It really likes you."

The clerk hurried back and was even more excited to see Sersha and Judy holding up the merchandise.

"I'd like this one," said Judy smiling brightly.

"And I'll take these two," said Sersha pointing to two very similar blooms.

"Oh, good," the clerk replied. "They are brother and sister. I was hoping they wouldn't get split up." She scurried away for more supplies.

Everyone bartered a deal that all three would be back to assist in the shop when the order for bulwarks came in. The clerk explained how they needed all the help they could get for those deliveries.

When the sales were complete, the three left the shop with huge smiles, and singing pansies in their lapels. Haley had even purchased a container, suitable to wear her flower in her hair.

"I don't know what mine can do yet, what about you Sersha?"

"I'm not sure, but this one keeps tickling my neck," Sersha replied giggling. "That tickles," she said to her flower, nudging it gently.

They proceeded past several shops and joined the guys at Anah's.

Haley began to laugh when they walked in. Judy and Sersha giggled when they spotted all three in front of full length mirrors, trying on all sorts of peculiar armor.

Valian had on a helmet, similar to the ones the guardians wore to the festival.

"It's you!" Haley laughed as she walked over and gave Valian a peck on his helmet.

Valian turned red and quickly took it off.

"Just trying on the latest gear," he explained. "Come over here. I've got something to show you," he said leading her away from the others, toward a display of swords hanging on the wall.

He turned to look at her. "I must apologize for what happened with the sorcerer before the meeting began. It's just that... he rubs me the wrong way. I don't know why, he just does."

"I know," Haley comforted him. "I am sorry for my little outburst, and I know it's not an easy thing for you to deal with, but I had to make my feelings known and understood. You two must bury the hatchet, and not in each other's heads," she urged with a small smile.

Valian smiled back. "Check these out," he pointed at the swords. "Do you like any of these?"

Haley scanned the wall. There were at least one hundred on display. She was impressed at the variety. There were long ones, short ones, and every one was made of fine polished steel, silver in color, however the handles were completely diverse. Most were adorned with magnificent displays of jewels.

There were plain ones, and fancy ones, and just a few were showpieces, not meant for battle.

One sword in particular drew her attention, a thin silver blade, medium in length. Its bronze handle wrapped around the hand for a firm grip, and was inlaid with emeralds and rubies designed to complement each other in finely laid out patterns.

"I like this one," she said. "It's exquisite. The hilt looks like dancing flames."

Valian lifted it off its holder and handed it to her.

161

Her eyes lit up as she took it. "It's so light!" She waved it around, getting a feel for it. "Wow, this is great! It's balanced so well, it feels like it's part of my arm."

Valian grinned as she handed it back.

"I do need my own sword, but this is much too extravagant," she commented, walking down the line. "Here," she said, picking up a simple silver sword with a plain bronze handle. "This one," she said waving it around.

It was a little more cumbersome than the one she really liked.

"This will do for now."

Valian took the sword and led her to the armor. "You need a breastplate that fits you better than the dragon skin one Sersha gave you before our trip to the islands."

Haley wrinkled her nose. "They're not very fashionable, are they? I like this," she stated, holding it to herself for sizing.

"You have excellent taste, my love. This is dragon hide; inlaid with titanium mesh plates, see?"

He turned the breastplate inside out to show her.

"Titanium? You know about titanium?" she asked.

"Where do you think humans got the idea?" he winked. "Why don't you go try it on?"

While Haley went into the changing room, Valian went to pay for the items. When they left Anah's, Henry had a new bow, arrows, and quiver. Valian splurged for a new shield; also titanium, inlaid with sapphire and diamond dust.

They flew a few trees over, to the Tea House. Haley had visited it once before, during a sail with Henry and Sersha.

The Tea House was a cozy bistro, two stories high. The main restaurant was downstairs, and upstairs was a bright room with large bay windows, and dozens of booths.

Everyone got comfortable and waited for a waitress.

Haley looked out at the view, as Valian and Henry discussed their new armor.

Suddenly Haley became rigid as she pointed. "Violet!" she burst out.

The others followed her finger, and sure enough, Violet's black hair flew out behind her as she zipped past.

Everyone scrambled out of the booth, leaving their purchases behind, and headed for the door downstairs. By the time they got outside, Violet was nowhere in sight.

"There are only two places I can think of she would go, her place or the palace," said Valian.

"I'd bet my bottom dollar it's the palace," Haley insisted. "Why else would she dare show herself?"

The group headed for the palace at lightning speed.

The courtyard was deserted as they rushed inside, and Valian recoiled at the sight before them.

Violet had the queen backed into a corner, a black blade pointed at her chest.

"Valian," the queen implored in barely a whisper.

Guardians surrounded the queen, their swords drawn.

Violet slowly turned her head. An evil calculated grin took shape as she eyed Haley and the prince. She sniggered.

"Prince Valian and his pet human, how quaint," she bullied.

Valian's eyes narrowed, his chest heaved. "You pitiful little fairy, how dare you hold the queen!" he roared at her.

"Careful," Violet sighed as if annoyed by his presence. "You have no conception of what you're dealing with."

"What the hell do you want?" Valian growled; crimson creeping up his face as his breathing increased and his anger rose.

"Oh, learning profanity? Your little pet is teaching you the important stuff, huh?" she sneered. "How predictable your human is."

Valian's jaw clenched tight.

Haley could see his facial muscles contracting. He looked like he was ready to burst, and she was petrified he was about to lose it.

"Violet," she appealed, "please, let's just calm down and discuss this rationally…"

"Silence you little rat!" Violet hissed at her, pointing her blade toward Haley. "I could kill you where you stand."

Valian started and Violet reacted by pointing her sword at him.

Haley flinched in fear.

"Violet, you're under the influence of obsidian…"

Violet erupted in laughter. "You silly girl, you don't have a clue do you?"

Haley stood her ground. "Enlighten me," she retorted.

Violet frowned at Haley's defiance. "I don't need to explain anything to the likes of you," she bragged. "You are insignificant."

"We shall see," Haley declared, not backing down.

For a split second Haley saw fear in Violet's eyes.

"What do you want, Violet?" Valian demanded again.

"You, Prince Valian, why are you wasting your time with that..." she motioned toward Haley, "when you can have me?"

She reached out and touched Valian's arm, running her hand up across his bulging biceps in a light caress, as she looked intently in his eyes.

Valian made no move to stop her as she walked around him enticingly, stroking his wings as she stepped back in front of him. "If anything, she is a child," Violet added.

Much to Haley's despair, Valian looked down at Violet and smiled.

Violet grew confident with her boasts.

Haley could see it in her eyes, and expressions, her body language. She was like a cobra, playing with its prey before the deadly strike.

The others stood watching, silently, shocked by Violet's attempt at seducing the prince.

Valian placed his hand gently on Violet's shoulder.

"Violet..." he began.

"Yes?" she answered in a tempting voice.

"You are indeed..."

She smiled up at him.

"Pathetic."

Violet stepped back, appalled at his words. Contempt and loathing seethed from her.

"Do you honestly think I would leave Haley for you?" he bellowed. "You are not even one tenth the woman she is! I wouldn't leave her for you if my life depended on it! Now, like I said before, what the hell do you want?"

Violet was outraged, and began to stutter, in search of a retort, but came up empty as she backed away, her black blade pointed at Valian.

"Fine! Have it your way!" she screeched at him, and turned back to the queen. "You WILL divulge the location of the gateway!" she demanded, pointing her sword at Lilia.

"I know not where the gateway lies," the queen said in defiance.

"You will do well to find it," Violet spit out, "if you ever want to see that stupid human boy again!"

Judy let loose a shriek that alarmed everyone, and made a move toward Violet, as the others scrambled to hold her back.

Violet sneered at Judy. "So this is the human mother. You could have done better, Ike," she belittled.

Ike was just as defiant as the others. "You're an idiot, Violet," he criticized. "The only one, who doesn't have a clue, is you."

Violet expressed her displeasure at the rebuke with a scowl, but remained still, trying to figure out what he meant.

Valian stood silent, as if waiting for Violet to drop her guard.

Haley could see this as well as the others and they continued to bombard Violet with questions and insults, but she held fast.

"Enough!" she yelled, and turned to the queen. "You will divulge the location of the gateway."

"As I've already explained to you, I know not where it lies."

"Then you will find it, unless you want the blood of that boy on your hands!"

"How dare you threaten the queen, you snake!" Sersha hissed. "You will destroy yourself with your own venom. How can you let Molock lead you around by the nose like that? Don't you have any self control?"

"Don't you dare show disrespect toward the master..."

"Master?" Valian hooted. "What are you, his little puppet? Is he pulling your strings?"

Haley snickered. "Very good my love," she responded as she walked over and gave him a very intimate kiss, then turned to see Violet's face turn scarlet with fury.

Violet, grit her teeth as she tried to keep her composure. "You know, it would be so easy for me to gut you like a fish?" she glared.

"That would be ill-advised," Valian countered. "You are outnumbered, and how can you accomplish your mission if you're dead?"

It seemed Violet couldn't think of a comeback and she began to tremble slightly. "You have until the next new moon, when I return. You'd better pray you have an answer or your kingdom will face the master's wrath."

The guardians stepped aside, clearing a path as Violet held her long black blade out in front of her and walked to the great arch door. When she got to the courtyard, she bolted.

"Go after her!" Valian commanded. "But just follow at a distance. I want to know where she's hiding. Don't be seen!"

The guardians took off as Valian rushed to his Mother's side. Everyone gathered around her as she sank into a chair.

"I'm getting too old for this," she sighed and wiped her brow.

"Mother, you don't look so well," Sersha stated with concern.

"I'm all right, just tired is all."

"What about the gateway?" Valian asked. "We can't let her know where it is. If we did, fairy world would become infested with corruption and the human world wouldn't stand a chance."

Lilia looked at them in contemplation. "Help me to the blue room," she winked at Haley. "This discussion must be held in private."

"Celio, Lonato, Troy, Theodore, please join us."

Valian helped the queen to her feet. She could barely walk, so he picked her up and carried her. His brow was creased with worry.

He set her down on one of the sofas and turned to Troy. "Go fetch Dr. Gretta right now, and bring her here."

Troy obeyed and left the room.

"That isn't necessary," the queen protested.

"Like it or not, you're going to be checked over," Valian dared to command.

Lilia smiled softly. "You are learning quickly my son. Haley is a good teacher."

Valian didn't return her smile, but continued to look solemn.

The others took seats and the room was as silent as a tomb as they pondered the situation.

Dr. Gretta arrived and promptly had the queen moved to a private room for an examination.

Valian paced the floor while Sersha stared out the window. No one knew what to say, but the worry and concern was clearly on everyone's face.

"What's taking so long?" Valian asked as he continued to pace.

The door finally opened and Dr. Gretta entered with a grave expression.

"Well?" Valian asked. "How is she?"

Dr. Gretta sighed. "She is dying."

Valian grew ashen. "Dying?" he repeated. "What do you mean she's dying? How can she be dying? She's immortal."

"I can't answer that Prince Valian. I can't find anything physically wrong with her, but her life force is fading and she is in a lot of pain."

Valian sat down, defeated. It was like all the energy was sucked right out of him.

Haley went to him and put her hand on his. She looked at the others. Sersha's face was white and expressionless. The group was at a loss for words.

"Can I go see her?" Valian asked.

Dr. Gretta nodded. "I have given her something to help her rest, but she should still be awake for a bit. Other than that, there is nothing I can do."

"Not a word of this to anyone," Valian instructed. "No one can know about this right now."

Dr. Gretta nodded and took a seat while Valian and Sersha left the room.

Everyone sat quietly, as if numb.

Twenty minutes later, Sersha poked her head through the door. "She's asking for you Haley."

"Me?" Haley asked getting up from her seat.

She followed Sersha across the corridor and entered the room. Lilia was propped against the pillow. Sersha stood by the door as the queen motioned for Haley to come to her bedside.

Haley glanced at Valian as she drew near. She saw sorrow reflecting back at her.

"Your Highness," Haley whispered.

"Come here, Haley. I've called you here for two reasons. I don't know how much time I have. The Doctor couldn't ascertain that. First, I want to apologize, for I have deceived you. I consider you part of the family so you must know… I am half human."

Haley's eyes grew wide.

"My mother was human. My father was a Manwan and completely taken by her, falling head over heels for her, and they wed, even though it was against Manwan law."

Haley's mouth fell open, and her heart pounded. Fear swept over her at the prospect of not being able to marry Valian.

"My father, being the king, amended that law, to make an exception, as long as the current king or queen gave their approval, which I do."

"Do you mean Valian is part human?" she whispered.

"Valian's father was of pure Manwan blood and took advantage of this law, and I married him. He became king when my father was killed in battle. We had a few glorious years together, and two beautiful children. Valian's father was also killed in battle, and on his deathbed, he bestowed upon Valian a gift."

Valian was taken aback. "A gift? What gift?" he asked.

"I don't know," Lilia answered. "It is a special power, and the only thing he would tell me was you could only use this power once."

"How do I know that I haven't already used it?"

"You haven't. You will know it when it shows itself."

Everyone was silent and in a state of shock at the queen's words.

"Secondly, I wish to give you my blessing."

She took Valian's hand, and Haley's hand, and joined the two over her heart.

"I proclaim that upon my death, Sir Valian, prince and guardian of Roan, you will become king. You shall rule Roan and all the lands of Wisen. You shall be fruitful in whatever you put your hand to, and will indeed be a wise king.

Milady Haley, I proclaim that when you are wed, you will be queen of Roan and all the lands of Wisen, and you will also be fruitful in whatever you put your hand to. You are a blessing to my son, and have shown him love, respect, and knowledge that will benefit the entire kingdom. I bless this union with all the powers within me."

A single tear rolled down Valian's cheek.

Lilia smiled at him. "Be not of a heavy heart my son, I am proud of the man you've become, and I have enjoyed every minute of our lives together. You will be an honorable king, kind and just. I foresee great battles and many victories in your future. You shall overcome."

"Oh, my queen," Valian said softly. "I have no words."

"I am sorry I kept this from you. Since I am half human, I am not completely immune to human disease."

"And neither am I, nor Sersha."

Lilia nodded. "It's all right, as long as we have human doctors to see us through."

Valian nodded and kissed his mother's hand. "You should rest," he said as he looked up at Haley.

Haley's heart went out to him. She wished she had some words of comfort for him, but none came to mind.

"Go," said the queen softly. "You have three months before the new moon, and you need to devise a plan to save that boy."

She closed her eyes and fell asleep.

The trio left the room and joined the others. Their forlorn faces told the story and they sat and told the news of the queen's fate, leaving out the part that she was part human.

The next few days were sad for the party, but produced many meetings with the Lords and Ladies of the court, while they awaited the return of the guardians that pursued Violet.

Valian called for a meeting with the witches upon the guardians arrival.

The queen held on with no change in her condition.

On the fourth day, Lilia actually got out of bed, stating that she felt quite a bit better and even had some color back in her cheeks. She spent most of the day with Haley, going over queen etiquette, duties and responsibilities, not to mention the queen's wardrobe.

Haley didn't know how to feel about the whole thing. She was appreciative, yet felt like she was intruding, and said so.

Lilia looked at her in a motherly fashion. "Don't be silly, I would have done this whether I was dying or not. It's tradition for a reigning queen to instruct her successor, in preparation for her coronation."

Lilia's words made Haley feel a little better.

"You're supposed to be enjoying this ritual," Lilia smiled.

The queen had Reed pull out all of her gowns, especially made for royal events, to let Haley choose any to her liking.

Haley began to try them on and view her reflection in the queen's wall of mirrors. Each one was as beautiful as the last, and she had a hard time choosing. Of course the ones she finally picked, needed alteration, and the royal seamstress was summoned for that purpose.

When she finally finished, she sat on the edge of Lilia's bed, struggling for the right words.

"What's bothering you?" Lilia asked.

The queen's compassion and tenderness was almost overwhelming, and Haley felt as if her heart would break.

"I am going to really miss you when you're gone."

Lilia patted her hand. "You are a strong woman, Haley, strong and confident. You're sure of yourself on so many levels."

"That's just it; I don't feel strong or confident. I'm so afraid that I'm going to make a mistake or disappoint Valian, because I'm not royal. I don't come from a royal family. I'm just a simple human girl, with worries and fears just like anybody else."

"That's true, you are human, but that's what makes you unique. That's what makes you strong. You have courage and drive, and you strive for what's right. Those are qualities we have sorely lacked for so long. You and your brother have allowed us to peek into your world of emotion, and shown us what we've been missing, what we have been deprived of. Yes, some of these emotions as of late, have been painful, but that's what makes us who we are. That is what makes us grow. So, you see, my dear, those are marks of a true queen."

Haley sighed, and gave Lilia a huge smile. "Thank you, Your Majesty, you have made me feel a whole lot better about all this, but you're gonna give me a fat head if you continue."

Lilia chuckled. "You go on now; you are coming along wonderfully with today's lesson. I don't feel like I'll need to give you much more instruction. You are an avid learner. One more thing before you go, you need to learn who you are. You have earned the right to be respected as Valian's wife. Never forget that, and never doubt yourself."

Haley curtsied and left the queen's bedroom with a lighter heart than she had felt in days.

She went to her room and freshened up. As she looked in the mirror, she held her head high, smiling. Her shoulders were back and straight as she posed. "Queen Haley," she said aloud, then began to giggle, and rolled her eyes at herself. "Never in my wildest dreams…"

Chapter 13
An Unexpected Confession

Two more days passed and still no word from the guardians. The group of six were growing anxious and antsy, waiting.

Valian asked Ike, Judy, Henry, and Sersha to join him and Haley for a private dinner at Mathilda's that evening. He reserved the entire place just for them, to get away from the palace for awhile and unwind a bit.

The old crone took the night off and left Buggsy in charge. Harvest was complete, leaving the fairy farm pretty much deserted, so he had come, looking for a job, and of course being the fabulous chef that he was, Mathilda hired him on the spot.

Buggsy let them in when they arrived, and locked the door behind them.

After heartfelt greetings, he led them to the private dining room on the left. It was the same room Haley and Valian had watched Violet grow tentacles out of her forehead, and Haley had to grin at the memory.

Buggsy had done a wonderful job decorating and arranging. It was dimly lit by candles on the only table in the room. The walls had been transformed into brick, in a rich burnt sienna, and were accented by small black lanterns. The room had an old world, Italian feel to Haley, and she smiled at the cozy atmosphere.

A fire blazed in the hearth across from the table. There were six place settings, three on one side and three on the other.

The men held out the chairs for the girls, and Haley giggled at Valian's attempts at being romantic.

Buggsy put on some soft music and promptly brought out an assortment of freshly baked breads and spreads, and filled each goblet with a sparkling concoction, Haley didn't recognize, then he disappeared back into the main bar area.

Valian raised his drink. "A toast; to my Mother, and to you my friends, and to our impending victory over the evil one."

Everyone raised their goblets.

The couples were seated across from each other, so Haley could look directly at her man. He was especially handsome in the glow of the candlelight and his pale blue eyes sparkled as he looked at her.

"Ike got together with Henry and I this afternoon to give us a few tips on being gentlemanly," Valian smiled. "How are we doing so far?"

Haley blushed, and had to smile back. "Prince Valian, you are, and always have been a gentleman."

The couples held quiet conversation as Buggsy came in with soups and salads.

Haley, Sersha, and Judy, were glowing by the time the main course was served, and Haley wondered what was in their drinks that caused her to feel so relaxed and warm. Her heart was light and she couldn't ignore the urge to giggle.

After dessert, Valian got up and walked to her chair, holding out his hand. "Would you care to dance, Milady?"

Haley took his hand and he led her to the middle of the room and put his arm around her waist and held her close, and they began to sway to the music.

"You look absolutely lovely this evening, my beloved," he said softly.

Haley felt the heat rise up her neck and begin to creep up her ears. She had never felt quite like this before, and again she thought to herself, "I wonder if this is what it feels like to be in love."

"I wish this night would never end," she whispered.

The others joined them on the dance floor, and Valian and Haley grinned as they looked over at Henry and Sersha. They were a little awkward toward each other, perhaps a bit nervous being so close together, but they were certainly enjoying it.

"Let's dance the night away," said Haley

She felt like Cinderella at the ball, in a beautiful gown, dancing with Prince Charming.

All three couples had a marvelous, relaxing evening together, and left Mathilda's just after midnight, flying hand in hand.

When Haley laid her head on her pillow, she let out a satisfied sigh and fell into a deep sleep, dreaming she was in her wedding gown, dancing with Valian.

She woke abruptly at four a.m. by knocking at her door. She slipped into her silk robe and asked who it was.

"It's the steward, Milady. Prince Valian requests your presence in the blue room at once."

She opened the door. Her steward wore an anxious look.

"What's going on?" she asked.

"The guardians have returned."

Haley hurried along the corridors behind her escort and went inside.

All eyes turned to look when she entered, then breathed a sigh of relief. Everyone looked nervous and on edge. There were at least a dozen guardians standing around the room. Their appearance startled her.

Everyone had tears in their clothes and were sporting various wounds.

Valian sat at the head of the table by one of the windows, with three other guardians, Henry, Sersha, and the Seers.

She quickly went to the open seat next to Valian, and was relieved she wasn't the only one still in pajamas.

"What's happened?" she asked looking at the guardians.

"Jones here was just about to tell us when you walked in," Valian answered.

"How did they get those injuries? Are they all right? Why aren't they healing?"

"Dr. Gretta has been summoned to check them out. She should be here any minute. As far as healing; every one of them elected to take off their given gems without informing anyone. We'll deal with that later. So as you can see, they had emotion overload and didn't know how to deal with it."

Haley sighed as Valian looked at Jones.

"All right Jones, let's have it, and don't leave out a thing."

Jones cleared his throat and lifted his drink with a shaky hand, took a sip, then began to explain.

"We set out after Violet like you instructed and spotted her flying over the Cimmerian realm. Having to keep our distance, it was difficult to keep her in sight, but we managed. We tailed her for three days. She didn't ever go to the dead mountain. By our calculations, we flew almost one thousand miles to a realm none of us had been to before."

He paused and took another drink and paused again.

"Go on," Valian instructed.

"Well, we were ambushed. It was like they knew we were coming. They were lying in wait. Violet escaped during the battle. We fought for hours before they retreated."

"Who retreated? Who were you fighting?" Valian asked.

"Witches!" Jones replied, swallowing.

"Witches?" Valian boomed, a horrible angry look on his face.

"Witches, I can't believe it," Haley whispered. "Are you sure?"

"Yes, of course. They were of the Rune clan. There was no mistaking their insignia. We saw the Rune medallions some of them were wearing."

Haley quickly reached down and pulled the chain from under her nightgown. "Did it look like this?" she asked, hoping upon hope his answer would be no.

"Yes," Jones answered. "That's it exactly."

"I don't understand this," Valian replied. "I never expected this. How could we have been so blind? They have been our allies for centuries. Why would they do this?"

Haley was deep in thought and Valian watched her, expectantly. Suddenly, her face grew pale and her eyes grew wide with dread.

"Oh, my God," she whispered and looked at Valian.

"What?" Valian asked with a look of doom.

"Hilda and Estelle are of the Rune clan."

The implication was too disastrous to consider, but it couldn't be ignored, and as it dawned on the group, fear filled the room.

"No. It can't be," Sersha appealed to them. "I refuse to believe it. Hilda and Estelle have been trusted friends for forever. I'll never believe it unless I've seen it with my own eyes."

Sersha was adamant and Haley prayed that she was right.

"I hope you're right," she replied, "but we must consider the possibility. If we don't, we could jeopardize everything. Valian, we have got to figure out a way to destroy Molock before he recruits more servants to do his bidding and destroys us."

Valian began to pace. "I'd ask for Mother's advice, but I don't think it wise for her to even know. I don't think she could handle the pressure, and it might make her sicker than she already is."

"I agree," Haley replied. "The only problem with that, if she's not told, what if Maximillion or Tilly try and contact her. She would be vulnerable and in danger."

"Yes," Valian agreed. "I didn't think of that."

"So, what do we do?" Haley asked.

"We will have to assign guardians to watch her constantly, with explicit instructions that no witches whatsoever are allowed to see her, and they are to use force if necessary."

Haley nodded. "I guess that's the only way."

Valian continued to pace as he racked his brain for answers.

Dr. Gretta was escorted in and began to examine all the cuts and scrapes, shaking her head in disapproval. "All this fighting," she muttered, going from one to the next.

Valian watched her with concern, and when she was finished, he called her to the table, dismissing everyone from the vicinity.

"Thank you for your assistance. I am about to give you a direct order, which you will follow to the T. Do you understand?"

Dr. Gretta nodded nervously.

"You will not repeat this to anyone."

The Doctor nodded again.

"We have been betrayed by the Rune clan."

Dr. Gretta gasped in fear.

"You will attend to the queen as if nothing has happened and nothing is wrong."

"Yes, Your Highness."

"You will no doubt see a lot more of these kinds of injuries in the coming days and months, but you will say nothing. Do you understand all that I have said?"

Dr. Gretta nodded again.

"I am going to order every Manwan to put their given gems back on, which will help them to heal on their own. Unfortunately, there are some who have removed their gems without permission," he said looking at the guardians in the room with disapproval.

"I don't know how many have disobeyed the order. I will send out a proclamation; under no circumstances are the fairies to remove their gems unless in my presence and my presence alone. On a personal note, Doctor, I want you to continue to check my mother on a daily basis and report any change, no matter how insignificant, and get that human doctor that treated me and sewed up my wounds to look at her. What was his name?"

"Dr. Cass, I believe."

"Yes, Cass. What do you know about him?"

"I know he keeps up to date on human methods of healing, and visits the other side on a regular basis," Dr. Gretta answered.

"What of his nature?"

"He seems like a personable fellow, keeps to himself, no family."

"I want you to send him to me. How long has he been here?"

"Only three years."

"Perfect. Send him at once."

"He's on duty at the Infirmary. It'll just be a few minutes."

Dr. Gretta hurried off, and Valian sighed with his face in his hands, rubbing his forehead.

Haley caressed his wing tenderly. "We'll get through this, I don't know how, but we will."

"I know we will, I can sense it somehow," Valian replied.

Dr. Gretta and Dr. Cass came in moments later and sat with Valian, Haley, and the rest of the group.

Valian dismissed everyone else. As they left, Valian turned to Dr. Cass with a sober look.

"Dr. Cass, we don't have a lot of time for in depth introductions. First I want to thank you for your assistance in my recovery from the injuries I sustained in battling the boar trolls. That in itself assures me you are quite capable. Dr. Gretta says you've been keeping up with modern human medicine on the other side."

Cass confirmed Valian's words with a nod of his head. "The methods used in healing in this day and age are very advanced. Take the common cold for instance; there really is no cure, however, the remedies…"

"I'm sure the explanation of the common cold is intriguing," Valian interrupted, "however, I'm afraid your expertise on that will have to wait for another time."

Dr. Cass looked a bit grieved at being cut short.

"My apologies, Doctor, this is of the utmost importance."

Cass looked at the prince, dryly, as if whatever he had to say would be uninteresting or blasé'.

Haley instantly grew annoyed with his attitude.

Valian hadn't seemed to have mastered the ability to read body language yet, as he continued being apologetic.

"Excuse me!" Haley butted in angrily. "I don't like your attitude. Not just your apparent indifference, but your lack of respect. This is the Prince of Roan who has summoned you here, and he runs the show. He makes the decisions around here, and he's the one who has allowed you to live here. You show him some courtesy or you can pack your bags!"

Valian and Dr. Cass were stunned by her outburst.

"I beg your pardon," Dr. Cass replied. "I was not aware you were in charge here."

Haley was furious at his boldness and presumptuousness.

"How dare you speak to me like that! I am Valian's betrothed, and will be queen…"

"Some day," Dr. Cass interjected.

Haley was enraged. "Listen you pompous little man…"

"Stop," Valian interrupted with a pleading look at Haley. "This bickering will get us nowhere." He looked at Dr. Cass. "Our apologies for this confusion…"

Haley was flabbergasted at Valian's lack of support.

"However," he continued, "she is quite right. She is my betrothed, and her word *will* be law soon. I trust her judgment, and I encourage you to show her the same reverence if you wish to continue to reside here."

"Please excuse my ignorance, Your Highness. I am not accustomed to the rules in relating to those with such authority."

"Apology accepted. Now, I have asked you here under the gravest of circumstances. The queen has fallen ill. Dr. Gretta can find nothing wrong. That is where you come in. I implore you to examine her as a human would examine another human. Try and discover her ailment."

Valian's request seemed to cheer Dr. Cass up, as his entire demeanor changed.

"Well, why didn't you say so in the first place? I'm sure I can find out what's wrong. Where is she?"

"Sersha, would you mind?" Valian asked.

"Follow me," Sersha instructed with a frown at the man, and led him from the room.

Haley hung her head. She was ashamed of herself at her barrage of anger, and embarrassed.

Everyone remained idle, watching her and Valian.

For the first time, the couple seemed at odds with each other in their silence.

Haley looked at Valian, and she felt bad, yet she still felt a twinge of betrayal at Valian's apology to Cass. She didn't like Dr. Cass, and didn't trust him, and she was disappointed that Valian couldn't read Dr. Cass's disregard for authority, but as she considered what happened, she was again ashamed at her reaction and lack of control. There was surely a better way to have handled it besides blowing up at the guy, and she certainly wasn't acting like a member of the royal family.

"I'm sorry, Valian," she whispered. "I guess I still have a few things left to learn about emotions, too."

"It's all right, my sweet. Its things like this that help us to understand each other better. We are teaching each other. I am learning from you continuously, but I also have things to offer as well. There is a time and place for anger, I have learned, but this was not one of them. I read Cass's attitude the minute he sat down. I didn't address it because I need him. If anyone can find out what's wrong with Mother, who better than a human?"

Ike, Judy, and Henry looked at Valian curiously.

"Why is that?" Henry asked.

Valian sighed. "You may as well know, but you must not breathe a word to anyone, do you all swear?"

Everyone nodded.

"My Mother is half human."

There were looks of bewilderment from the group.

"What?" Henry asked.

Valian spelled it all out, the queen's father, her husband, the whole story.

Everyone was dazed at the news.

Valian began to pace the floor again.

Haley sat quietly, staring off into space, when the rumble of thunder captured her attention. She got up and went to the window. All she could see was darkness. She could hear the wind as it began to pick up, and the sky lit up far in the distance as if a flash bulb went off.

"Another storm," she said quietly as Valian joined her at the window.

"Molock is at it again," he said softly. "I just know it. He has something to do with these storms."

The sun never did come out that day. Reed and Jack came in around seven a.m. and brought breakfast, but no one seemed very hungry. Sersha stayed in the room with the queen and Dr. Cass. Sersha seemed to have had her suspicions as well as Haley.

Around noon it began to rain. The sky was dark and overcast in dark gray and blue clouds. Thunder continued to echo throughout the land and the lights in the tiny houses in the trees continued to burn. Fires were lit in the hearths sending out ribbons of smoke that were quickly smothered in the deluge. With the rain, came a chill that was difficult to shake.

Jack piled on the logs in the fireplace, but it didn't help their dampened spirits.

Dr. Cass walked in at two o'clock. All eyes turned to him. His face was grim, but there was just a hint of jubilation in his eyes.

"I can't find anything physically wrong, except it seems her hands are rather stiff, and she complains of feeling like she's on fire and in much pain. She is definitely ill."

"What do you think it is?" Valian asked anxiously.

"I can't tell without further tests."

"Well do them," Valian ordered.

"I can't do them here, I don't have the equipment."

"The infirmary…" Valian began.

"The infirmary doesn't have what I need."

"Well…" Valian paused as he deduced Dr. Cass's meaning.

"No," Valian appealed. "We can't."

"What?" Haley asked.

"The doctor is suggesting she be taken to the human side."

"Yes," Dr. Cass concurred. "If you want to find out what is wrong."

"We can't."

"Why can't you?" Haley demanded.

"We can't take her over there, it's not safe."

"Well, send a couple guardians along," Haley suggested. "Valian we must take her there. If there's any hope they can figure out what is wrong. It might be her only chance!"

"The idea makes me very nervous," Valian admitted.

"Nervous or not, you do want to help her don't you?"

"Of course I want to help her, Haley!"

"Well, what are we waiting for? The sooner we get her there, the sooner she can come home."

Valian sighed. "I don't like this."

Sersha walked over and put her arms around him. "We have to trust him," she said calmly. "Haley's right, this might be her only chance."

Valian looked down at his sister, almost pleadingly and nodded. "All right," he said quietly. "We'll assign our very best to watch over her. You know she's not going without protest, I can promise you that."

Jack walked in with a tray of fruits, and cheeses and set them on the table. Just as he was about to leave, Valian called to him. "Sir Jack."

Jack was startled and his long ears drooped as he turned around. "Yes, Your Highness?"

"Jack, I would like you to go and find Celio, Lonato, and Dinora and bring them to me."

"Yes, Your Highness," Jack sighed with relief and left the room.

"They are three of our very best. They shall accompany her."

Sersha nodded in agreement.

"They are only to know she is ill," Valian instructed."Sersha, brief them when they arrive. I'm going to break the news to Mother."

Celio, Lonato, and Dinora came in a few minutes later. Sersha and Haley brought them up to speed on their assignments. They were stressed at the news their queen was sick and even more alarmed at the thought of being on the other side without the Prince.

Haley took comfort when she saw all three wearing their given gems. "At least we won't have to worry about them wigging out with uncontrollable emotions," she thought to herself. The minor emotions they were displaying now would have been much more severe without the gems.

"Mother was not very cooperative," Valian said when he came in.

"How did you convince her?" Haley asked.

"I reminded her that she might possibly want to be around to see her future grandchildren," he smiled deviously.

Haley laughed quietly and blushed, rolling her eyes.

"Well it worked didn't it? I told her she had no choice since she is incapable of ruling in her condition. I am legally the one in charge and gave her an order."

Haley smiled. "You can be quite shifty when you want to be. Where did you learn that?"

"I don't know. Maybe it comes naturally."

"Ah ha," Haley giggled.

"How are we going to get her to the other side?" Sersha asked.

"The posterns would be the easiest," Henry suggested.

"What about Hilda, and Estelle?" Haley asked. "How do we know we can trust them?"

"We don't have much choice," Valian replied. "We're gonna have to take our chances."

"I pray you're right," said Haley. "Our parents could be in danger."

"I'm telling you, you're wrong about those two," Sersha re-iterated. "Celio, did you see anyone you recognized during your battle with the witches'? Maximillion, Tilly, Hilda, or Estelle?"

"None, Your Highness. I'd never seen any of them before."

"Besides the witch's crest, was there anything else that would indicate they were of the Rune clan?"

"No, Your Highness… now that you mention it, there was something a bit peculiar."

"What?" Valian asked.

"Every one of them had a greenish tint to their skin."

"Something else," said Dinora. "There were females engaged in battle. If I'm not mistaken, females of the Rune clan are forbidden to fight in battle."

Valian broke in to a wide grin. "Yes! That's true!"

"Then it couldn't have been the Rune clan," said Haley suddenly energized.

"Greenish skin," Valian repeated. "If I didn't know any better, I'd say they were related to the wicked witch of the west."

"Ha!" Henry responded. "I knew the Wizard of Oz was gonna come into this eventually!"

"Serious?" Haley asked with a raised eyebrow and a smirk.

Valian smiled. "Munchkin land isn't that far from here, just a few realms west."

"Why am I even surprised?" she laughed. "Does that mean Glinda is real?"

"Yes, but her name is not Glinda, its Tia."

"Tia," Haley repeated at a loss for words. "We'll have to visit sometime."

"And I suppose scarecrows can really talk," Henry said grinning.

"Correct again, but buzzards, not crows."

"Scare buzzards? Unbelievable."

The twins shook their heads in skepticism.

"Are you honestly asking us to believe that?"

"Have I ever lied to you?" Valian asked.

"Wow," Haley replied. "I guess we should expect the unexpected… all the time, Henry," she grinned at her brother.

"All right, on to serious matters," said Valian. "We shall all go to the other side to make sure all is well and taken care of. Celio, you, Lonato, and Dinora will remain with Dr. Cass and see to it Mother is protected at all times. Your wings shall remain shrouded until your return. Dr Cass, you do whatever needs to be done, but keep it short and sweet if you can."

The doctor nodded. "There is a hospital in Spokane. We can have her tested there. If there's anything to be found, they will find it."

Valian nodded.

"Mom and Dad sure will be surprised to see us," said Henry.

"I'll be right back," said Valian. "Doctor, will you come with me? We'll need to get the queen's transport prepared."

They left the room and came back a half hour later with what Henry called a glorified wheelchair. It was shaped just like a lounge chair, but it had no wheels. It hovered, stationary, a couple inches off the ground, and moved with just a touch on the handles.

"Mother is sleeping. We'll wait until she is awake before we move her. Let's take this time to discuss meeting with the witches."

"What?" Haley asked.

"We've already decided the witches that fought the guardians weren't of the Rune clan, and that was Mother's plan upon their return."

"I know. I don't trust Maximillion."

"I'm not particularly looking forward to it either," said Valian, "but they are our allies and they haven't done anything to prove otherwise."

Haley sighed. "You're right."

Valian walked over to a pretty piece of artwork hanging from the ceiling by the door. It was a long, thin, bronze plate with all kinds of meaningless symbols. Sitting on a tall stool next to it was a gadget that looked like a wooden spoon. He picked it up and struck the bronze plate which made a soft reverberating sound.

Reed and Jack came in through a side door, hidden from view by a silk screen.

"So that's how they suddenly appear out of nowhere," Haley thought to herself.

"I didn't realize what this was," she said running her hand over the bronze plate.

"There's one in every room," said Valian, "each with a different sound."

"I've seen the one in my room; I just thought it was a decoration."

"Reed, can you track down Theodore and give them this message?" he asked as he wrote a message on a scroll, rolled it up, and waved his hand over it. "Jack you find Troy and take him to see Theodore. The rest of us will be leaving for a couple of hours. We'll be back in time for the evening meal in the blue room here, and set two extra places at the table."

"Yes, Your Highness," the duo echoed in unison.

"Oh, the queen will be coming with us, just so you know."

The two bowed and left the way they came.

"What did you say in the message?" Haley asked, already knowing the answer.

"To bring the Sorcerer and Tilly for a private meeting to discuss what we are going to do about Molock and his nasty little apprentice."

"Do you have any ideas?" Henry asked.

"Yes, a few. We'll discuss them during the meeting," he explained at Henry's inquisitive expression.

Henry frowned and exchanged looks with Haley.

She answered him with a shrug of her shoulders.

"When Maximillion and Tilly arrive, we will not mention anything about the queen other than the fact she is indisposed. We'll have dinner, and exchange pleasantries, and afterward try and figure out a game plan, agreed?"

Haley gave a thumb's up, and everyone nodded.

Sersha went across the hall and peeked in on the queen. She came back a moment later. "She's awake. Ike, Judy, could you assist?"

"Absolutely," said Ike. "I've been feeling kind of like a fifth wheel around here, not knowing what to say or do."

"Not at all," Valian replied, leading them next door.

Lilia was sitting up, and looking cranky.

Haley couldn't help but smile at the queen's feistiness.

"I don't like this, Valian," Lilia grumbled. "Not one bit."

"My apologies, my queen. I understand this may be a bit of an inconvenience for you, but it is for your own good, not to mention your subjects. How could I possibly stand before them and say I didn't try and help you?"

Lilia rolled her eyes. "Oh, you are a clever one, my son. You have a flair for trickery," she smiled at him. "I don't know that I like your ease with it."

"Might come in handy," Valian responded with a snappy comeback and grin. "Now come on," he said reaching for her.

The queen held out a trembling hand, and Valian, and Ike lifted her out of bed, and laid her on the lounger, covering her with blankets.

"My bag," said the queen with a glance in the corner.

Haley picked up the queen's bag, and handed her an umbrella. "It's raining rather steadily."

Lilia smiled gratefully.

The group wheeled her out to one of the many private verandas as Celio, Lonato, and Dinora arrived.

"Are you ready, Ike?" Valian yelled over the din of thunder.

"Yes!"

"We'll have to use Hilda's postern! The one next to Mathilda's is only an exit! Let's go!"

Valian and Ike beat their wings and began to rise, each one holding a side of the lounger with both hands.

Lilia held up her umbrella, covering them both.

The others followed behind, ready to assist if needed.

The flight was slower than usual to accommodate the queen.

They landed at Hilda's doorstep, and Valian quickly rapped the gargoyle knocker.

Hilda opened the door, and her mouth fell open at once. "Heavens to Betsy, come in!"

Everyone rushed inside.

"We've come to use your postern," said Valian breathing heavily. "Please tell no one of this. The queen is ill and we need to get her to the other side."

"Yes, of course, this way."

Hilda led them down the hall past the stairs to her bedroom. Her postern was an extravagant piece of work. It was made of gold in carving arcs, and swirls, studded with emeralds all around the edges of the frame. The picture was a moonlit night.

"Will this come out at Estelle's?" Valian asked urgently.

"It will now," Hilda answered with a wave of her hand.

"Thank you," Valian said quickly, steering the lounger ahead, and into the center.

He faded at once into the blackness.

Ike looked at Judy. "Come on," he said grabbing her hand.

The others followed.

Sersha and Haley were the last.

Hilda took Sersha's hand. "All my hopes," she said grimly.

Sersha squeezed her hand. "Thank you," she replied as she stepped through the frame.

Haley flashed Hilda a half smile and followed. She found herself staring into candlelight.

Estelle was rummaging in one of her dresser drawers while the others stood waiting. She was wearing an off white night gown with little purple flowers on it, and her frilly nightcap was lopsided, her hair sticking out in tangles.

She stood up and turned; her hands full of candles. She handed one to each, and lit them with a wave. "Goodness sakes, you are all wet." She snapped her fingers, and towels flew off the shelves next to the bathroom.

Valian immediately began to blot the queen's face and arms.

The look of alarm on Estelle's face told Haley the queen didn't look good, and she bent down to look upon her and gulped.

Lilia seemed to have aged. There was just a hint of gray in her hair at her temples, and her skin seemed to have drooped slightly under her eyes.

To anyone else it may not have been noticeable, but to her, she spotted it immediately as Estelle did.

Haley looked up at Valian with dismay.

Valian's face drained of color as he looked back. He seemed to have to force himself to look at his Mother. A tear trickled from his eye as he tucked the blankets further around her face.

"We must act quickly," he said turning to Dr. Cass. "Where is this place, this Spokane?"

"About an hour or so," the doctor answered, almost cringing.

"An hour? We can't fly that far with her!"

"I'll go wake up mom and dad," Henry volunteered and left the room.

"Why didn't you tell us it was so far?" Valian demanded angrily.

"Valian," Haley said softly. "Take it easy. He didn't know," she continued, looking down at Lilia. "We'll get her there in the van. Dad has been to Spokane loads of times, he knows the way."

They could hear Paul and Carol's thumping as they descended the east tower.

Paul was buttoning his shirt when he came in. He took one look at the queen and turned. "I'll get the van ready."

He hurried through the foyer and out the door.

"Ike and I will go..."

Before Haley could protest, he cut her off.

"Haley, Sersha, you stay and explain everything."

"Stay and visit with Ernie," said Ike at the hopeful look on his wife's face. Judy let out the breath she was holding and hugged him.

Paul came back in. "Let's go."

They hustled out the door with Queen Lilia in tow, with Celio, Lonato, and Dinora behind them.

The rest of them stood in the arched doorway and watched the van disappear through the shroud hiding the estate.

Haley turned to the others. "Let's pray everything goes well."

They went inside and gathered in the kitchen.

Estelle put on a pot of coffee while Carol and Judy began cutting up some cantaloupe and made toast.

"How is Ernie?" Judy asked.

"He is good," Carol replied. "He has been a delight to look after. I went to the school and picked up his homework for two weeks. I told them your whole family had come down with the chicken pox."

Judy smiled. "That was clever."

"Well I didn't want him to fall behind in his studies."

"What about Ike's homework?"

"No one brought it up, so I didn't want to press the issue."

"Can I go see him?" Judy asked.

"Of course, he's just at the top of the stairs, second door on the left."

Judy smiled and left the kitchen.

Estelle stopped and turned around. "What is wrong with the queen? She looked terrible."

"We don't know," answered Sersha, glancing over at Haley. "Dr. Gretta couldn't find anything, so we thought we would try a human doctor."

"How long has she been like this?" Carol asked.

"Just a day or so," said Sersha. "After Violet's visit… she just seemed drained and weak."

"Violet's visit?" asked Estelle.

"Sit down, it's a long story," Sersha instructed.

Between Sersha, Haley, and Henry, who had been busy stuffing his face, they relayed what happened at the palace.

"That little imp!" Estelle exclaimed in disgust. "She has a lot of gall to pull a stunt like that."

"She's wearing an obsidian stone, Estelle," Haley added.

Estelle's eyes grew round. "Then she's … involved with Molock."

"That's not all," Sersha interjected. "There's a band of witches in league with her. They were lying in wait and battled with the guardians as they pursued her."

"No! Who were they?"

"Well, some of them were wearing the Rune clan crest…"

"What?" Estelle exclaimed. "The Rune…"

"They weren't of the Rune clan," Sersha interrupted. "I imagine the medallions were stolen. Celio said they had a green tint to their skin."

"From munchkin land, I might have known."

"And, Violet didn't even go to the dead mountain, but led them to an unfamiliar realm a thousand miles out," Sersha added. "Which means, Molock has moved. That's where the guardians lost her."

Estelle drew in a deep breath. "This is disturbing. We have to do something. The longer we wait, the more time Molock has to get more servants."

Haley thought about that statement for awhile as Estelle and Carol began frying up sausages and eggs.

Judy came back to the kitchen grinning. "He looks great," she commented. "He looks so peaceful, and so much like a little boy when he sleeps."

"He's been a joy," said Carol.

"So what did I miss?"

"We were just talking about Molock," Haley answered.

"Molock!" Judy snarled. "I'd like to get him and hang him up by his buster browns, and that Violet too! The nerve; taking my son, performing her magic on him. She better hope the queen gets her hands on her before I do!"

Judy stopped abruptly when she realized what she said. "I'm sorry, Sersha. I'm sure the doctors will figure out what is wrong. I wonder if they're there yet?"

"They must be by now," said Haley.

"What do you suppose is wrong with her?" Estelle asked.

"I don't know," Sersha answered, staring off into space. "She's in a lot of pain and very stiff, Dr. Cass told us."

"And her legs have a case of the twitches," Haley added.

"Twitches?" Estelle repeated with a solemn look.

"Why? Do you know something?" Sersha asked, sitting up straight, and leaning forward in her seat.

"Well," Estelle began, turning her back to them. "Those are signs of Parkinson's disease, but that is a human condition."

The others exchanged nervous looks.

"I've heard of that," said Haley.

"What is it?" Sersha asked, growing nervous.

"It is a condition that attacks the brain," Estelle answered. "It affects a person's coordination, motor skills, and speech, but she couldn't possibly have that, she's a fairy. It's not a contagious disease that could have been passed to her; she's a fairy, like I said."

"Is it... fatal?" Haley asked softly.

"Yes, eventually. It is a progressive and debilitating disease."

The others looked at Estelle expectantly, waiting for an explanation.

"Parkinson's begins with symptoms like tremors, stiffness of the joints, loss of smell, skin problems, and speech difficulties."

Estelle looked at their faces. "What? You don't think she has it do you?"

Sersha looked at the others in contemplation.

Haley could see she was struggling, deciding if she should say anything.

"She might," Sersha answered.

"But that's not possible…"

"My mother is half human," Sersha whispered.

"Half human?" Estelle whispered back.

Sersha began to explain everything the queen told them about her being half human and her father's relationship with her.

"Oh dear, she may very well have it," Estelle responded softly.

They ate a very early breakfast in silence, each buried in their thoughts.

Ernie came down to the kitchen promptly at five a.m. and was delighted to see Judy, telling her all about the neat things about the estate, and about Casey and her puppies, and the great library.

"You're having a good time then?"

"Yes, except I'm not allowed to leave the estate."

"That's all right, honey, your dad and I won't be long,"

"Ok," Ernie said, extremely chipper, digging into his breakfast.

Paul, Valian, and Ike pulled into the drive a couple hours later.

"It's a good thing we had Valian along," Paul said as he kissed Carol. "I'd forgotten he blocked the driveway."

"By the way, how have you gotten out of work?" Ike asked.

"I took three weeks of vacation. Dr. Malcolm didn't even think twice, of course I've been staying in touch by phone."

"Are you ready?" Valian asked Sersha and Haley. "Don't forget, we have dinner guests tonight."

"How could I forget?" Haley grumbled.

As they said their goodbyes, Ike peeked into the library to see Ernie. His head was buried in a book, and he barely looked up. "Hi Dad," was all he said with a quick smile, and went back to his reading. Ike smiled and joined the others at Estelle's bedroom door.

"What about the queen?" Estelle asked.

"She's in capable hands, and she's stable. They are giving her an I.V. to get her fluids under control, and they'll let us know as soon as they can. Paul will explain it all to you."

Estelle nodded and gave Valian a thin smile. "Fare thee well," she said as the group disappeared into her dark and stormy postern.

They emerged next door to Mathilda's and hurried up the street.

Ike wanted to get a change of clothes to take to the palace, and they said their hi's and goodbyes to Norman and Mable, and tried unsuccessfully to dodge the raindrops as they headed to the palace.

It was barely noon when they arrived, which gave everyone the opportunity to rest and get cleaned up. A messenger from the Tea House had come that morning to drop off their purchases.

Haley's breastplate had come as well. She tried it on before her bath and was pleased with the fit. She picked up her new sword and admired how she looked in the mirror. "I look like one of those female warriors from a comic book," she laughed to herself. She ran a hot bath and had a nice long soak, then decided to have a short nap before dinner.

When she woke it was four-thirty. She went to her closet to pick out a gown, and was surprised to see the gowns she had gotten from the queen hanging there, clean and pressed. She was thrilled, but sadness filled her heart at the thought of the queen sitting in the lounger, looking so weak and vulnerable.

She took a deep breath and let it out slowly, trying to shake off her thoughts. She wondered how the meeting with Maximillion and Tilly would go. She was hoping for the best, but was expecting the worst, given the princes' history.

Her steward arrived and escorted her to the blue room.

She was pleasantly surprised to see Valian and their guests sitting at the table, laughing about something.

"Maybe this will go smoothly after all," she hoped.

Valian and Maximillion stood as she neared the table.

"Good evening," said Maximillion with a polite smile. His smile seemed genuine, but something lurked behind it, barely noticeable.

"Good evening, Prince Maximillion," Haley answered. "Good evening, Madame Tilly," she nodded.

Tilly nodded back as Valian pulled out Haley's chair and pecked her on the cheek.

"It is so good of you to come," she continued, practicing her role as a princess, with pleasantries.

"It was nice of you to invite us," stated Tilly, raising her goblet in respect.

Sersha and Judy flowed into the room, wearing new gowns and looking fabulous and feminine.

Haley suddenly wished she had chosen one of the queen's gowns to wear, but it seemed inappropriate.

Henry and Ike were right behind them.

When everyone was seated, Reed and Jack came in with shrimp cocktails.

The beginning of dinner was a bit awkward, but soon the table was filled with small talk.

It seemed to Haley, everyone was trying to avoid the reason they were there, but as they finished their peach pie, Valian got right down to business.

He looked at Maximillion and Tilly in earnest.

"Since your discovery of Violet being Molock's new apprentice, the situation has escalated. The enemy's intention is to locate the gateway."

Valian paused for reaction.

"Molock intends to penetrate the other side," Maximillion commented.

"It looks that way."

"How do you intend to stop him?" the sorcerer asked.

"With your help," Valian answered. "Haley had an idea a while back I think may be our only salvation."

Haley turned to Valian, taken off guard.

"Medusa…" Valian didn't need to finish his sentence.

Maximillion looked at Valian as if he'd lost his marbles. "What is your idea?" asked the sorcerer as he stared at Haley.

"Legend has it; Medusa has been dead for ages. The plan is simple, bring back Medusa's head and use it to destroy Molock."

Valian sat back and waited for some feedback.

"It is an interesting plan, however how are we to get past the creatures that guard her resting place?"

"Creatures?" Haley questioned.

"I had no knowledge there were sentries," Valian responded.

"Yes," Maximillion replied to Haley, his voice lowered to a mysterious tone. "It is recorded in sacred scrolls; Medusa's resting place is guarded by the dead. All those souls she stripped from men and beasts are bound to act as sentries, never having peace or rest while she lies entombed."

Haley shuddered as the sorcerer lingered in the moment, almost reveling in her fear.

"It is said their bodies remain intact, wandering aimlessly throughout her tomb, and open their mouths in silent screams of despair and loneliness, for they cannot see each other. They have heightened senses in everything about them, but they are sightless, in mourning for their freedom and to rest in peace."

The entire room was silent as the grave as the group took in every word.

"And how are we to get past them?" Haley whispered.

"That's the trick, isn't it," Maximillion smirked. "How do you plan on getting there?" he continued. "The sea spans thousands of miles. You couldn't fly there if you wanted to. You wouldn't even make it an eighth of the way before you'd tire."

"I've already thought of that," Valian quipped. "We will build a ship. I have already sent our finest to the shores to begin construction."

"You don't have the time to spend building a ship before the new moon," Tilly objected.

"I sent them weeks ago, right after Haley suggested it. I'd say they have but a weeks' worth of work left before completion."

Maximillion nodded. He seemed impressed with Valian and his intuition. "When do we set sail then?" the sorcerer inquired.

"The sooner the better," Sersha piped in. "I say as soon as the last nail is hammered."

"I agree," Haley replied.

"I have many strong men to crew her, but not enough," Valian stated. "Have you any able men?"

"I have six that are experienced in steering a vessel."

"It's settled then," Valian sighed. "Get plenty of rest, and we'll send out a messenger to let you know when she's ready."

Valian held out his hand and Maximillion shook it, then he and Tilly were escorted to the courtyard where they took flight into the drizzle.

The group relaxed in the blue room and continued to talk about dinner and the journey ahead. Haley was happy that Valian used her idea about Medusa, but also nervous about it.

"Medusa," Henry stated, "now I've heard everything. Who would have believed all those stories we've heard, the fairy tales and myths we've grown up with were all true."

"Mind boggling, isn't it?" Haley agreed. "Have any of this crew of yours ever sailed a ship before?" she asked.

"Only two that I know of. They were fishermen before they joined the academy."

"Good," Haley responded.

She sat silently by the fire, watching the flame fairies doing loop-d-loops. "What about Lilia?" she asked.

"I've instructed Lonato to bring word of any change. Hopefully it will come before we have to leave."

Haley nodded.

"You know," Henry began, "mom and dad aren't going to be very happy when they find out how much school we're going to miss on this little trip."

Haley didn't respond. She knew the conditions her parents set down and she didn't want to think about it, "and besides, this is too important," she thought to herself. "A chance to rid the fairy world of the evil one. This just has to work."

"How are we going to get past the sentries, Valian?" she inquired.

"I'm not sure. I believe there is information about Medusa in the library."

Haley's face lit up. She loved libraries, and books, and all the history. "Let's go see!" she offered hopefully. There were hundreds of books lining the shelves in the royal library. Haley took in the smell of the old and faded covers and pages. She could lock herself away in this room for days and never grow tired of it.

Valian scanned the rows until he found what he was looking for, an ancient book with a very loose binding. All the color had faded from the cover. He blew the dust off and began to turn the pages.

"Ah, here it is."

He began to read aloud how Medusa was the subject of a lovers' quarrel. "The reigning king and queen of the age had a horrific fight over the beautiful handmaiden Medusa. The queen accused the king of being promiscuous and became extremely jealous, putting a curse upon Medusa and banishing her to the Desert Mountains in the Desolation realm; swearing that she would never see daylight again. You see, Medusa's beauty surpassed the queen's by leaps and bounds. Her hair was golden as the sun. Her skin was fair, and without flaw, and her eyes were as blue as crystal clear waters. The king called her Lady Fair which the queen despised. It says here the queen gave the king small doses of the venom from a coral snake until he became sick and had taken to his bed, falling unconscious. She then sought out Medusa and found her singing by a small pool in the royal gardens and cast the curse upon her and instructed her own loyal bodyguards to bind Medusa, blindfold her and cast her into a cave so high in the cliffs, no one dare try to scale it, less death befall them. The story goes on to say when the king finally recovered, he was so distraught at the disappearance of Medusa, he cursed the queen and his entire kingdom, proclaiming they would never know another day of peace, then took his own life. The kingdom was besieged by war and the entire population was wiped out and lay barren."

Valian looked around at everyone, mesmerized by the tale. He sighed heavily.

"There isn't anything mentioned about Medusa's sentries."

Haley pondered the story, when she suddenly had a revelation. "Do you remember what Maximillion said, the sentries would never know rest or peace while Medusa was entombed?"

The others responded with blank looks.

"Don't you see? We need to remove her from her resting place. We will have to bargain with the sentries, tell them they will finally be free, to move on, and to rest!"

"Wow, Haley you're a genius!" Henry let loose with enthusiasm.

The dimples in Valian's cheeks began to take shape as he smiled that smile that made her go weak in the knees. "I concur," he replied. "How do you do that?"

"Like I've said before, I've read too many mystery novels," she giggled.

"Well at least we have a plan," Sersha commented, "but how are we going to even get that far without conflict?"

"We'll have to cross that bridge when we come to it," Valian sighed again.

"Well I'm beat," Haley yawned.

Jack and Reed came in and began clearing the dishes as the group went to their rooms.

Haley re-played the entire evening in her mind as she drifted off to sleep.

Chapter 14
Preparation for the Quest

The following morning at breakfast, Lonato brought news of the queen. She was not afflicted with Parkinson's disease.

"They diagnosed her with something called Fibromyalgia. It is a painful disease, but her vitals are good, and the doctors have given her medicine to relieve some of the pain," Lonato smiled.

"So she's going to be all right?" Valian asked.

"For the most part," Lonato replied. "The syndrome will never go away completely, as there is no cure, but they said she would be able to live a relatively normal life, she'll just have to manage the pain of her illness. She asked the doctors for a list of natural ingredients she can use instead of the medicine they gave her."

"When will she be able to come home?" Haley asked.

"Now," Lonato answered. "They are checking her out sometime this morning."

"This morning?" Valian uttered. "We don't have time to get there…"

"I stopped at the Miles estate on my way back," Lonato interrupted. "Mr. Miles is already on the way. I cleared the driveway and closed it behind him. Celio can take care of the rest."

"Very good, Lonato. Well done." Valian let out a long breath. "We'll wait for her, and see to it she is comfortable, then I want to fly out and see how the ship is progressing, anyone want to come along?"

Everyone but Sersha agreed. "I want to spend the day with Mother," she stated.

"In the meantime, let's all go shopping. We are going to need a lot of supplies.

The entire group headed for the shops and boutiques.

There was just a slight drizzle as they leapt from the balcony.

They stopped at Henry's Hardware; run by a very old human. He had light gray eyes and hair, and a long white beard that hung down to his exposed belly button. His white t-shirt was at least two sizes too small, but it didn't seem to bother him.

He walked slowly, hunched over from an old back injury, and he had a high voice that cackled when he talked.

Haley saw he had a habit of scratching his left ear.

"He's a bit deaf in that ear," Valian whispered to her.

Haley could see that right off as he kept saying "eh?" whenever anyone spoke to him.

His shop was chuck full of everything you could ever want from a hardware store, and Henry Miles walked around, looking important since it was called "Henry's Hardware."

The group walked up and down the aisles, contemplating what they might need.

"The builders will have already stocked the ship with the basics," Valian was saying as he examined a cord of rope. "We can never have too much," he continued, throwing it into the basket Haley was wheeling along behind him.

She pointed out they should have an extra set of tools.

They collected several hammers, nails, screwdrivers, pliers, and wrenches. Valian grabbed a couple of saws, water canteens, wool blankets, and pillows.

By the time they finished at Henry's, they had three full carts.

"Why don't you and the girls go down to the forest floor to the food market and begin loading up on what you would like," Valian suggested turning to young Henry to bid Henry to barter their purchases.

The girls landed on the forest floor in front of the food market. There were four shops, side by side, just opening for business.

Dry goods lined the shelves in the first shop, next to it, outside the door; various fruits in trays on long tables were displayed. Further down were vegetables of every sort, and finally a butcher shop, filled with thick steaks, roasts, smoked hams, and dried and smoked meats.

Each took a different shop.

"Remember, get things that won't spoil too quickly, stuff that we can store for an extended period," called Haley walking into the dry goods shop.

The shop had everything under the sun, dried beans, wheat flour, and sugar in ten pound gunny sacks. There were dried apricots, banana chips, pineapple, raisins, and plums. She spotted bags of rice, jars of bullion, dry cereals, and oatmeal. She was overwhelmed with so much to choose from and wondered who was going to do all the cooking on board.

With a sigh she began grabbing things, randomly when a thought came to mind of her mother telling her on many occasions as they shopped, "stick to your list and don't buy spur of the moment items." Haley put back the dried chocolate squares and moved on.

There was an annoying fairy that kept buzzing past her, watchful, as if she suspected Haley might steal something. Haley ignored her and continued on, but the fairy wouldn't let up.

Just as Haley was about to say something, Valian walked in.

The fairy let out an excited squeak, and approached him, curtsying and bubbling with nervous fever.

Haley couldn't help but smile at her, being all flustered, and when Valian walked up and kissed Haley on the cheek, the fairy's face turned from excitement, to disappointment, then anxiety.

"She's probably afraid I will say something to Valian about her incessant whirring about," she thought.

Haley said nothing as she and Valian headed up the isle together.

Valian turned. "Excuse me, miss," he began, glancing at the flustered fairy.

The fairy froze as if petrified.

"Have you any cocoa?"

The fairy began to fidget, glancing around the shop as if she'd forgotten where it was, then suddenly flit to the end of the isle and picked up a tin of cocoa and held it out with trembling hands, unable to speak.

Valian walked up the aisle and smiled at the fairy as he took the tin.

She giggled anxiously. "Is… is… is there anything else I can get for you, Your Highness?" she stammered.

"No, that will be all," he replied.

Valian took care of their purchases, and as they walked out the door, Haley glanced back and saw the fairy zip to the back of the shop, whispering excitedly to the clerk.

Haley giggled as they went next door to find Judy. "You have an amazing effect on people," she laughed. "She was absolutely star struck."

Valian grinned.

They finished with their shopping and instructed the shopkeepers to have their items delivered to the ship.

"That's at least a three day trip, if not more for such a big delivery," Haley commented. "It took us three days to get to the sea, and we weren't loaded down with hardly a thing."

"Oh, we're not going there sweetheart, that was an ocean, we're going to the eastern shores, to the sea, that's only an hour from here, as the crow flies," Valian replied.

"Ocean, sea, what's the difference?" Haley grinned.

"Oceans are much larger than seas," he grinned back.

"Great, I'm glad we won't have to travel far. I want to get this journey over with as soon as we can."

"I know what you mean."

Everyone gathered in the royal dining hall for lunch. The room was filled with the usual chatter as fairies helped themselves to steaming bowls of soup and delicious sandwiches. It was just the kind of food that's good to eat when it was cold and rainy.

Half way through their meal, a guardian came in and whispered in Valian's ear.

Valian leaned over and told Haley the queen had arrived via a side entrance, close to her royal bedroom.

Haley passed it on to Sersha.

The group quickly finished their food and went to see her.

She was sitting up in bed, and smiled as they all walked in. She had a lunch tray on her lap, and was buttering a roll.

"That hospital food was nasty," she replied as they gathered around her. "Why on earth they would serve such rotten food to sick people is beyond me."

She looked a whole lot better than when she left. The color was back on her cheeks, her beautiful eyes were bright, but Haley couldn't help noticing the stiffness in her hands as she laid her butter knife down.

"You look wonderful Mother," Valian complimented. "You really threw is a scare there."

"Oh, I'm fine," Lilia replied, but it seems my humanness has caught up with me."

No one knew how to respond to her comment and shifted nervously.

The queen looked at all the somber faces and she smiled reassuringly.

"Honestly, I feel just fine, the pain comes and goes. The doctors said I will always have these episodes, and that I would have to learn to manage it."

Her words didn't have their intended effect.

"I'm not dying; I have a manageable disease. Now, would you all please put on some happy faces for me?"

Valian grinned. "You certainly sound like your old self," he chuckled.

That lightened the mood, and before long everyone was jabbering and filling the queen in on all the latest developments.

"Medusa, eh? I never would have thought of that. As I've said before, you will make an excellent queen someday, Haley. You are smart, witty, and a joy to have around. I like your plan. Have you given any thought as to how you are going to get past the sentries?"

Shock and surprise were popular responses with the group at the question.

"You know about the sentries?" Valian asked in amazement.

"Very much so." She began to laugh, and looked at Valian and Sersha. "Your father, rest his soul, told me a story once about the time he and his good friend Skipper went looking for Medusa. They were just boys, curious and adventurous. One day they decided they would sneak into Medusa's cave and steal her treasured shield, a very special shield which never left her side."

"What was so special about it?" Sersha asked, taking a seat on the edge of the bed.

"Legend has it that the shield will cause whoever holds it to become invisible. I suspect that is how she was able to overcome many of her victims. Anyway, your father and Skipper decided to sail the Eastern Sea and come back with their prize; heroes in their cunning."

She began to laugh again as she continued.

"They constructed a crude little boat which promptly filled with water and sank a quarter mile from shore. Lucky for them it sank there and not a thousand miles from home."

Everyone smiled, but Haley was busy processing this news.

"Do you suppose this shield is real?" she inquired.

"Oh yes, we have plenty of documentation of its existence in the archives, didn't you check the archives?"

Valian's face turned crimson. "No," he admitted, "but you can be sure we will before we depart."

"Do you think the shield will still be there?" Haley asked.

"I don't see why not," Sersha interjected. "Mother said it never left her side."

"What are you thinking, Haley?" Valian asked.

"If someone could sneak in and get that shield, they could get Medusa's head and sneak out. The sentries would be none the wiser."

"I don't know, it would be very dangerous, not to mention risky," said Valian. "I think I like your other idea better, about bargaining with them. How could they refuse our offer, a chance to finally be free from what must feel like an eternity of captivity?"

"That would be a tempting offer," said Lilia. "Go check the archives and let me finish my lunch, and then I need to rest for a bit."

Valian kissed his mother's hand and bowed. "It's good to have you back safe and sound."

"Before you go, on my bureau is a list of herbs. Can you take it to Dr. Cass, and have him collect what is needed and send it to Reed to prepare? There should be instructions on the second page, thank you."

Valian picked up the list and bowed again. He passed the list to one of the guardians to deliver to Dr. Cass with the queen's instructions, and then proceeded to the archives.

The group gathered at a round table and waited while Valian searched. He came back with a box and set it down, then began going through its contents.

First he pulled out an old compass, and blew the dust off. "What is this?" he asked, turning it over in his hand.

Henry took it. "It's a compass," he grinned. "It shows what direction you're going, see?" he pointed. "North, East, South, and West."

"What's wrong with using the stars in the heavens?" Valian asked.

"You mean you know how to follow the stars?" Judy asked in wonder.

"Sure, doesn't everybody?"

"No," Henry answered. "It's not common practice in the human world. I did have an astronomy class in school, but I thought it was boring."

"Boring?" Valian exclaimed, "I have always found the heavens fascinating." He reached in and took out a wooden flute. He scowled as he studied its markings and holes.

"It's a flute," said Haley.

"I know it's a flute," Valian replied. "Sersha plays flute beautifully," he continued, handing it to her.

Sersha wiped it free from dust, and began to blow into the mouthpiece softly.

The others listened to the pleasing melody, enraptured. "Wow, that was very lovely Sersha," Henry gazed at her. Sersha's face turned rosy red as she beamed at him.

Lastly, Valian pulled out a very old book, and flipped it open. The yellowed pages were filled with handwritten entries. He skimmed the pages and came to a section about the flute.

"It says here that the flute was used to appease Medusa. Its sound enchanted her, and captivated her to the point where she was spellbound and couldn't move."

"Interesting," Haley responded.

"I guess we don't need the flute," Valian commented.

"Yes, please, bring it along. I love the music of the flute. Sersha, will you play it again sometime?" Henry interrupted. Sersha nodded in reply.

"Look here," Valian said, pulling out three loose pages.

"That's sheet music," Haley uttered. "Can you read it?"

"Only a couple of times in my life have I read sheet music," Sersha answered, taking the pages. "It's been a long time. I'll study it and see if I can remember."

Valian continued to search paragraph after paragraph, thumbing through the pages. "This is intriguing, look, here's a drawing of her."

Everyone leaned in to get a look as Valian read the caption.

"It seems as though she could control the sea, and could wreak havoc, having a terrible power over the forces of nature."

The others weren't listening, but stared at the hideous face looking back at them.

"Geez Louise," Henry whispered. "I feel like I could turn to stone just looking at her picture."

"She gives me the creeps," Haley commented, rubbing her arms. "I'm glad she's dead."

"Amen to that," Valian agreed. "She will still be a danger though. We won't be able to look upon her, at least not directly. Let's go check out the ship, see how it's coming along."

Sersha stayed behind as the rest took to the skies.

It didn't take long to reach the eastern shores. The scent of saltwater reminded Haley of the trip she and Valian had taken to the islands.

The ship builders were putting on the last boards, covering its skeleton.

Haley was impressed. It was a grand vessel, roughly fifty feet in length. Its stern was round and wide. Her white sails were rolled up on five separate masts and she came to a sharp point at the bow.

Skilled carpenters had carved intricate designs on her sides, and the likeness of a fairy stood watch over their impending journey.

The group climbed aboard and toured her innards.

The rooms where the crew would bunk were small, but there were two large rooms for the captain's quarters, each with silk curtains dividing the rooms in half, one half for the men, one half for the women with three beds on each side.

"Who is the other room for?" Haley wondered out loud.

"I assume it's for the sorcerer," Valian replied.

The galley was quite large, and already equipped with cooking gear. Large pots and pans hung from the ceiling. The cupboards were jammed with dishes and eating utensils.

The adjoining room had a long table like a booth with its seats lining the walls. Lanterns hung overhead, with smaller ones mounted on the wall in just the right places. Round windows presented an ocean view, and tall cupboards stood empty, waiting to be filled with all the food.

Back on deck, Haley wondered where the cannons were, and asked Valian about it.

"Cannons? We won't be needing cannons… do you think? We're not exactly going into battle, just taking a long cruise."

Haley shrugged her shoulders; after all, the crew was gifted with magic.

"She's a fine ship," Valian said, slapping her mast. "Solid, and strong. Well done," he said to the carpenters.

"I just wish it would stop raining," said Henry.

Haley breathed in deeply. The smell of salt air, and freshly cut wood mingled together, playing tag with her nose as though competing for her pleasure. She suddenly heard a soft swish, and turned around just as Maximillion, Tilly, and six others landed on deck.

"Ahoy mates!" Maximillion called out with a huge grin. "She's looking good Valian, old chap."

The sorcerer's disposition befuddled everyone on board. They didn't know whether to smile back or run.

"Prince Maximillion, good day to you," Valian began. "What brings you out in the inclement weather?"

"We stopped at the palace to have a chat. Princess Sersha said you would be here. We wanted to check out how things were coming along with your ship, and by the looks of it, she'll be ready to sail soon."

"Yep, it's going well I think. Would you like a tour?" Valian offered.

"I'd love one," Maximillion replied as Valian led them below deck.

Haley, Henry, and the Seers exchanged puzzled looks.

"What was that all about I wonder," Henry chimed in.

"Beats me," Haley answered with an eyebrow raised in suspicion. "That man confuses me. Just when I think I can read him, he does an about face. I still don't trust him. He's up to something."

"What?" Ike asked.

"I don't know, but I think we're all going to have to be on our guard during this trip," Haley answered.

The rain began to let up slightly as Haley walked the deck from end to end, taking in its beauty and solid construction.

Horse drawn carts began to arrive, loaded down with the supplies from their earlier shopping spree.

Everyone pitched in, and helped unload, carrying bags, boxes, and sacks to the galley.

The women showed the deliverers where to place things as Valian and the witches' came in from the sleeping quarters.

"Yes, I'd say she is seaworthy," said Maximillion grinning.

"Perhaps you would care to join us for dinner tomorrow evening, a celebration of sorts, our sending off party."

"We would be delighted," Tilly responded. "What time?"

"I'd say, sixish," Valian answered.

"Sixish it is," Maximillion smiled, looking around at everyone. "Till then," he bowed to Valian and Haley, and swiftly moved up the stairs, mounted his broom, and shot toward the sky with his crew behind him.

"Well that was certainly interesting," Valian commented, watching the witches turn to pin pricks in the distance. "He seemed to have changed his tune a bit."

"I'd say he was a little over zealous," Haley objected. "Why would he suddenly be so pleasant after all we've been through with him? I still don't trust him," she complained.

"Now, my flower, I think we should allow him the benefit of the doubt for now, don't you?"

Haley threw him a doubtful look. "I'm just sayin'."

"You worry too much, love, but if it makes you feel any better, I'll have Celio, and Lonato just keep a watchful eye, all right?"

Haley smiled. "Thank you, that does make me feel better."

"I think we've seen enough for now. Shall we?"

"Wait," Henry interjected, "we have to give her a name."

"You're quite right," Valian responded. "Any suggestions?" All he got back were blank looks.

"How about we think about it for awhile?" Henry frowned. The party agreed to mull it over and headed back to the palace.

The afternoon grew darker, and it began to thunder. "You know, I love a good storm, but this is getting old." Haley was saying as they landed and went inside to the fireplaces in the dining hall to warm themselves.

The wind began to pick up as yet another storm front moved in. Lightning lit up the sky in continuous strikes. Haley stood in the great arch, looking out as she toweled off her hair and face. Valian came and stood beside her.

"I've seen a lot of thunderstorms before, but I've never seen lightning like this," she said, taking Valian's arm. "It's frightening. Do you really think its Molock?"

"I can't think of any other reason," Valian replied. "I don't think Wisen has ever seen the likes before. It is widely believed that Molock has powers beyond comprehension. It is hard to figure out because anyone that has ever gotten even remotely close to him has died or gone mad. His secrets died with them."

Haley stood quietly, watching the sky. Even the clouds looked different. "I have an idea," she said softly as she looked up into Valian's pale blue eyes. "I think we should get together with Zeb and Ike, just the four of us. See if we can't spark their memories. You must have some kind of magic that can do that."

"I'm afraid not, but…" Valian paused. Suddenly his face lit up. "I don't know why I didn't think of it before."

"What?" Haley inquired.

"There is a seer that lives in the bluebell meadow, on the edge of the Woodland realm. It is said he is all seeing, and has powerful magic. He dabbles into a darker kind of magic, things most creatures wouldn't dare attempt. We could take Ike and Zeb to see him and see if he can do anything to bring back their memories."

"Yes! I think we should. It can't hurt to try. After dinner, let's take Ike to the Bonner house and see if Zeb will agree, besides, I haven't been there yet to see their place."

Valian nodded. "What's the worst that could happen?"

"What is his name?" Haley asked.

"Merlin."

"Merlin? As in Merlin the magician?" she burst out in disbelief.

"The one and only," Valian smiled.

Haley just shook her head in wonder.

The couple went to check on the queen just before dinner.

Sersha was sitting at the foot of the bed, weaving quietly as Lilia napped.

"How is she?" Valian whispered, tip toeing toward the bed.

"She's weak, but doing better," Sersha whispered back. "Here," she said softly, handing Haley a silk gown. "This is the special gown I promised you."

Haley took it in her hands. It was the thinnest, softest material she'd ever felt.

"Oh my," she whispered, "this is exquisite, it's so light and airy."

It was a beautiful midnight blue and deep plum color in a tight floral design. Sersha handed Valian the tunic she made for him in the same rich colors, but not as feminine in its design.

Valian kissed his sister on the top of her head. "It's magnificent," he replied.

"So, how was the ship?" Sersha inquired.

The three sat quietly, discussing the fine craftsmanship, and sturdiness of the vessel, and how the witches showed up, and Maximillion's change in demeanor.

"Yes, they stopped in to see you, and I figured it couldn't hurt to let them know where you were. They were bound to show up sooner or later."

"Well I have to say, it was more of a pleasant visit than we expected, right my sweetness?"

Haley didn't comment, but raised her eyebrows in response.

"You believe something different?" Sersha asked.

"I just think we should be wary, that's all."

"I would heed Haley's suggestion," said the queen softly, startling them.

"Mother, I didn't know you were up, did we wake you?"

"No, I was already awake when you came in, just resting my eyes. I would trust Haley's intuition. She's good at reading people. I worry about you all taking this journey. You have never undertaken such a quest. You must be cautious, and ever mindful of your surroundings."

"We'll be fine, Mother," Valian interrupted her.

"You of all people should know of the dangers you will face," Lilia butted in with a stern look.

"Have you already forgotten what happened to you in the forest with Iris? You can't be so careless. You have precious cargo going with you, and you can't afford to be sidetracked by something which could be avoided in the first place. You have little time to find Medusa before the new moon."

Valian lowered his head, embarrassed at the queen's rebuke.

"Don't get me wrong, my son, I trust you, but you tend to jump ahead, without contemplation. You haven't mastered the skills Haley and Henry can offer you yet. Vigilance, Prince Valian. Stay alert, focused, and watchful. I promise you, your patience will pay off in the end."

"Yes, Mother. I admit I can be presumptuous at times."

"Stick close to your betrothed. She can help you. Protect her and her brother fiercely… and keep your temper in check. Rash behavior benefits no one but your adversary."

"Your wisdom is just, my queen," Valian bowed to her.

"So, what are your immediate plans?" she asked with a motherly smile.

Valian and Haley explained their idea of taking Ike and Zeb to see Merlin.

"That's a wise move," Lilia replied. "You must take care in dealing with Merlin. He is very crafty, but dabbles in things that ought not to be dabbled in. He'll expect compensation for anything he does."

"Like what?" Valian inquired, frowning.

"Rumor has it, he's fond of the drink."

"Huh?" said Valian.

"The drink. Rum. It's hard to come by in this neck of the woods, but I'll bet Estelle could get her hands on some for you."

"Rum," said Haley. "Yuck. Anyone who can stand to drink hard liquor has to be out of their mind."

The others looked at her in surprise.

"How would you know?" Valian asked with a raised eyebrow.

"I snuck a taste when my dad wasn't looking once," she admitted, wrinkling her nose. "It made me sick, and I went and threw up. Never again, and I don't recommend any of you try it either. I was young and stupid."

Valian chuckled. "Young? Yes. Stupid? Never. It was natural curiosity."

Haley cocked her head. "Very good, Valian."

There was a knock on the door.

"Come in," Lilia answered.

Reed entered with the queen's dinner.

"All right, everyone go have your dinner, and good luck with your meeting. I want a full report when you return."

The group left for the dining hall. There were only six Lords and Ladies in the room. The storm kept everyone else at home.

The soft gong sounded, and only two brownies came in, rolling a cart stacked with covered plates. The head chef apologized, informing them that most of the kitchen staff stayed home, fearful of the lightning.

"That's understandable," Valian reassured him.

The brownies served the prince first, then the others and then quickly scurried back to the kitchen.

They ate in silence, very much aware of the torrent raging outside.

"Maybe we should wait until the storm subsides," Haley whispered.

"Those were my thoughts as well, but we just don't have the time to wait," Valian whispered back.

Haley sighed and picked at her food. She was wary of the storm.

Minutes later the head chef hurried back into the room with a peculiar look on his face, and set a clear bottle on the table in front of Valian. "This just came for you," he said, and retreated back to the kitchen.

"This must be the rum," Valian remarked, unscrewing the cap, and taking a whiff. "Phew!" he uttered, putting the cap back on.

Haley burst out laughing. "I've never heard you say "phew" before!"

Something must have tickled her funny bone because she couldn't stop giggling, and tears rolled down her cheeks as she held her stomach.

Valian didn't know what to make of her outburst, but it was contagious as everyone else began to laugh.

Maybe it was nerves because of the storm that had everyone in stitches. Their jolliness finally wore off, and several excused themselves, heading for the arch doors, still holding their stomachs.

"Nothing like a good laugh," Valian said, rubbing his belly as he stood, grabbing the rum bottle.

"I'll go get my wrap," said Haley, hurrying down the corridor. When she returned, Henry, Ike, and Judy looked at them questioningly.

"We're just going on an errand. You don't mind if I borrow Ike for awhile, do you?" Valian asked Judy.

"No..." Judy answered, a little confused.

"It'll be all right, we'll be back soon."

"Come," Sersha said, taking Judy by the arm. "Let's go play a game I invented."

"Oh... ok," Judy responded as Sersha led her from the room. "Coming, Henry?" Sersha asked with a wink.

"I'm right behind you."

Valian, Haley, and Ike headed into the pelting rain, and quickly dove under the canopy for cover. The cold rain blasted them in the face like tiny frozen pin pricks. They held their arms up to shield their faces, but it didn't do a whole lot of good.

"It's hailing!" Haley cried out, trying to keep control as the wind whipped around her.

The Bonner cabin was on the fringe of the outskirts. A lone lamp cast a bright light inside, and Valian quickly pounded on the door.

Zeb answered, his face cast in shadow. He grinned as soon as he saw Valian's muscular frame in the doorway.

"Come in," Zeb said quickly.

"Haley!" Susan and Rosie cried out, rushing over, almost tackling her.

Haley smiled and hugged the girls as Ike entered behind her and shut the door.

"What in the world are you doing out on a night like this?" Sarah exclaimed, walking over and giving Haley a big hug.

"Well for one thing, I've never seen your place," Haley answered, surveying the large living room.

"Well, it's not the Taj Mahal, but it's comfortable. We did have a few things added after we returned from your place," Sarah added, pointing out the carpeting. "Zebulan made all the furniture himself of course."

Susan and Rosie went to their bedrooms in the loft and came back beaming, their baby dolls in their arms.

"My, you've taken very good care of them," Haley exclaimed.

"Let me show you the rest of the place," Sarah said proudly, leaving the men in the living room.

"Very nice!" Haley complimented.

The kitchen was painted a soft yellow with hand sewn curtains in the two windows, and to Haley's surprise, a modern day stove, fridge, and washer.

"Where's your dryer?" Haley inquired.

"Oh, I'd rather hang out the clothes," said Sarah. "There's just nothing like the smell of fresh dried clothes from the outdoors."

Haley glanced out the window, just as lightning struck really close, causing them to jump. Haley saw briefly, other buildings in the back.

"These darned storms," Sarah replied, her hand on her chest. "I've never seen storms like these."

Haley looked at her gently. "It'll be all right. You know, it's like looking in the mirror," she gazed at Sarah.

"I know," Sarah agreed. "If we had been twin sisters, we would have had a lot of fun growing up," she giggled.

Haley smiled, then turned serious. "We have another reason for stopping by."

A worried look crossed Sarah's face.

Haley explained her idea about the possibility of finding out more information about Molock.

Sarah breathed a sigh of relief. "I thought you were gonna say you wanted Zeb to help find, and fight Molock."

"Rest assured Sarah; we would never put Zeb in harm's way, or have him have to face Molock again."

"You don't think bringing his memory back will hurt him, do you?" Sarah asked.

"I don't think so. It might actually help him by answering some of the questions he may have about what happened to him."

Haley helped Sarah pour some lemonade for everyone. When they got back to the living room, Haley could tell Valian had spilled the beans about their plan.

Zeb asked Sarah to join him in the kitchen.

Haley went up to Valian.

"They have both consented," he said softly, looking over at Susan and Rosie, playing quietly by the fire.

"I don't much like the idea, I have to be honest, but I'll do anything if it will help lead to his destruction."

"It'll be all right, Ike. We'll be right there," said Haley.

Ike returned her kindness with a half hearted smile.

Zeb came out of the kitchen, followed by Sarah. "Let's get this over with," he said, grabbing his hat and coat.

"Where ya goin', papa?" Rosie asked, getting excited at the prospect of her getting to go along.

"Sorry, my honey," he smiled, picking Rosie up and rubbing his whiskers against her cheek. "Not this time. Papa is going to help the prince on a quick errand. I won't be long," he said with a glance at Sarah.

Sarah nodded. "Hey, girls, how about we roast some marsh mallows?"

"Yay!" they cried, their attention diverted.

The group quickly rushed out into the rain. Valian and Ike each took one of Zeb's arms and flew into the deluge, Haley close behind.

Chapter 15
Re-living a Nightmare

I t only took a few minutes to arrive in the bluebell meadow. The bluebells were of course very large, and hung their heads shut tight against the pelting rain and hail.

They made their way through the flowers and were suddenly standing in front of a huge grass covered mound with a rotting wooden door.

Valian rapped four times, pausing between each knock.

The door creaked open slowly, revealing a dimly lit hall and one of the most beautiful creatures.

She had soft brown, wavy hair that almost touched the floor. Flowers and vines intermingled, intertwined in her locks. From what Haley could tell, she wore no clothing, but was covered in all the right places in greenery and flowers. She had soft, round brown eyes, and an almost overwhelming gentleness about her. Perched on her shoulder was a sleeping mourning dove.

Haley was sure she had seen her walking through a dew covered meadow with animals following behind her when she and Henry had arrived in Wisen for the first time.

Valian bowed. "Milady," he said softly. "We have come seeking Merlin's wisdom on an urgent matter. May we seek an audience?" he asked, handing her the rum bottle.

The creature didn't speak, but motioned for Valian to follow, and led the group down the hall to a wonderful large room that nearly took Haley's breath away.

There were several sitting areas with soft velvet furniture, neatly arranged. Vines and flowering bushes grew right out of the grass floor, separating the areas. Dozens of lanterns and candles glowed softly, flickering as they passed by.

The creature motioned for them to sit, and left the room.

Haley sat and took it all in, with pleasure.

There was an open aviary that ran the entire length of one wall, filled with sleeping birds of all types, and in the center of the room, night birds nestled together at a wonderful pool, with a cascading little waterfall, tumbling softly.

Haley watched several birds as they stood in the water, drinking. Their long legs made them look like little storks. She could hear the hum of crickets, and could smell a sweet, light fragrance she didn't recognize. It didn't take long for the group to warm up as the room was quite balmy.

Haley looked at Valian, wondering what was going to happen. "Who was that?" she whispered.

"She is Mother Earth," Valian replied softly.

Haley's mouth dropped open.

"She is in charge of every creature, and looks after them. She is most tender and loving when it comes to any animal, but her wrath is terrifying lest anyone harm a hair upon her charges. It is said she can change form in an instant, and become a frightening beast. Death comes quickly to those foolish enough to abuse or hurt an animal."

"My kind of woman," Haley replied.

Haley could feel her approach as Mother Earth entered and motioned for them to follow.

She led them down a long flight of stairs. Haley figured it was at least three stories. She looked into the huge underground chamber with wide eyes.

The walls were dark, solid granite with so many lanterns that Haley didn't think she could count them all.

The cavern was filled with table upon table, with all sorts of weird looking cauldrons, glass tubes, beakers, and burners heating up bubbling pots of strange looking liquids, spewing odd smells. It looked like the laboratory of a mad scientist.

Movement caught her eye as a figure emerged out of the shadows.

Merlin looked exactly as she imagined him, like a very old wizard with long gray-black hair and beard, dressed in black robes. The only thing that kept him from looking totally spooky was his bright blue eyes that seemed to turn green and back to blue again.

He was a man of few words, mostly just listening as Valian laid it all out for him.

When Valian finished speaking, Merlin motioned for the group to be seated on a very long, black couch where they all fit quite nicely.

Merlin snapped his fingers and a chair suddenly appeared out of thin air, facing them. It was more like an elaborate throne than a chair.

He proceeded to one of the tables and returned with what resembled a tiny white teapot with a long spout.

"I will administer this elixir, but you, Prince Valian, will be the one to question them. If things start to get out of hand, I will pull the plug, agreed?"

Valian sighed deeply and nodded.

"Who shall go first?" Merlin asked.

"I will," Zeb blurted out, as if wanting to get it over with quickly. "I will go first."

Merlin produced a shot glass the size of a thimble and filled it from the teapot.

Zeb accepted the glass, tipped it to his lips and swallowed.

Immediately his eyes glazed over, and his breathing slowed considerably.

Everyone watched in almost fearful anticipation as Valian was directed to sit on the throne.

With a glance at the others, he leaned forward.

"Zebulan, can you hear me?"

"Yes."

"Zeb you are here with me, Haley, and Ike. You are safe among your friends."

"Yes," Zeb answered with a pleasant smile.

"Zeb, we want you to picture in your mind, the day you approached the cave of the dead mountain, when you were searching for Sarah."

Zeb's smile disappeared, looks of dread, confusion, and weariness crossed his face.

"Where are you Zeb?"

"Marsh," he whispered. He began to move his legs as if walking slowly, like he had little strength. He batted the air as if warding off something buzzing about his head. Sweat began to bead up on his face.

"Bad smell," he said, cupping his nose, all the while still lifting his legs in mock steps. "There are black pools, bubbling thickly. Where am I? I'm scared," he whispered, wiping his brow.

Suddenly he ducked, putting his arms over his head, shielding himself.

"Bats!" he cried out in horror. He began to sob.

"Zeb, you are all right," Valian said, his voice raising an octave. "You are still here with Haley and me."

Zeb's face relaxed very little.

"Where are you now Zeb?"

"There's a cave." His face went blank. There was no emotion present whatsoever.

"Keep going Zeb. Tell us what you see."

"I am in a tunnel. It's red in here. I am going through a cold room. There is a putrid smell. There are bones on the floor."

"Keep going Zeb."

Zeb's breathing began to increase. "There is another cave ahead. I don't want to go in, but I can't stop. There is evil here."

Zeb suddenly froze, his mouth hanging open. The terror on his face made the hair stand up on Haley's arms.

She looked at Valian and was surprised to see he was affected too.

"It's all right, Zeb. What do you see?"

Zeb's mouth moved, but it took a moment for his voice to work. He bowed his head. "I can't look at it."

"Zeb, you are safe here with Haley and me, now you can do it, what do you see?" Valian asked again with authority.

Zeb looked up then quickly bowed his head again. "It is so beautiful, and terrifying," he sobbed. "It has a body that keeps changing its form. First human, then… something so horrid, I… don't know the words to describe it, and it's speaking to me," he panted, covering his ears.

"What is it saying Zeb?" Valian asked, trying to keep an even tone.

"It's lonely. It wants to keep me here... forever. It wants me to find others and bring them here to... to..."

"To what, Zeb?"

"To torture them for its pleasure," he wailed. Tears streamed down his face. "It wants to make the fairies suffer in pain, to die a slow agonizing death."

Everyone was dead quiet, afraid to go on, afraid to learn more.

Valian wiped the beads of sweat from his face.

"Why does it want to kill the fairies?"

"It hates the fairies because they are free, and full of light. It's something it can't stand. It wants to get to the human side where it thinks it will escape this torment of goodness, and corrupt the world, and become a god over men."

Zeb hung his head. His entire body shook and he was racked with sobs of grief.

"Wake him," Haley begged. "Please Valian, wake him before his hope is gone."

Valian looked over at Merlin standing just behind the throne and nodded at him.

He looked over at Ike who was white as a ghost, with his eyes so wide, Haley thought they would pop out of their sockets. It was almost as if Ike was re-living his memory as well.

Haley laid her hand gently on his shoulder, causing him to jerk out of some kind of trance. He looked at Valian, almost pleadingly.

"Don't worry Ike; I don't think we will need you."

Ike looked relieved, but the color didn't return to his face.

Merlin went to the table again, and came back with a wet, steaming towel and another shot glass.

"Wipe his head and face," he instructed, handing the towel to Valian.

Valian took the towel and draped it over Zeb's head, then moved it down over his face and began to wipe.

"Wake," Merlin commanded.

Zeb's terrified eyes opened.

"Drink this," Merlin said, lifting the glass to Zeb's mouth, helping him to swallow.

The glazed look in Zeb's eyes was gone, but he continued to shake uncontrollably. He looked worn out, beaten, in the bowels of despair. Everyone was quiet as he tried to recover from his broken state.

Haley looked at him with pity. She felt sorry for him. Sorry they put him through it, and sorry for his pain.

"Zeb?" Valian said quietly.

Zeb slowly looked up and shook his head. "I feel like something inside of me has died," he told them.

"Are you ok?" Haley asked.

"At the moment, no, but I'm going to be. That was the worst thing I have ever experienced."

"I am so sorry Zeb, to have put you through this," Valian apologized. "I don't think any of us here understood the reality of what we are dealing with. It is difficult to comprehend something we know so little about, and now seeing you here, like this, breaks the heart, and for that I am truly sorry."

"You didn't know," Zeb consoled the prince. "How could you or anyone else? We are dealing with perfect evil, a being so full of hatred and loathing without end. It has no reason, or hope, just an unending thirst for mayhem. Its power is so overwhelming; I can understand why men have gone mad. I am a strong willed man, and I believe that was the only reason I survived. It was my only weapon. The weak minded wouldn't stand a chance."

Everyone grew quiet, each one thinking about what Zeb said, what they were up against.

"I'm tired," Zeb said softly, rubbing the back of his neck.

Valian stood and looked at Haley, and Ike. "Let's get him home. Thank you, Master Merlin. You have helped to shed some light on our plight."

Merlin nodded once, and motioned to the stairs.

The group ascended, helping Zeb along in his weakened state.

Mother Earth was waiting at the top to show them out.

The lightning hadn't let up, nor the pounding rain.

Valian and Ike picked Zeb up and flew back to the Bonners.

Sarah ushered them in by the fire. She took one look at her weary husband, and steered him into the bathroom, where a hot tub of water was waiting. When she came back out she brought them each a hot cup of cider.

Valian was about to explain what happened, but Sarah cut him off.

"I know what happened. I can see it in his eyes. He saw the evil one."

Valian nodded.

"Did you get what you were looking for?" she asked

"Yes," Valian answered, "for the most part."

"Good," Sarah said with a stern tone. "Then I hope you won't mind if I ask you to leave now. Zeb needs to rest."

"Of course," Valian responded apologetically.

They saw themselves out as Sarah went back to the bathroom and shut the door.

No one talked as they flew back to the palace. They warmed themselves by the fire in the dining hall, rubbing their hands together.

Reed came in with towels, and ember potions, and drew up a few chairs.

"Thank you Reed," said Haley sitting down, scooting her chair closer to the fire. She took a sip, and sat back, staring into the flames. "I feel so sad;" she said quietly, "like our team just lost the ballgame."

"I know what you mean," Ike agreed. "It was like I was there myself."

Haley looked over at him, listening.

"I only remember bits and pieces, but it was horrible. I can imagine what Zeb was going through."

"Was it the same for you?" Haley asked.

"I don't think it was as bad for me. Zeb was already in despair, searching for his family. I was searching for wealth and riches. I was easy to control, but not Zeb. I imagine Molock had to fight tooth and nail to turn him."

Valian sighed heavily and took a long drink.

"How do you feel Valian?" Haley asked.

"Worn out. Drained. I didn't realize the scope of what we're up against. I know Molock is evil, but I never felt it like this before. And I'm angry. Angry at myself for dragging you into this mess. Angry that

Molock thinks he can take over and destroy people's lives, just because he wishes it."

"We're not alone," said Haley. "We have each other, we have our weapons, and we have a plan. Have you ever heard that old saying; together we stand, divided we fall? Or the bigger they are, the harder they fall? We're a family, and families stick together. We will stand together. We will put up such a fight; Molock won't know what hit him! Our greatest weapon? It's love, and family, will power, determination and perseverance!"

Her voice grew louder as she went on. "Steadfastness, fortitude, and mettle! Darn! He's got me fired up!"

Valian looked at her in wonder.

"That's what we need," she continued. "We need to light a fire under everybody's butt, get them riled up, and get some spunk into them. Take those given gems off! Forget playing it safe, let their emotions run wild and do what they were designed to do! Make us fight for what is right, and just, and true!"

She had risen from her chair, and was letting loose all the pent up fear and frustration.

"It's time we got off our rear ends, and showed that creep what we're really made of!"

Her face was flushed, and her eyes shone more brightly than ever. Her courage was catchy as Valian stood and shouted.

"Yes! That's the spirit! That's what we need! Our gems have made us complacent. Prevented us from being our true selves. We are warriors! Guardians! Have we become so smug, and comfortable that we've forgotten our purpose?"

"Damn the torpedoes!" Haley began to laugh.

Valian cocked an eyebrow. "What?"

Ike wore a huge grin. "You two are nuts," he laughed.

Valian picked Haley up, and twirled her around. "You're a sharp and intelligent woman! We've been walking around with blinders on for far too long. Our race has so much potential!" he pointed out.

The sudden sound of clapping interrupted their little tribute to fairy kind, and they discovered the queen standing in the doorway.

"How long have you been standing there?" Valian prompted.

"Long enough," she answered, walking stiffly over to one of the chairs by the fire. "I take it your visit with Master Merlin was successful?"

"I don't know that I would call it success, but yes, we found out everything that was possible."

"Good, good. And Zebulan is faring well?"

"He'll make it," Valian answered. "He has a strength."

"What about you?" she glanced at Ike.

"I'm pumped," Ike declared. "Molock is gonna have a real fight on his hands, I can tell you that, if these two here are any indication of what you're made of," he motioned to Valian and Haley.

The queen smiled and stood. "You are well on your way. Goodnight, and don't stay up too late."

"I think I'll join her, and hit the sack," said Haley.

She gave Valian a peck on the cheek, and went to her room.

Morning greeted Haley with a sunbeam across her face. She smiled and stretched, not wanting to get out from under the warm blankets, the room was so cold.

She threw the covers back, and grabbed her robe and went to the window.

There were several inches of fresh snow blanketing everything in sight. She was thrilled as she gazed up at the sky. There were sunbeams here and there, but the clouds were dark and ominous.

She hurried and showered and got dressed, and almost ran down the corridor to the dining hall.

The fires were blazing and welcoming, and she was hurrying toward them when she spotted Henry and Sersha sitting in the corner, talking quietly.

"Did you see that snow?" Henry asked cheerfully when he spotted her.

Haley grinned. "Isn't it wonderful? Good morning you two. You're up early."

"We all turned in early," Sersha explained. "So what happened last night? How'd it go?"

"We really didn't find out anything we didn't already know," Haley answered. "Master Merlin gave Zeb a special elixir. He went under some kind of hypnosis, and relived the day he went into the cave of the dead mountain. It hit him pretty hard. It was terrible to watch."

They paused quietly for a moment.

"We must do everything in our power to destroy Molock. If he gained any kind of control, there would be no hope. The sooner we can set sail the better."

"Sersha and I were talking… and we think we should pay a visit to the cave."

"What…?"

"Listen, the guardians said Violet didn't go to the cave. That means Molock has moved. Maybe we'll find a clue."

Haley thought for a minute. "You know, that idea is not half bad. Who knows what we might find?"

Haley walked over to the fireplace and let the heat soak into her body.

"Good morning, Haley, my love," came Valian's voice behind her.

She turned and wrapped her arms around him. She felt so at home in his arms, so safe. "Couldn't we just stay like this for a couple of days?" she suggested.

"Um, I'd like that," Valian hinted.

"Did you see the snow?" she asked.

"Yes, that's why it's so cold in here. Someone forgot to close up the arches last night."

"Huh?"

Valian walked over to the columns. As he stood under the canopy, he rotated his arm in a wide arc.

Suddenly a wall of glass appeared. It was white with beautiful designs that looked as though they had been heated by a blow torch perhaps, melted clear in great arcs and swirls.

Almost immediately, the hall began to warm as all three fireplaces were lit.

"What beautiful windows," Haley sighed. "Valian, come over and listen to an idea Henry and Sersha had."

When Henry and Sersha finished explaining their thoughts, Valian stood up, rubbing his chin. Haley cocked her head and stared at his face. It was red and seemed chapped.

"Darling, are you all right?" she asked, getting up and rubbing her hand across his cheek. "It's rough," she uttered in surprise. "It's stubble! I thought you said you couldn't grow facial hair."

"We're not supposed to be able to… I don't think. This feels weird," he replied, sitting down, still rubbing his face.

"Wow," Henry said curiously. "A side effect?" he continued. "Who knows what's possible now that you stopped wearing your gem."

"Yeah, maybe you're right," Valian said in bewilderment.

"So, about the cave," Henry began, "what do you think?"

"I think it couldn't hurt to have a look. We don't have any other plans for today except our little dinner party tonight. We'll take Celio and Lonato with us, just in case."

The brownies came in to set the tables as the four sat comfortably in the corner, chatting.

Ike and Judy were escorted in, and they joined the group.

Ike declined the invitation to go along, which wasn't really a surprise to Haley. Judy seemed to be relieved.

"I think I'll take Judy over to Mom and Dad's today," he announced.

"Good idea," Haley commented. "Give them our love, will you?"

They finished breakfast then went their separate ways to get dressed in warmer clothing.

When Haley stepped onto the balcony to wait for the others, she took in a deep breath. "Ah," she sighed.

The air was very cold, and froze the inside of her nose.

Valian, Henry, and Sersha joined her minutes later. Haley had to smile at Sersha's furry hat, boots, and muffler.

"You look toasty."

Suddenly a snowball went whizzing past Valian's ear, startling him, and he looked down and smiled at a dozen fairy children having a snowball fight.

"All set then?" Valian asked, looking at everyone.

The four leapt from the balcony. About a mile from the palace they were joined by Lonato and Celio, and it began to snow, fat, lazy flakes, just the way Haley liked it.

It was a pleasant flight until they got to the Cimmerian realm where it turned an ugly gray in the sky and grew darker.

"Snowflakes are wasted here," Haley grumbled.

It became a bit warmer as they neared the black, bubbling pools, and Haley hoped she'd never have to smell that putrid odor again.

They flew over the pools and landed, making their way around the large, black boulders. The memory in Haley's mind of her last journey here came flooding back. It was such a creepy place, the snow just made it more depressing.

Soon they were standing in front of the mouth of the cave.

Valian pulled six torches out of thin air, and drew his sword. Celio and Lonato followed suit. "No sense in taking chances."

"Your mother would be proud," Haley beamed.

They cautiously proceeded inside.

Haley wasn't as afraid as she thought she'd be, and remembered she wasn't really afraid last time either. The feeling of hopelessness and dread were thankfully absent.

The darkness was illuminated by a red glow, revealing several passages ahead.

"Let's split up," Valian suggested. "It's obvious he isn't here. We'll cover more ground and finish quicker."

Valian and Haley chose the center passage. Their torches revealed wet stone walls. They could hear the sound of dripping as they began to descend. The floor was made of dirt, compacted, like stone from many years of treading. They could smell that same nasty scent, like rotting eggs, making their eyes water as they entered a large cavern. A green glow lit the room full of huge stalagmites, and the glug glug of a bubbling pool of muck puffed its rotten foul stench into the humid air.

They entered a small alcove and Valian paused, looking at the floor, appalled at the sight of bleached white bones, scattered everywhere, some in piles three feet high. "This is strange," Valian's voice echoed. "Could Molock possibly be carnivorous? Meat eating? That would indicate he has a solid form; that he has to eat to survive."

"This way," Haley directed him to a door on the right. They entered a rectangular, dark, cold room. Valian raised his torch high.

Long chains lined all the walls. "This is where the fairies I rescued were bound." Her heart was heavy as she remembered.

Old, dried up fairy wings littered the floor, and blew in every direction as Valian walked the length of the room, like pieces of feather light straw. "Is this the key?" he motioned to a rusty skeleton key hanging on a hook. Haley nodded.

Valian sighed heavily. "Come on, there's nothing to see here."

They made their way back to the cavern and looked around the abandoned room. Valian turned quickly, raising his sword at the shuffling sound coming from the passage Sersha and Henry had taken. A soft light appeared and became brighter as the two emerged. They both looked excited as they caught their breath. Henry blurted out, "We found a toilet! And a huge, huge bed… it was made completely out of obsidian stone!"

"Seriously?" Haley exclaimed.

"Yes! And we found a room covered in bones!"

"Well, I'll be," Haley murmured. "You may be absolutely correct," she said to Valian.

"Why would Molock need a toilet and a bed unless…" Sersha paused, a look of amazement crossing her face, "he was human…"

Everyone was quiet as they listened to the drip, drip around them.

Celio and Lonato emerged from their passageway. "We didn't find anything," said Lonato.

"I think we've seen enough. Let's get back and give this news to Mother," Valian suggested.

"You don't have to ask me twice," said Henry, grabbing Sersha's hand, leading the way.

It was good to get out of the Cimmerian realm. As soon as they crossed into the Spicewood realm, the difference was like night and day. The snow continued in large, fat flakes, whisked away on whatever direction the winds would take them.

Haley took Valian's hand and they flew slowly, weaving back and forth like a couple, skimming across the ice on skates, with a swaying rhythm, keeping perfect time with their movements.

Henry and Sersha held hands and smiled at the harmony between their siblings.

Celio and Lonato were all business, heading up the rear, keeping a watchful eye on their charges.

Once they crossed the Woodland realm border, Henry and Sersha veered off toward Mathilda's while the others went on to the palace. "I'll fill Mother in!" Valian called after them.

The snow changed over to sleet and they got back just in time before getting soaked.

Valian and Haley promptly went to the queen's royal bedroom, but she wasn't there. They found her in the blue room, all cuddled up under a blanket, sitting in a lounger next to the fire.

"Mother, it's so good to see you up and out of your room."

"Actually, I'm feeling pretty good. Reed mixed up my second batch of herbs, and it's really doing the trick. I feel almost perky."

Valian pulled up a couple more loungers by the fire and filled the queen in on everything they learned during their visit to the dead mountain.

She sat quietly when he had finished.

After several minutes she still hadn't commented and Valian looked anxious. "What do you think?" he asked.

"If your thinking Molock is human, you must proceed with care. He must be destroyed before he finds a way to the other side. Make haste to find Medusa's head. The gateway is sealed and hidden, but you can be sure he has his servants out looking for it."

"Where is it Mother?"

"I don't have any idea. The gateway is where the rift began to tear our two worlds apart. It was shrouded, tens of thousands of years ago, long before I was ever born. The immortals from that time are long gone, in the heavens. They left this world and moved on to spend eternity in another place, where they can see the goings on here, but won't interfere."

She paused and looked in her son's eyes. "Just find that head."

"We will. I promise we will, and we'll return and put an end to this."

"Why don't you two get some rest and get cleaned up. Our guests will be arriving in a few hours."

The couple excused themselves and retired to their rooms.

Haley went to her closet and began to pack her gowns and shoes. She put her breast plate in a bag and laid out her sword. All her toiletries were packed in a special case, except for those she would need in the morning. Finally satisfied, she lay down and drifted off.

She woke several hours later, totally refreshed and eager for the party and setting sail the following morning. She decided to wear one of the queen's gowns for dinner, and chose a soft, cream colored, lacy gown with a high collar and a beautiful bustled train.

She showered and got dressed, putting her hair up in a delicate wrap.

As she looked at her reflection, she felt beautiful and special, and honored to be considered part of the royal family, even though she wasn't yet.

Just as she slid on the matching slippers, her steward announced he had arrived to escort her. He smiled when she opened the door.

"If you don't mind my saying it, you look radiant."

The color in her cheeks deepened as he bowed. She took the top of his hand and he walked her down the corridor.

As they neared the dining hall, she could hear the voices of a large crowd, laughter, and merry making. When she stepped through the doorway she had to catch her breath at the décor.

Someone had taken great lengths in decorating the hall to look like the sea. There was even a mock ship with white sails, and someone had charmed one wall, sending waves crashing to the shore. It was like looking at a giant movie screen.

Palm trees, ferns, and exotic flowers were everywhere. The hall was dimly lit by dozens of candles and lanterns, and smelled heavenly.

Fairies stood around in small groups, conversing, clinking their goblets, and enjoying the party like atmosphere. All heads turned as Haley walked into the room, and everyone nodded their heads as she passed. Smiling, Haley returned their nods of greeting.

Valian was standing by one of the fireplaces and she squealed with delight when she saw who he was with. Her parents had wide smiles when they saw her.

"Mom! Dad!" She ran to them.

"Oh honey, you look so beautiful," Carol exclaimed, giving her a hug.

"I'm so glad you're here," said Haley. "Thank you," she looked lovingly at Valian.

"We couldn't leave without your parents there to see you off," he grinned.

Henry, Sersha, and the Seers came in and joined them at the fire with hugs of welcome.

Haley looked over and saw Maximillion and Tilly just arriving with Hilda and Estelle.

"What did you do with Ernie?" Haley asked her father.

"Prince Valian here, sent two guardians to entertain him while we're here," Paul explained to the group.

The witches walked over to a table and sat down.

"Excuse me a moment," said Valian.

He walked over to them and informed Maximillion they had seats reserved at the head table for them.

Maximillion shook Valian's hand and tried to hide the surprised look on his face.

The dining hall was all a buzz with chatter, then began to quiet down as the prince headed for his seat. Everyone followed suit and remained standing as the soft gong announced the queen's arrival.

She flowed into the room, accompanied by an escort on each side, wearing an emerald, satin gown and a simple crown of gold. She stood at the head of the table and motioned for everyone to be seated.

"Welcome to all," she began. "We are here to pay tribute to these brave souls," she motioned to the crew. "They are about to embark on a great quest, and if successful, will mark the end of Molock the Merciless."

The hall couldn't have been quieter.

"Tonight we celebrate their impending victory," she finished, raising her goblet in a toast. "To success!"

The clinking of goblets, echoed through the hall as the queen took her seat. Music began to play, reminding Haley of the big band sound that was so popular when her mother was a young girl. It was a grand evening, with no talk of their mission, just light hearted gaiety.

The brownie servants were in and out continuously bearing trays, clearing plates, serving each course in a very orderly fashion. Haley paid them no mind, but just sat, taking it all in. Her smile never left her face as she enjoyed the company of her parents, surrounded by all the people she loved and cared about.

Valian asked her to dance between courses on several occasions, as her parents sat, beaming at the couple. Then when Henry asked Sersha to dance, Carol's mouth fell open and she had a look of melancholy about her. Happy, yet sad. As though she were about to lose her other child to the pangs of love.

Fairies started to depart as the party began to wind down. After inviting everyone to the eastern shores for a send off in the morning, Queen Lilia was escorted to her royal bedroom.

Valian and the rest of the crew gathered at one of the smaller tables in the back of the room and went over final plans. They agreed to meet at the ship at nine a.m., during high tide, and Valian reminded Maximillion and Tilly not to forget any provisions they themselves couldn't provide for them.

Everyone bid each other goodnight and turned in early.

Haley walked her parents to their room and sat with them for a few minutes. She wished them well and made them promise not to worry, that she and Henry were in good hands, then went off to bed.

She slept hard and had no dreams to interrupt her slumber that night.

Six o'clock a.m., and she woke with a start, looked at the clock and sighed with relief. She had been so worried she would oversleep.

It was raining again with gray overcast skies. She was delighted when she looked out the window to see everything covered in a thin layer of ice. Every branch, every leaf, and every single structure sparkled.

She hurried to the shower, dressed, and rang for her steward.

When he arrived, she directed him to take her bags to the dining hall to be delivered to the ship, and went toward the blue room. Peeking in, she saw no one and went on toward breakfast. Her parents and the rest of the crew were just beginning to fill their plates when she joined them.

Lonato came over with his gear and told them the queen had already eaten, and was on her way to the ship, that she would meet them there.

Breakfast was fairly quiet, everyone busy thinking about what was to come. Eight o'clock came all too soon and everyone began to leave for the ship. They leapt from the balcony, into the light rain in twos. Haley was surprised to see such a large turnout, despite the rain.

Maximillion and Tilly had arrived minutes before with their crew and were busy loading their personal supplies.

The queen sat in a tent by the shore, in her glorified wheelchair, covered in blankets. She called the group inside for final words of encouragement and goodbyes, until Valian, Haley, Sersha, and Henry were the last ones standing.

She handed each one round, smooth, blue stone. "I don't know how much good these will do, but at least we'll be alerted if anything should go wrong. I will be checking on your progress in the sacred sphere. I've never tried to see anything that far away before."

She smiled at each one.

"Fare thee well, as Hilda would say. May the celestial spirits be your guide… and I love each and every one of you. Now go, and return as quickly as you can."

All four gave her a hug and left her in the tent, tears rolling down her cheeks.

Author's Note

I recently had the pleasure to step back in time up in Virginia City, NV. I love the great state of Nevada and love its rich history. It's a place where the days are hotter than blazes and the nights can be downright cold. Where there are tumbleweeds, the scent of sage, and dust devils the size of twisters towering high in the sky. I can only imagine what it was like during the gold rush in Virginia City. There is so much to see and experience, from gunfights throughout the day to the hundreds of motorcyclists that come for Street Vibrations and Hot August Nights.

Through my mother-in-law, Nancy Patterson, I was introduced to a wonderful lady at the Bucket of Blood Saloon, also named Nancy, who stopped in to see David John and the Comstock Cowboys, a group that can whoop it up with foot stompin' guitar pickin' and banjo playin' music, almost every weekend during the summer.

Nancy runs a shop in Virginia City called, Fred's Closet, specializing in Old West, Victorian clothing rentals. Nancy and Fred were kind enough to dress me and let me cruise Virginia City for the day.

The following pictures were the result. I had a blast! If you ever want to feel how it was back in the old west, a visit to Virginia City is a must, and look up Nancy and Fred and take your visit to a whole new level.

Visit: fredscloset.net

On the way home, David and I ran into a magnificent herd of wild mustangs grazing in the hills. I couldn't resist getting out of the car and getting up close to take some photos. What a great ending to a perfect day. Check out my website to see all the photos in color.

Visit: bonnersfairy.com

This is one of the outfits Nancy picked out for me.
What fun! I never realized how complicated it was to
dress a woman back in those days. I loved the hat!

This was the outfit I wore all day. Putting on the bustier was an experience. Fred tugged and pulled on the ties in the back literally taking my breath away, but it sure held things in nicely!

Here is a picture of David John from the Comstock
Cowboys, and I, standing outside the Bucket of Blood
Saloon. I never miss an opportunity to go up and see them
play. The energy the Cowboys create is contagious.

Here is Fred, of Fred's Closet, and I, inside the Bucket
of Blood Saloon, ready for some gun slingin'.

Wild mustangs!

What a Stallion. He stood by himself while
the rest of the herd grazed below.

Mother and child.

Just amblin' down the road.

This was taken in one of the many forests in Lake Tahoe, CA, just across the road from my mom's house.

The smell of the pine is still strong in my nose. I love Lake Tahoe!